MYTH HUNTER

Myth Hunter

MYTHICAL MENAGERIE SERIES BOOK 1

Suneé le Roux

Strawberry Moon Press

Copyright © 2023 Suneé le Roux

For permission requests, contact the author at
contact@suneeleroux.com.

This book is a work of fiction. Names, characters,
places, incidents and dialogues are used
fictitiously. Any resemblance to actual people,
living or deceased, is coincidental.

ISBN (Paperback): 978-0-620-87538-7

AUTHOR'S NOTE

The stories that make up the *Mythical Menagerie* series were written in serialised short-story form. Each story contains its own complete arc while contributing to the larger narrative of the series as a whole. Think of them as very large chapters in a single story.

This collection brings the episodes of the first series together into one continuous reading experience.

This novel makes use of UK English spelling and syntax.

TABLE OF CONTENTS

PART 1

BEGINNER'S LUCK

"**S**hit!" I swore as I stumbled and fell flat on my face.

I lay there for a few seconds, contemplating life, love, the universe and everything else, all the while getting soaked to the bone by the incessant drizzle that had turned the streets of London into a slippery nightmare. It took me a while to realise that both my hands, currently stretched out before me as if in supplication to some uncaring, yet doubtlessly chortling, deity, were touching bits of paper. I clutched onto them as I pushed myself to my feet, ignoring the stares of passersby, none of whom had even the slightest decency to offer a hand.

In my right hand was some kind of wanted advert. I scrunched it up and pushed it into the pocket of my tweed jacket.

Of more interest was what I held in my left hand. A fifty-pound note! I stared at it dumbly, numbly, not believing my luck. A stupid smile crept across my face. I got to eat steak tonight!

That smile twisted into a scowl when I saw the reason for my fall. The sole on the right foot of my best pair of loafers gaped wide open. My sock was sticking out. Not exactly the impression I wanted to make at tomorrow's interview. Not that it would make any difference, I imagine. I could show up in a suit made of hundred-pound notes and I would still not get the job. The financial world was unforgiving, especially if you'd made the sort of mistake I had made.

Still, I had to try. Giving up meant not eating,

and forfeiting on this month's rent. And, worst of all, having to listen to yet another one of Mother's tirades.

I surveyed my surroundings, trying to get my bearings again while absentmindedly scratching my stubbly chin. I had just crossed Westminster Bridge on my way home from an interview in the South Bank. Big Ben towered over me, like some giant from myth; silent, judgmental, implacable. Both tourists and Londoners swarmed past me, indifferent to just one more well-dressed twenty-something hoping to somehow survive in this pitiless city.

I squinted as a trickle of water dribbled from my sandy blond hair into my eyes. A rainbow arched over the Houses of Parliament and descended towards the Tube station where the sign for a shoe repair shop caught my eye. I pulled my jacket closer about myself and hurried towards it.

A bell jingled as I walked through the door, the strong odour of shoe polish and sweaty feet assaulting my nose. A man slightly older than me looked up from behind the counter where he was busy repairing someone's footwear. His red hair blazed like a furnace in the darkness of the tiny, windowless shop, reflecting the light from a single spotlight that provided just enough illumination for him to work by. An easy smile crossed his freckled face, blue eyes twinkling with merriment as he greeted me with a distinct Irish lilt.

"What can I do for you?"

I pointed at my offending shoe. "Think you can fix this?"

The man held out his hand and I passed him the shoe, feeling ridiculous standing there in my slightly soggy sock. He stroked his short-cropped beard thoughtfully as he inspected the grinning sole. "Expensive brand," he noted. "You really should take better care of these."

"Can you save it?" I asked, knowing full well I couldn't afford to replace it.

"Sure," the redhead said. "Ten pounds. Come back tomorrow."

"Tomorrow? You want me to walk home barefoot in the rain?" I asked, looking pointedly towards the door where the inlaid glass had steamed up, obscuring the view outside.

The man shrugged.

"Look," I said. "I need that shoe. Is there any way you can fix it now?"

"Sorry, mate," he replied, nodding at the pile of shoes lying on the countertop already. "Got a bit of a backlog here. But..." He reached below the counter and pulled out a pair of white trainers with a green four-leaved clover embellishment adorning the sides.

"My own design," the shoemaker said proudly.

"How much?" I asked. Unfortunately, the days where I refused to wear anything that wasn't a high street brand were long gone.

"Twenty quid."

I sighed. Those fifty pounds were dwindling fast. I handed the note over and sat down to try the trainers on.

"What name should I put on your slip?" the man asked as I tied the shoelaces.

"Ambrose Davids."

"That's... unusual," he said diplomatically.

"You can thank my mother for that," I replied, taking a few steps in my new trainers. They did fit remarkably well. Not particularly stylish, and paired with my brown tweed suit downright ridiculous, but they would have to do for now.

He handed me my change and the slip.

"Thanks," I said in way of farewell. I opened

the door and stepped out of his shop.

Thankfully, the rain had stopped, replaced by a bitingly icy wind. I thrust my hands into my pockets and remembered the other piece of paper I had picked up earlier as my fingers brushed across it. I pulled it out and stared at it.

Instead of the wanted ad I had first assumed, it was a flyer promoting an information session for jobseekers. No further details, just the location, date and time. I looked at my watch and swore again. The session was in fifteen minutes, and about a mile from here. Heedless of the stares once again directed my way, I set out at a jog.

The easiest route was through St James' Park. Ducks quacked as I ran past, dodging pedestrians and cyclists alike. I was out of breath by the time I sprinted past the old war memorial on Waterloo and dripping with sweat when I finally reached Piccadilly Circus, barely sparing a glance for the statue of Anteros and the crowd of camera-wielding tourists around it. By the time I found the unobtrusive door of the venue hidden in a side street, I was already ten minutes late.

The door clicked open when I pressed the buzzer, revealing an empty landing area and a narrow staircase. I took the stairs up two at a time and entered a darkened room on the second floor where a dozen or so people were already watching a slide show. I sat down in the back row, waving apologetically at the presenter in the front as she continued talking.

The woman looked to be in her early twenties too, with dark chocolate skin and a waterfall of black curls framing her face. Her accent was as English as my own, but the African-print scarf wrapped around her throat hinted at a more exotic background.

"As you can see," she was saying, "we are

interested in creatures of a more... shall we say, unusual... reputation." She pointed at the screen where a picture of a winged horse on an old Grecian vase was displayed. "We specialise in animals of myth, folklore and fantasy. Your job would be to locate and acquire these creatures on our behalf. This does not come without an element of danger, but you will be handsomely compensated for any risks you may need to take. All we ask is that you deliver the creatures into our care alive and unharmed. Any questions?"

"Yeah." The guy in front of me raised his hand. "What have you been smoking, lady?"

I glanced at the faces around me as laughter bubbled throughout the room. Almost everyone looked sceptical, some shaking their heads in amusement, others frowning in annoyance. One or two even glanced at their watches, barely bothering to hide their yawns.

"I assure you, we are not crazy. These creatures may be scarce, but they are as real as you and I." The presenter looked calmly at the sea of disbelieving faces staring at her. "And they are in danger. They need to be protected."

The man scoffed again, turning an incredulous gaze at the surrounding people. "Is she serious?" he asked of the room. He picked up his coat and stood up. "I'm out of here, lady. Thanks for the fairy tale, but I have mouths to feed. I wouldn't want to send my children off to find the gingerbread house in the woods." More laughter followed as he strode out of the room. One by one, the rest of the people stood up and left, too.

"What a waste of time," a woman said to her friend as they shuffled past me.

The presenter made no move to stop them, but her shoulders slumped a little as she bent over her laptop and turned the presentation off. She flicked a switch on the wall, bathing the room in fluorescent light. Her eyes widened when she saw me still sitting in my chair.

"Was there something?" she asked, a small frown creasing her forehead.

I stood up, not sure how to explain to her I was desperate enough to go in search of fairy tales if it meant I could eat something other than dry bread the rest of this week. Hell, for a small stipend I would swim the length of the Thames in search of selkies or whatever imaginary creature they wanted right now, no matter if I ended up on Sky News tonight.

"Well, uh..." I hesitated as her brown eyes met my own. She looked me over with one eyebrow raised quizzically. I must look a mess, I realised, all sweaty from the jog here and wearing a water-stained suit. I ran a hand self-consciously through my windblown hair.

"I like your shoes," she said, a small smile playing across her lips. She held her right hand out and I shook it automatically. "Amari Kerubo of the CPPCC. And you are?"

"Ambrose Davids," I replied. CPPCC? Sounded like a remnant of the old Soviet Union. Father would have been looking for conspiracy theories right about now. He'd always had an active imagination.

"Well, Mister Davids," Amari said as she reached into her laptop bag and pulled something out of a side pocket. "I sense you are not quite as sceptical as the rest, so I will give you this." She placed a silver whistle in my hand. "Blow it when you have something we might find interesting."

I stared at the whistle. She had to be kidding me. I suddenly wondered if there was a hidden camera somewhere and my sister would soon show all her friends on YouTube how her brother had fallen for some obscure practical joke.

I looked back at the woman. She raised an eyebrow at me again. I mumbled my thanks and shoved the whistle deep into my pocket, wondering how much I'd be able to flog it for. Without another word, I turned around and left too. This really had been a waste of time.

✳✳✳

With twenty quid in my pocket, there would be no eating steak tonight, I thought gloomily as I made my way home on foot. I stopped at a hole-in-the-wall fish and chips shop in Mayfair and ate the greasy fare while walking. I could probably have afforded to take the Tube, but I didn't want to waste the money. No idea when I would get more. Besides, I enjoyed walking, especially now that the rain had cleared up and the wind had died down. Also, I had to admit that these trainers were exceptionally comfortable. At least that was twenty quid well spent.

The light was fading by the time I entered Hyde Park. There were shorter routes home, but I always walked through the park when I had the chance. Something about the trees and the smell of wet grass. It cleared my head.

It was becoming all too apparent that this job interviewing business was not going well. I'm not even sure why they had called me in this morning. They had hardly asked me any questions. Only the one, really - how? How had I made such a crucial mistake? I had shrugged and given them a non-committal answer. The truth would have been too embarrassing, especially in that sterile white boardroom in front of a panel of black-suited and stern-faced brokers.

The sound of a large splash drew me out of

my reverie and I stopped short, surprised. I had crossed over into Kensington Gardens and was walking along the path parallel to that part of the Serpentine known as the Long Water. Bushes obscured my view of the lake and I held my breath as I strained to hear what was going on.

Another splash. It sounded too big to be a water bird, and it was too cold and dark for some nutcase in a swimsuit to be out. Gripped by curiosity, I scaled the low fence and pushed past the greenery. My eyes were drawn immediately to a pale figure in the water.

A young woman was floating on her back in the middle of the lake. Her face was pallid under the light of the full moon and her long white dress billowed around her motionless body.

"Help!" I shouted, looking around to see if there was anyone about. Not a soul in sight.

I hesitated at the water's edge. It had never occurred to me that knowing how to swim might one day be a necessary skill. The girl floated, pale and unreachable, like some morbid Lady of the Lake, and me, Arthur, building up the courage to jump in and rescue her.

"Did you off her, then?" a voice behind me said and I nearly jumped out of my skin.

I spun around. It was a teenager, his hoodie pulled low over his eyes so I couldn't make out his entire face, hands thrust deep into his pockets. Probably came here to smoke a joint where no one would see him.

"No, I did not *off* her," I replied irritably.

"Better call the cops then." He shrugged and turned around, heading towards the path again.

"Hey, wait," I called. "Can you swim?"

"That water looks freezing." He disappeared behind the bushes without a backward glance.

"Unbelievable," I muttered, shaking my head

in the direction in which he had left. Then, remembering the need for urgency, I pulled my mobile from my jacket pocket. I dialled Emergency Services and explained the situation. When I ended the call, I turned towards the lake again.

The girl was gone.

✕✕✕

Three hours later, someone handed me a mug of strong coffee while I sat under a blanket and watched the search-and-rescue team fine-comb the lake. They had found no trace of the girl so far, not even a body.

"Mister Davids? May I have a word?"

A woman wearing dark-rimmed hipster glasses stood before me. Her brown hair was swept back into a ponytail and she wore a thick black coat against the evening's cold.

"Detective Inspector Miller, Metropolitan Police," she introduced herself, flashing her badge at me. "Did you say you saw the body of a girl floating in the lake?"

"Yes. I mean no, she wasn't dead." I wrapped my hands around the empty mug, trying unsuccessfully to warm them with the residual heat. I stifled a yawn and wondered when they would let me go home. "I heard splashing before I saw her, so she must have been alive."

"Splashing of a body being dumped into the lake?"

"No." I hesitated. "It sounded… playful."

"Playful."

I nodded, feeling uncharacteristic heat rise to my cheeks. She was looking at me as if she could read all my past offences in my eyes. I resolved yet again to return that dust-covered library book at the back of my closet as soon as possible.

"Did you hear anything else? Any voices? Did the girl cry out for help?"

I shook my head. "No, it was deathly quiet, apart from the splashing. When I saw her, she didn't move, just, sort of, floated. And then she was gone."

Detective Miller's eyes bored into me. "Mister Davids, the police are very busy. We really can't afford to waste time on pranks or hallucinations."

"What?" I spluttered, standing up and dropping the blanket to the floor. "I'm not making this up! There really was a girl in the lake. If I could swim, I would have tried to pull her out myself. Look," I said, dragging a hand through my hair. "There was another kid who saw her. Teenager. Dark hoodie, baggy pants. Ask him, he'll confirm my story."

The detective levelled a stern gaze at me before her face softened. "Alright, Mister Davids. I believe you. I think you should go home now. You look exhausted. We'll contact you if we find anything."

I *was* exhausted. I nodded gratefully and handed Detective Miller the empty coffee mug. She took it wordlessly, her lips drawn into a thin line and a small frown wrinkling her brow, but I was too tired to pay much attention.

It was after midnight when I pushed the door of my flat closed behind me. I didn't bother to undress before falling onto my bed. I was asleep within seconds.

※ ※ ※

I woke up groggy the next morning with a vein in my temple throbbing like it was a drummer at a Christmas parade. I squinted at the light streaming in through the window where I'd forgotten to close the curtain last night. With a gargantuan effort, I rolled over and peered at my bedside clock. It was past eleven already.

Shit. I'd missed my interview.

I'd really been having the rottenest luck lately.

A flashing light from my mobile lying on the nightstand drew my attention. Two missed calls. I dialled into my voicemail and winced as the nasally voice of Mister Curry, my landlord, blared over the speakerphone.

"Davids! You're a week late on your rent. If I don't get the money by the end of today, I'll have the locks changed, you hear me?"

I deleted the message.

The next call was from Cassie. My sister's perky voice was almost drowned out by background noise. She must have been in a club when she'd called.

"Hey Am, just wanted to know if you're dead or something. Haven't heard from you in a while. Just because that cow left you, doesn't mean your family aren't still here for you. Anyway, call me when you get this message, alright? Love you!"

I groaned as I put the phone down. I wished Cassie hadn't reminded me of 'that cow'. I looked at the picture of Rachel still standing on my bedside table. Then I turned it over, opened the drawer and pushed it in next to the engagement ring I had never had the chance to give her. I slammed the drawer shut, pulled the covers back over me again, rolled over, and went back to sleep.

※※※

It was much later that day when I finally emerged from my apartment. I hadn't bothered to shave or shower and still wore my rumpled suit jacket and white trainers.

I needed to pick up my interview shoes. Although, to be honest, I probably needed a new plan now. No one in the finance industry was going to hire me again; not here in London, and probably nowhere else in the country, either. Still, I wanted my shoes back. They were the last remnants of my old life.

The sky was a pale, empty, grey. The surrounding buildings were grey too, everything from the Houses of Parliament to the high-end stores I was walking towards. It seemed as if the only bit of colour left in the world was the rainbow hanging over the shoe shop.

The bell jingled as I closed the door behind me. The red-haired man looked up and smiled in recognition.

"Ah, Ambrose Davids. How are the trainers treating you?" he asked in his strong Irish lilt.

"Fine, fine," I said, distracted. I noticed he was wearing a red waistcoat with a four-leaved clover pinned to it. A picture from my youth flashed before my eyes and I inhaled sharply. I'm embarrassed to admit it took me this long to realise it, and even then a few moments passed before I let myself believe it.

I reached into my jacket pocket and pulled out the whistle I had all but forgotten about.

The man's eyes widened in alarm.

"Now hold on, Ambrose," he said, his arms raised as if I were threatening him with a gun. "Let's not do anything rash here. The Council doesn't know I'm here, and I much prefer it that way."

"You're a..." I hesitated. Saying it out loud would be ridiculous. And yet... "Leprechaun?"

The man sighed, his shoulders slumping as he lowered his arms. "I prefer Tuath, but alright then, if you insist. What gave me away? Was it the pin?" he asked, frowning.

"The rainbow," I replied, dazed by the revelation.

"That darn thing," the redhead said, shaking a fist at the ceiling. "I can't tell you how many times I've tried to hide it, but it just keeps popping back up."

"Look, um… Mister Leprechaun…"

The man winced. "My name's Daniel Brady."

"Alright," I said, nodding my head as if this conversation was completely normal. "Daniel, I'll level with you. I'm not sure who the Council is, but a woman told me that if I blow this whistle and bring her anything mythological, or anyone I guess, they'd pay me, and I really need the money right now."

Daniel's face lit up. "If it's money you need, you can have my pot of gold."

I stared at him dumbly.

"And three wishes," he added. "That's a fair trade for my freedom, don't you think?"

"Uh…" I clearly wasn't handling the situation very well.

"Give me a second, I'll be right back," Daniel said, and turned towards a door at the back. He glanced over his shoulder. "Don't blow that whistle, alright? I'll just be two seconds." Then he disappeared into the back.

I don't know what I expected. Him returning with a cast-iron pot filled with gold pieces? A nervous giggle escaped my lips before I could stop it. It was just so absurd. I definitely didn't expect him to return at all, but he was back within seconds, carrying a cheque book.

"Sorry about this," he said as he scribbled on it. "Haven't quite got the hang of Internet banking yet." He grinned as he handed me the cheque.

My eyes bulged. That was a lot of zeros.

"You're giving me all this just so I won't blow this whistle?"

"And three wishes," he said, nodding. "Redeemable anytime you want them. Just three, mind, none of that wishing-for-more-wishes nonsense."

I clutched the cheque, unable to believe my luck. If this were true, everything was about to change. A ray of hope melted the grey from my thoughts.

But something niggled at the back of my mind.

"Who is this Council?" I asked. "And why are you afraid of them?"

"The Elder Council," Daniel replied, his voice lowered, as if afraid they might hear him if he spoke any louder. "They mean well, I'm sure, but I don't need their help. I can get by on my own. I much prefer freedom over safety. Don't you agree, Ambrose?"

"Sure," I said, entirely unsure and none the wiser. "Thanks," I said, lifting the cheque up. I turned around to go, startled by the bell as I opened the door again.

"Hey Ambrose," Daniel called. "Don't forget your shoes."

✳✳✳

The full moon gazed down on me by the time I stumbled out of the pub. After the best meal I'd had in ages, and a few too many beers to wash it down with, I was in the mood for a stroll.

I had never been as nervous as I had been while standing in front of the glass window at the bank, waiting for the cashier to cash my cheque. I was certain something would go wrong. She'd look at it and laugh at me for falling for a scam, or phone security and have me arrested or something. But as I stood there, sweating through my shirt and rumpling my unwashed hair even more, the lady had efficiently and disinterestedly completed all the necessary admin and sent me on my way again.

I couldn't believe my luck had finally changed.

The first thing I did was transfer the rent money, just to get Mister Curry off my back. Then, the financier in me won over and I sensibly paid off all my student debts as well. I felt like Atlas without the world on my shoulders.

I considered buying a sports car next. Instead, I went to the nearest pub to celebrate.

The brisk evening air had sobered me up a bit by the time I reached the lake in Hyde Park on my way home again. I shuddered at the memory of last night, which seemed surreal now. Could I have imagined the young woman in the water? It had probably been an illusion conjured up by my stressed out mind. An overactive imagination did run in the family, after all.

Then I heard splashing again.

I was over the fence before I'd had time to think about it.

The girl I had seen floating in the lake last night was sitting on a rocky outcrop, bare feet tracing circles in the water. Pale blond hair flowed down her back in wet ringlets and a lacy white dress straight out of the Victorian era clung to a figure that had me swallowing nervously. Her skin was almost translucent in the bright light of the full moon. She must have heard me, because she looked up from her reverie and fixed eyes the colour of a morning mist upon me. I felt my heart rate quicken and my knees turn to jelly. She was beautiful. I wanted nothing more in that instant than to walk over, take her in my arms and kiss her until we were both gasping for breath. I took a tentative step towards her.

The girl slipped gracefully into the water.

"Wait!" I said before I could stop myself.

To my surprise, she turned towards me again, her pale hair fanning out behind her in the water.

"Who are you?" I asked, slowly advancing, hoping not to startle her again. She remained in the water, watching me closely, but did not retreat. "I mean you no harm," I said as I reached the edge of the lake. I bent down and sat on my haunches, all fear of the water forgotten as I stared into those entrancing eyes.

The girl remained silent, but she stood up in the waist deep water, rivulets running down her wet dress. She smiled enticingly and beckoned me closer with one finger as she slowly walked backwards, deeper into the lake.

I needed no further urging. I was in the water before I knew it. Somewhere in the back of my mind, I vaguely realised that it was getting deeper and deeper - it was up to my chest now - but I hardly noticed. I cared even less. I could almost touch her.

She reached her hands out to me, longingly, and I stretched towards her. Our fingertips caressed.

And then the girl grabbed my wrist and pulled me under the water.

I gulped water as my head went under the surface. The shock forced my eyes open and I watched, horrified, as the moonlight retreated and we plunged deeper and deeper into the lake.

I struggled, tasting bile, and flailed wildly, but her grip was like iron. I could not escape.

And then my hand was free and I was floating, floating. I looked around. The girl was gone and I was hovering in darkness. Far away, a dim light beckoned. I kicked feebly, half-heartedly.

I was drowning.

Well, shit. Just when it seemed like things were finally going my way again.

It was probably for the best. It would hardly be a great loss to the world. I was a failure. Mother would most likely be relieved to be rid of the embarrassment I had become. Rachel... Well, she'd hardly care. The only one who would miss me would be Cassie.

Sweet Cassie. I never did phone her back. I wish I could tell her how much I loved her too.

The world disappeared in a burning white light. I stumbled over something and seconds later heard it crash, splintering into pieces. I caught myself on the edge of a couch just as my vision cleared. A broken lamp lay on the floor. There was water everywhere. I was drenched.

"Ambrose!"

I looked up to see a girl a few years younger than me standing in the doorway. Her short brown hair was tied back into a half-pony and her green eyes were wide with shock. It took me a few seconds to realise it was my sister, Cassie. I was standing in her living room, dripping puddles onto her carpet.

"What the hell happened to you? You're soaked," she said as she recovered from her own fright.

I stood there, gulping air, not quite sure what had happened.

"I love you, Cassie," I finally managed.

Her worried face broke into a smile. "Gosh, you're drunk, aren't you? How did you get in? Never mind. You must be freezing." She darted out of sight and returned almost instantly with a towel, which she threw around my shoulders. I shivered, my teeth rattling.

"Stay here," she ordered, and disappeared into the kitchen.

I was still too dazed to protest. The embers of a fire were still burning in the hearth and I edged closer, warming myself. Cassie returned a few minutes later with a hot cup of tea. I inhaled the heavenly aroma gratefully, cradling the warm cup in my chilly hands.

By the time it was empty, Cassie had brought a pillow and a couple of blankets out and placed them on the couch.

"I don't have any clothes that will fit you, but you can take those off and put them in the tumble dryer. Just please be dressed by the time I get up tomorrow morning," she said, an impish smile dimpling her cheeks.

She kissed me on the cheek and left me standing in the lounge, wondering what the hell had happened and why I wasn't floating face down in that lake right now.

※※※

White arms reached out to me, pulling me deeper, deeper into the murky depths. Pressure on my chest. I can't breathe! Bubbles escaped my nostrils. I opened my mouth to shout for help and water streamed in, choking me. I flailed about, trying to swim for a surface that didn't exist.

I fell off the couch and landed on the floor, hard.

That woke me up.

I lay there for a minute, drenched in sweat and staring up at the ceiling while I regained my breath and tried to calm my racing heart.

Finally, I pushed myself to my feet, still entangled in blankets, and called out for Cassie. No answer. I headed to the kitchen to retrieve my clothes and found a note on the microwave: "Had to go to class. Breakfast inside. Don't be a stranger."

I dressed quickly, shrugging into my still-damp jacket and white trainers. At least the rest of my clothes were dry and, when I opened the microwave, a plate of scrambled eggs on toast waited inside. It smelled delicious. Bless her.

With warm food in my belly, I felt ready to face the world again.

I went back into the lounge and perused Cassie's bookshelf. It didn't take me long to find what I was looking for: Father's old notebook. I pulled the heavy leather-bound tome from the shelf and wiped the dust off the cover. I set it down on Cassie's coffee table and opened it somewhere in the middle. A musty smell tickled my nose, and memories of Father floated to the surface.

James Davids had been a renowned professor of literature when we were little. He had specialised in ancient texts and had been fascinated with mythology. While other kids our age were learning about the wizarding world or chanting *hakuna matata* like they had any worries, Cassie and I listened to bedtime stories about the gods and goddesses of ancient Greece and Rome. Instead of playing cops and robbers, we acted out scenes from the Mahabharata, or pretended to save the world from Ragnarok. I asked for a Pegasus for my fifth birthday. Cassie had a crush on Sir Galahad all through her teenage years.

We eventually figured out it was all make believe, but for Father... it became more real. He became obsessed, claiming all the myths were true. He published a paper that made him the laughingstock of the academic world and the university sacked him, saying they couldn't be associated with someone as delusional as he clearly was.

Mother divorced him a year later.

Not long after, he disappeared completely.

Cassie and I were both inconsolable when the police declared him missing, presumed dead. That was three years ago.

I hefted the book into my lap and flipped through it. Father's neat handwriting covered the pages, hardly leaving any white space empty of notes or citations. He was meticulous in his research and methodical in his writing. I cross-referenced his entries on lakes and beautiful women and applied it locally to England, and found what I was looking for.

I sat back on the couch, exhaling loudly. The girl in the lake was an asrai, a water nymph.

I hardly believed it. Father had been right all along.

A thought struck me, and I quickly turned to his entry on leprechauns. My breath caught as I read: "Mischievous, but generally harmless. When captured, these descendants of Celtic gods often offer a pot of gold and/or three wishes in exchange for their freedom. Beware: their bargain is only good from sunrise to sunset on the day it was made."

I grabbed my phone, which had luckily survived submersion relatively unscathed, and opened up my internet banking app. Shit. All the money that had wiped away my worries yesterday was gone.

I jumped to my feet, tucking Father's notebook under my arm. I needed to have a talk with a certain redheaded shoemaker.

✖✖✖

"You have some nerve!" I stormed into the

shoe shop and stopped short as both Daniel and the old lady whose footwear he was examining gaped at me. "Sorry," I muttered. "Didn't mean to interrupt." I busied myself looking at the shoes on display while the cobbler and his customer finished up.

I avoided eye contact as the old lady turned to go, but I felt her disapproval weigh down on me like a hand-knitted blanket. When the doorbell announced her departure, I turned to the redhead.

"The money's gone," I accused.

Daniel Brady smiled in that comfortable way of his and said: "Of course it's gone. Didn't think it would be there forever, did you?"

I stared blankly at him. I had assumed our bargain had been permanent. It had never occurred to me that there had been an expiry date on the money.

"But you seem like a sensible fellow," Daniel continued. "I'm sure you used some of it wisely."

"Yeah, I guess," I said, the wind completely out of my sails.

"And one wish down too. Must have been an eventful day for you."

I frowned. "I used a wish yesterday?"

He nodded. "Sometimes a little extra luck helps, doesn't it?"

It suddenly dawned on me. I had wished to see Cassie again. That's how I had escaped from drowning. Why hadn't I realised it before?

Daniel watched me closely, his blue eyes sparkling with amusement. "I suspect you're still struggling to believe it," he said. "Mortals often do."

I looked at the red-haired man before me as if seeing him for the first time. He really was a creature from myth. "Are all the stories true, then?" I asked.

Daniel tapped the side of his nose with one finger, a mischievous twinkle in his eyes. "Not all of them, but some are. If you continue working for the Council, I'm sure you'll see things you'd never have believed true."

The Council! I'd almost forgotten about them. Without the rest of the pot of gold, I still had to earn some money, or be in the same desperate situation next month. Perhaps the Council was the answer to my problems. A plan started forming in the back of my head.

"Thanks, Daniel," I said, a smile returning to my face. I held two fingers up. "I'll be keeping you to those wishes," I promised him as I opened the door again on my way out.

"I'll count on it," he said, grinning from ear to ear.

※※※

"Planning on wiping away the evidence, Mister Davids?"

I turned to see Detective Inspector Miller smiling at me, small wrinkles at the corners of her eyes just visible underneath her dark-rimmed glasses. I noticed her eyes, too. They were green, like moss on a forest floor. I snorted. Like I knew what moss on a forest floor looked like.

"Something funny, Mister Davids?" she asked again.

"Detective Miller," I said, trying to hide my momentary embarrassment. "I didn't expect to run into you here at Tesco." I glanced around the shelves of the household products aisle, wondering for a split-second if she really thought I was guilty of something.

"Please, call me Sarah. I'm off duty now. And even detectives need to go home some time to clean their apartments, Mister Davids."

"Ambrose," I said, suddenly grinning. Was she flirting with me?

"Although I've never seen anyone examining sponges with such detail before, Ambrose." No, not flirting, teasing.

I ran a hand through my hair, eyeing the shelves again. "It's just that there's so many to choose from. And what I had in mind... It needs to be super-absorbent. Can't risk any spills." I glanced her way, wondering what she'd make of that.

"Here," she said, reaching past me to take something off the shelf. I couldn't help but notice she smelled of oranges. It reminded me of Spain in the summer. "The guys in Forensics swear by this." She handed me a dense yellow sponge that looked like a two-year-old Twinkie. I turned it around to look at the price tag and sighed. Typical.

"Hey, I know twenty pounds is pretty steep, but you wanted the best," she said.

"No, you're right. Thank you." I flashed her my most winsome smile.

"Well," she said, adjusting her glasses and breaking eye contact. "I'd better get going."

"Wait!"

She looked at me with those moss-green eyes and suddenly my throat was as dry as a Finance 101 lecture. "Uh..." I floundered. "Did you ever find that guy in the hoodie? The one I told you about at the lake."

She laughed then, and swiped her arm out to indicate the surrounding shoppers. In our aisle alone, there were three teenagers in hoodies and baggy pants. It could have been any of them at the lake that night.

"I see your point," I said sheepishly.

"See you later, Ambrose Davids," she said, a smile still lingering on her lips as she walked away.

⁂

As luck would have it, it was the last night of the full moon and, according to Father's notes, my last chance of glimpsing the asrai. I hid behind some bushes next to the lake, hoping to find the pale woman again. This time, I would be ready for her. She wouldn't catch me so easily tonight.

I didn't have to wait long. The surface rippled and the asrai emerged, water streaming from her long blond hair and her lacy white dress clinging to her body. My palms were suddenly sticky and I had to remind myself that the last time we met she tried to drown me. Still, I could hardly tear my eyes away from her. I was incredibly aware of my own breathing.

I watched as she made herself comfortable on the rocky outcropping and started running her hands through her hair, working the tangles out. One of her feet dangled in the water, sending ripples outwards into the lake.

Slowly and as quietly as possible, I inched closer. The asrai looked up and I froze. She cocked her head to one side, listening. I hardly dared breathe. My foot started cramping. After what felt like ages, she returned her gaze to the ripples in the water.

I moved closer again.

"Three nights in a row have we met," the asrai said. Her voice was as soft as a burbling brook. She turned to where I stood, half crouched, frozen in place, and her grey eyes met my own. "It must be fate that brought you here."

"Fate," I croaked as I stood up. I coughed to clear my throat and worked some saliva into my mouth. "Or luck."

The asrai glanced down at my white trainers and back up at my face again. "You are luckier than most."

I took a tentative step towards her. She was almost within arm's reach.

"Will you join me in the lake again?"

For a moment, I was tempted. I imagined our bodies entwined, nothing between us but the cold water, my hands in her hair, her lips on mine. Then the memory of darkness enveloping me scared me back to my senses.

"I think not," I said, taking her hand and pulling her towards me.

She folded into my arms as if she belonged there. She laid a hand on my chest and looked lovingly into my eyes. I imagined what our children would look like.

It took all my willpower to place the Council's whistle on my lips and blow it. There was no sound, and for a second I thought nothing had happened, but fear flashed unmistakably across the asrai's face.

"You have a cold heart," she said, her voice suddenly hard as ice.

An arctic chill stabbed through my chest and I reared backwards, gasping. I stumbled over something and fell, pulling her along with me. We tumbled to the ground, but as she hit the earth, the asrai's form dissolved into a puddle of water.

Ignoring the cold shivers that spasmed through my body, I pulled the sponge from my jacket pocket and quickly soaked the water up until not a drop was left on the ground.

"A sponge?"

I looked up to see Amari Kerubo, the woman who had given me the whistle, standing over me. Her arms were folded across her chest and a smile played across her lips. "Now why hadn't I thought of that?"

She held a hand out and helped me to my feet.

"Well done, Mister Davids. Few men can withstand the allure of an asrai. I'm impressed."

Another shiver ran through me and I placed a hand on my chest where the nymph had touched me. Even through my jacket, I could feel her frozen hand imprinted on my skin.

"Ah, not completely unscathed, I see," Amari said, wincing. "No cure that we know of for that, I'm afraid. But come, let's get you someplace warmer at least."

She said something then, a word I didn't recognise, and the world around me dissolved in a white light.

※ ※ ※

When I could see again, we were in a windowless room, warmed by a crackling hearth fire that cast a cheery glow over the room's furnishings. The walls were covered in shelves housing books that looked hundreds of years old, and a large mahogany desk stood in the middle of the floor.

"Better give me that sponge, Mister Davids," Amari said, holding her hand out. "Wouldn't want our little water nymph to dry out now, would we?"

I handed her the sponge gladly.

"I'll be back in a few minutes. Please, make yourself comfortable. I won't be long." She nodded towards a leatherback chair next to the fire and, as she closed the door behind her, I lowered myself into it, stretching my hands out towards the warmth. The shivering had stopped, but I still felt cold. I suspected that wouldn't change any time soon.

I swept my gaze across the study. With its dark wood shelves and thick Persian carpet, it seemed a comfortable refuge. I could see myself sitting here on a rainy day, getting lost in a good book.

Suddenly I was curious. I wandered over to the nearest shelf and examined the titles on the spines of the books. My eyes widened in amazement. Father would have loved this. *How To Trim a Harpy's Wings* stood next to *Of Winged Beasts* and *The Minotaur: Man or Monster?* Some books were in languages I recognised, although I've lost most of what little Greek or Latin I'd learned, but here and there were tomes that looked to be hundreds, if not thousands, of years old, written in languages that I could make no sense of whatsoever. I was about to pick up a book that looked particularly ancient, when Amari's voice rang out behind me.

"Please don't touch those, Mister Davids. They are incredibly old and one of a kind. It would be a tremendous loss if you damaged any of them."

I took a step backwards. "I know how to handle ancient texts, Miss Kerubo."

"Yes," she said as she walked past me and seated herself at the desk. "Your father taught you well, no doubt."

I gaped at her. "You knew my father?"

"I know of him," she corrected me. "Now, let's get down to business, shall we?" She pointed at a chair in front of her desk and I sat down.

"The Council is most grateful for the retrieval of this particular asrai. She has caused a few incidents over the years."

"Incidents?"

"Drownings."

"Ah."

"As such, the reward is a little more substantial than you would normally expect for a water nymph."

She handed me a cheque. For the second time this week, I had trouble believing my eyes.

"This is very generous. Is there an expiry date

on it?" I asked, making sure this time.

Amari laughed. "No, Mister Davids, but I can see you've been burned before. Don't worry, you can trust the CPPCC to deal fairly. Unlike some others you may have encountered recently."

"What is this CPPCC? If I'm going to be working for someone, I'd like to know what I'm getting myself into."

Amari looked at me, considering. Then she stood up suddenly. "Alright, Mister Davids -"

"Please, just call me Ambrose," I interrupted her as I also rose.

She smiled. "Ambrose. I rarely do this, but I like you, so I'm going to show you something few mortals know exists. Please follow me."

She ushered me out of her office and into a long corridor. Lights suspended from the ceiling every few feet illuminated walls of polished stone and a smooth stone floor. Somehow, I had the impression we were inside a mountain, as if a great weight was suspended above our heads.

"The CPPCC is an acronym for the Council for the Protection and Preservation of Cultural Creatures. In the mythical world, we're also known as the Elder Council," Amari explained as we walked. "The Council was formed centuries ago and has had many functions over the years, but for the last century or so, we have focused all our efforts on finding mythical creatures and housing them in a safe place."

We stopped in front of an iron door. Amari paused with her hand on the door handle. Her dark eyes studied me intently for a moment, her expression serious.

"What I'm about to show you is not something you should share with anyone else, Ambrose. Promise me you will keep this a secret."

"I promise," I said, my curiosity piqued.

"Then, as the Keeper, I welcome you to the Repository."

She opened the door and a cacophony of sounds assailed my ears. I stepped through onto a balcony that overlooked a huge cavern. The space was filled with enclosures, much like those at the London Zoo, but instead of monkeys and lions, the pens contained what were undeniably mythical creatures.

My jaw dropped as the creature in the nearest pen turned and looked at me. It was huge, at least ten feet tall, and in the middle of its bald, wrinkly head was a single, bloodshot eye. As we stared at each other, the creature's mouth twisted into a grin, exposing razor-sharp teeth. It licked its lips at me.

I shuddered and looked away, and saw a burst of sunlight penetrating the cavern ceiling from high above. I followed it downwards and blinked in amazement. Standing as if in a spotlight, a snow white unicorn grazed upon an enclosed grassy knoll. She whinnied and shook her mane, and I wanted to rush over and run my hand along her flanks.

"Look over there."

My eyes tracked the direction of Amari's pointed finger towards a recessed enclosure that was bathed in shadow. Water cascaded down rocks into a small pool. The asrai I had captured was sitting on the edge of the pool, staring up at me. Her pale face showed no emotion, but her eyes blazed. An icy shiver ran through me again and I wrapped my arms around myself for warmth.

"She might hold a grudge for a while," Amari said, "but she'll thank you for bringing her here in the end."

"Why do you keep them here?" I couldn't help but wonder. A twinge of guilt clouded my mind for a second at the sight of the caged asrai, and then I remembered how she had tried to drown me.

"For their protection. Few people know this, Ambrose, but each mythical creature is linked to one very specific trait. You know, unicorns have long been associated with-"

"Purity," I said, remembering Father's stories. "Which is why they only let virgins touch them."

"Right." Amari smiled, genuinely pleased at my knowledge. "So while some creatures share traits, unicorns are the only ones who bring purity to this world. Which is why it's vital that we preserve them. Can you imagine a world that no longer had purity in it?"

The question was rhetorical, I hoped, but it made me think. "How many unicorns do you have?"

"Only the one. Una has been with us for a very long time. As far as we know, she's the last of her kind." A hint of sadness tinged her words, and I looked at the unicorn in alarm. I suddenly understood the importance of the Repository and my work for the Council.

I nodded at the asrai, my contribution. "And what about her? What trait does she gift to the world?"

Amari laughed. "I thought that would be obvious. Desire, of course. The waters all over the world are filled with nymphs, so little chance of that trait ever vanishing."

I grinned. "So what happens now?"

"You are now officially an employee of the Elder Council, Ambrose. You form part of our pool of Freelance Procurement Specialists. Now you bring us more creatures. Sometimes we'll send you an assignment, but we'll take whatever you can bring us. The more creatures we can preserve, the better the world will be."

I nodded in understanding.

"I'll see you soon, Ambrose Davids," Amari said. Then she uttered another strange word and the world melted away in a white light. I closed my eyes against the brightness.

⚹ ⚹ ⚹

The sun setting over the Thames painted the South Bank in shades of red and orange. I was on my way to one of my favourite restaurants to meet up with some friends. It had been quite some time since I'd had a night out and I was looking forward to seeing everyone again. After the incident at work, and then the breakup, I had avoided company, but now I felt ready to socialise again.

My mobile rang and I grimaced as the caller ID identified the number.

"Hello, Mother," I answered.

"Ambrose, your sister tells me you have a new job. Is this true?"

I sighed. "Yes. It's freelance. They call me a Procurement Specialist."

"Freelance? And since when do you know anything about procurement? Don't tell me you're someone's personal shopper now. I didn't send you to business school so you can buy shoes for the rich and famous."

"That's not what I'm doing," I said, counting to ten under my breath. "Besides, it pays well. You'll be happy to know that all my bills have been paid this month and I am completely debt-free."

"Ambrose!" I pulled the phone away from my ear lest my mother's shriek do permanent damage. "That's wonderful. This disaster has taught you one lesson then, at least."

I was just about to step off the sidewalk next

to the river to cross the street when something in the water under Tower Bridge drew my attention.

"I have to go, Mother. We'll talk again soon."

"Ambrose-"

I disconnected the call, too intrigued to worry about manners right then. I stared at the water until I saw the head bobbing up to the surface again. It was a seal. Its brown pelt gleamed almost golden in the fading light. As I watched, the seal swam closer to the embankment. It looked around and I ducked out of sight. When I looked again, the animal was gone, but a naked teenage boy stood on the shore, his golden brown hair dripping water down his back. He scrambled towards a drainage pipe.

I smiled at my luck. Who would have thought there really were selkies in the Thames? I gripped the whistle in my pocket.

"Hey, Davids?"

I nearly leaped six feet into the air. I'd forgotten why I was here. I turned around to see a bunch of my mates standing just outside the restaurant door. They beckoned and I hurried over.

I shook hands with everyone, grinning and hugging. The group parted and my heart lurched into my throat. Rachel stood there, talking to one of our friends. Her face lit up when she saw me and her smile ignited all sorts of conflicting emotions. I hadn't known she would be here. I stood frozen as if I'd just looked into the eyes of Medusa.

"Davids!" A hand clapped me on the back. I blinked, returning to the present.

"Jake," I acknowledged my old squash partner.

He shook my hand enthusiastically. "Good to see you back in the land of the living, Davids," he said, grinning from ear to ear. "We need to get a game going again. You're getting fat in your retirement."

"Sure, Jake," I said, laughing.

"Let's go in and I'll tell you the most hair-raising story you'll ever hear. Picture this: an evening so late it's actually early at the stock exchange, the Hindenburg omen, and a salesman that wouldn't take no for an answer."

Pausing at the top of the steps, I shot a look over my shoulder towards the river again. The boy would be long gone by now. But I knew about him now. I would find him again later.

Someone brushed against my arm as they passed me on the steps.

"Coming, Ambrose?"

It was Rachel.

I nodded, slowly, hesitantly, and followed her into the restaurant. My luck had changed recently. Who knew what would happen next?

PART 2

BANSHEE'S WAIL

When I came to Paris to forget about love, I hadn't quite expected to find myself in the arms of another woman on the very first night.

And yet here I was, dancing a jig with a pretty girl under the first of the Pont Neuf's many arches. Moonlight cast eerie shadows in the mist blowing off the Seine, enveloping us in a world of our own. A strangely silent world where the music was all in our heads, and yet we danced to the same rhythm; she with reckless abandon, barefoot and apparently with no regard for bruises or blisters, while my two left feet, ensconced in my lucky four-leaf clover trainers, somehow kept pace without mishap.

She laughed as I twirled her from one arm to the other, her wispy white dress twisting about her body while her long platinum hair flowed in the breeze. Grey eyes sparkled and I smiled back. It felt good to forget for a little while.

Trust me to travel to the City of Love to try to forget about the woman I had left behind in London. Not that she would give me a chance to forget about her. Even now, my mobile phone was vibrating in my jacket pocket. One guess who'd be calling me, and if you guessed my ex-girlfriend Rachel, you'd be right. I ignored the buzzing and concentrated on the steps of the dance again.

Two more pirouettes and then the girl let me go. I gasped for breath, grinning like an idiot with sweat dripping down my temples, feeling warm again for once. I clutched at a cramp in my side, then quickly straightened up as I saw her watching me, suddenly serious again. Her pale eyes seemed to bore into my soul and for a second I let myself wonder about the absurdity of dancing with strange women beneath bridges in the moonlight.

You'd think I would know better by now.

Finally, her face relaxed into a smile again and she waved me on. I exhaled loudly, a sudden surge of relief releasing a tension in my shoulders I hadn't even realised was there. I bowed courteously, like some awkward gentleman of yore, before continuing on my way towards my hotel on the Ile Saint-Louis.

I paused to admire the Notre Dame in the moonlight. The famous cathedral, with its imposing architecture, loomed over me like Mount Doom. It felt like eyes were watching me; weighing and measuring, and finding me wanting.

I shuddered.

The atmosphere had been very different this morning when I had passed through the cathedral's grand doors, fresh off the early train from London. Its hallowed halls had been filled with tourists then, more than usual apparently, as pilgrims from all across the country had come to see the special exhibition. The jostling and the queuing were worth it, though, to see the legendary Cross of Calais with my own eyes. The bejewelled masterpiece had glinted in the rainbow light cascading down from the Rose window, sparkling golden and setting my imagination on fire. It was said that the Cross could heal any ailment. I wondered if it could lift my curse, but locked away beneath a bulletproof dome of glass, there'd been no way of knowing for sure.

Another chill ran through me and I wrapped my jacket tightly about myself, leaving the cathedral and its ominous mood behind.

It didn't take long to reach my hotel, a grand

old building that cost more per night than an entire month's rent for my little flat in Bayswater did. I nodded at the clerk at the desk before taking the lift to my room. Closing the door behind me, I turned the heating up and climbed into bed.

I yawned. It had been a long day of sightseeing, but there was time for reading just one more entry in Father's journal. I opened the heavy leather-bound tome where I had last left off at the letter G and read for about ten minutes before my eyelids became too heavy to hold up. I put the book down and turned the light off.

The last thing I heard as I drifted off to sleep was my mobile phone buzzing once more.

※※※

The damn phone buzzed again, setting the cutlery on the little bistro table to jingling. I picked it up and glanced at the caller ID. Rachel. Who else? I let it go over to voicemail and dropped the phone into my jacket pocket, where it continued to vibrate and sour my mood.

Rachel had been calling me almost non-stop since I had dropped everything to come to Paris on short notice. Apparently, she didn't understand the concept of needing some space to think about us.

Did I really want there to be an *us*?

Ever since that night at the restaurant, she had tried to convince me to get back together again. I wasn't sure what had made her change her mind. I was still almost as disreputable as I had been when I'd lost my job. On the surface, nothing much had changed.

But in reality - everything was different now.

I'd seen things few people would ever believe: nymphs, selkies, unicorns, the stuff of legends.

They were all real. And they lived among us. Hell, I played a game of squash with a leprechaun every Tuesday. It didn't get any weirder than that. I doubt Rachel would find me half as respectable as she wanted me to be if she learned what my new job really entailed - finding and catching mythical creatures for a mysterious menagerie.

A cold shiver ran through me, and I suppressed the urge to place a hand on my chest. Instead, I pulled my jacket even closer around myself and drew a scarf out from my backpack, wrapping it tightly around my neck. I glanced out the window. The sky had turned a little murky and it looked like it might start raining soon.

Unfortunately, this chill had nothing to do with the weather outside.

The asrai's curse was still going strong and I wasn't sure how I was going to make it through winter this year. I dreaded the first snowfall and what it would do to my already freezing digits. Amari had said there was no cure for the nymph's touch, so I had to make peace with the fact that I would be cold for the rest of my life. Perhaps I should move to Jamaica, or Africa, or somewhere along the equator where the weather at least would be in my favour.

"Le Monde, monsieur?" a waiter interrupted my melancholy reverie, offering me a selection of newspapers.

"Anything in English?" I asked.

He thrust *The Times* at me, nearly knocking my boiling cup of tea off the table. Ignoring the waiter, I took a sip and sighed contently as the warm liquid glided down my throat.

I wasn't really interested in the news, but I skimmed the headlines just in case anything out of the ordinary pointed me toward something the Council might be interested in. Not that I needed the money right now. My first pay cheque had been extremely generous. Enough to keep me going for many months if I didn't live too extravagantly. But you never knew.

I flipped past the political features - honestly, things were weird enough without worrying about what was going on in the US right now - and paged towards the back where the science and local news were reported.

A bold headline caught my attention. *Let There Be Light!* I read with growing fascination about a new type of LED light that generated artificial sunlight. The Solar Simulator, as its inventor had dubbed it, replicated all the inherent properties of sunlight so realistically that it even tricked the brain into thinking that its glow came directly from the sun.

I sat back, cradling my cup of tea for warmth. If I had one of those, I could whip it out whenever I felt cold. I scanned the article and almost whooped with joy when I saw the LED was already for sale. I needed to keep an eye out for it. It was worth a shot, and probably a lot less hassle than moving halfway around the world after the real sun.

A short buzz sounded from my pocket. A text message this time. I pulled the phone out and looked at the display.

-- You can't keep avoiding my calls. We need to talk.--

I thrust the phone back into my pocket without responding and signalled the waiter for the bill. The man's animosity was almost palpable as he brought me the slip. I guess I could hardly blame him. Apart from being English, I also committed the offence of looking completely out of place in this rather posh café, what with my stubbly chin, tweed jacket, jeans and white trainers.

I took my wallet out and watched the waiter's eyes widen as I riffled through the stack of hundred euro bills. I stood up to leave and pushed a fifty into his hand.

"Keep the change."

I was out the door before he regained his composure.

I looked up at the clouds gathering in the sky. Murky had turned into threatening by now. I had better find something to do indoors before I got drenched. Perhaps it was time to go see the lady with the enigmatic smile.

※※※

"That's it?" I mumbled. "This is what all the fuss is about?"

Honestly, the Mona Lisa was highly overrated. It had taken me the better part of an hour just to get inside the Louvre, luckily entering its glass pyramid just as the first raindrops started falling, and another hour or two of wandering around inside before I finally found the room containing the minuscule marvel. The place was packed with tourists, all elbowing each other to get a closer look at Leonardo da Vinci's masterpiece. To say it underwhelmed me would be an understatement.

"Ambrose?"

I turned towards the familiar voice and smiled at the woman wearing black-rimmed hipster glasses standing beside me. "Detective Miller. What a pleasant surprise."

"Oh please, Ambrose, I thought we'd moved past the formalities long ago. Call me Sarah. How did your industrial strength sponge work out for you?"

My hand strayed towards my chest at the

memory of the asrai's touch, but I fiddled with my scarf instead, pretending to think about it. "It did the job quite admirably."

Sarah laughed, and I had to keep myself from staring at the twinkle in her moss-green eyes. "Glad to hear it. So, what brings you to Paris?"

I exhaled loudly. Where to start? "Oh, just a quick breakaway," I replied evasively. "You know what they say about change..."

"That it's painful and should be avoided at all costs?" Sarah teased.

I chuckled. "Maybe."

She turned towards the tiny painting that was the centre of everybody's attention. "You enjoy art, do you?"

"Not in the slightest," I admitted. "I like it if it's pretty. Otherwise, it's probably art."

Another laugh. "Then you're definitely in the wrong part of Paris, my friend."

"It's not that I don't like it," I said, suddenly feeling sheepish. "I guess I just don't understand it. One painting looks pretty much the same as all the rest to me."

Sarah's hands swept through her dark hair, pulling it back into a makeshift ponytail before releasing it again. I watched, mesmerised, as it cascaded across her shoulders.

"It might just be your lucky day today then," she said, drawing my eyes back to hers. "I'm going to give you a tour of my favourite pieces."

"Um... okay, thanks, I guess," I said, not really sure if lucky was the right word.

She laughed again. "Don't look so alarmed. Trust me, you're going to find this fascinating." She grabbed my hand and pulled me out of the room.

Sarah's tour was indeed interesting, although I admit my focus was less on the art than on her hand in mine. I watched her face light up whenever we reached a piece she liked. Her eyes sparkled as she regaled me with tales of Renaissance artists, painting pictures with her words that were even more vivid than theirs. Her enthusiasm was infectious and, although each new painting she showed me was still baffling at first, I hung on her every word while she explained why she loved it so much. I was entranced.

I stopped of my own accord in front of a large painting depicting an ethereal young woman holding a hand out to a man who, frankly, looked terrified at the sight of her. The woman's white clothes wafted about her body in a way that reminded me eerily of a Victorian dress spread out around a body in a lake.

"Ah, yes," Sarah said as she joined me. "*La Dame Blanche*. She's a figure from folklore."

"Not one I'd like to meet, judging by the look on that guy's face."

"No, not if the tales are true. The White Lady invites young men to dance with her. If they do, she lets them go unharmed. But if they don't... well."

"Who wouldn't want to dance with that?" I joked, nodding at the ghostly girl in the painting. It suddenly occurred to me that I had done exactly that last night, and my arms broke out in goose bumps. Coincidence. It had to be.

"You know French folklore has much in common with Celtic myths? The White Lady is France's version of a banshee. If she shrieks at you, you'd better know trouble is heading your way," Sarah said, an ironic smile playing across her lips.

I looked at her as she studied the picture. "How do you know all this?"

Sarah turned towards me. "Everybody knows

about banshees, Ambrose."

"No, all of this." I held out my arms to indicate the museum in general.

"Oh," she said, adjusting her glasses. "I used to study art. Before I joined the police force. I actually come to Paris every year just to visit the Louvre."

I gaped at her. "Just the Louvre?"

She nodded, a faint blush suddenly colouring her cheeks. "Can you believe I've never even been up the Eiffel tower?"

My phone buzzed in my pocket. I checked it out of habit and winced at the message popping up on the screen.

--We're meant to be together, you know that. Let's talk about this.--

"Right," I said, thrusting the phone back as deep as it would go and striding off towards the nearest window. The clouds were mostly gone and the sun shone wanly outside. I turned towards Sarah again. "I'm taking you sightseeing."

⁂

Sarah loved the Jardin des Tuileries with its statues and manicured lawns. We ate ice cream while riding on the carousel at the Place de la Concorde and then walked along the Seine, admiring the houseboats. She wanted to take a cruise on the river, but I took one look at the water, shuddered, and steered her towards that most famous of Parisian landmarks on foot instead. By the time we had taken the lift to the second level of the Eiffel tower, the sun was dipping towards the horizon. We ended the evening with dinner at a little three-star Michelin restaurant.

"You really know how to show someone a good time," Sarah said as the waiter poured us each a glass of wine.

"Paris isn't meant to be explored alone," I answered. "I'm glad I could see it with you."

She smiled and placed her hand on mine. "Why *are* you here alone?" Her green gaze was intense.

Just then, my phone buzzed again, and I couldn't help but glance at the text.

--Thinking of you. Call me.--

"It's... complicated," I said with a sigh. "Something happened at work a while ago, something that cost me my job. Rachel, my girlfriend at the time, couldn't face the humiliation, I guess. She dumped me soon after." Sarah frowned, but she nodded as if she wanted to know more. "And then... I got a new job. And now she wants to get back together again."

"And do you want to get back together again?"

I ran a hand through my hair, considering. "No, I don't think so. But that's why I'm here. To think it through. I bought her a ring, you know. Before it all happened."

"That's pretty serious." Sarah removed her hand from mine and took a sip of wine, her green eyes focussed on me and her gaze intense. I knew it probably wasn't a good idea to be discussing all of this with her, here, now, after one of the best days of my life. But I felt safe with Sarah. It didn't feel like she was judging me. And it was good to get it all off my chest.

"It felt serious then. It doesn't anymore. How can things ever be the same when I know she could leave me just as easily as that?"

Sarah nodded in understanding. "What are you doing now? When I ran your file, it only said you were unemployed."

"You ran my file?" I suddenly remembered that Sarah was a detective. How could I ever explain to her what I did for a living? She'd laugh in my face or have me committed. Possibly both.

"Just after that incident at the lake. I needed to know who I was dealing with. If you were a serial killer or not." Her eyes twinkled mischievously. "Luckily your profile didn't come up with any red flags."

"You thought I was a serial killer?"

"No, but I had to make sure. Someone drowns in that lake regularly. Men usually, but that didn't mean the killer, if there were one, couldn't make an exception."

"I can't believe you thought I could be a killer."

"I never did, but I had to make sure. Part of the job description, you know."

I eyed her suspiciously. Was she making fun of me again?

"How did you become a detective anyway," I asked, trying to move the focus away from me. "Didn't you say you studied art?"

A frown swept across her face and she looked away, as if remembering something painful. "My brother went missing a few years ago."

I felt that familiar twinge whenever I thought about my father. "I'm sorry," I said. This time it was my hand enveloping hers.

"It was a long time ago," she said, as if that made any difference. "He was taking a year off to travel, so it happened abroad. The police couldn't find anything, couldn't tell us what happened. Just another crazy traveller who'd disappeared. They said he'd probably show up, stoned on a beach somewhere, but he never did. It left a hole, you know, not knowing."

I nodded. I knew all too well.

"Anyway. I thought that if I could help somebody else find someone they had lost, it would make things better. It wouldn't bring Ben back, of course, but I would have made a difference in someone else's life at least. I'm the youngest detective on the Force, you know. I wanted it badly, so I worked my butt off and gained my badge in less than two years." She adjusted her glasses and flashed me a sardonic smile. "Of course, that was before I knew how much paperwork came with the job. Had I known that from the start I would have stuck to painting."

I grinned.

"I'm a freelance writer," I said. "You wanted to know what I do. I write."

She cheered up immediately. "Anything I would have read?"

"Well, there was this article in *The Times* about the nymphs in Greek mythology -"

"I read that!" she said, her face lighting up. "It barely scratched the surface about their depiction in fine art. It was very disappointing."

"I told you I know nothing about art," I said, a little defensively.

She smiled again, a gesture of peace. "I didn't know you'd written that. I would have remembered if you had, Ambrose Davids."

"I use a pseudonym," I admitted. "My father was pretty well known in classical circles. I didn't want to have anything I wrote ridiculed because of his reputation."

"What happened to him?"

I sighed. "He went missing too."

Sarah's face paled visibly. "You're kidding." She sat back in her chair, momentarily at a loss for words. "What are the odds of us having this in common?"

"Slim to none," I joked.

"I really wish we didn't. I wish it were something silly, like a preference for superhero movies or an obsession with chocolate. Tell me you love Adele too," she demanded.

"Oh, I'm her biggest fan," I said with a straight face, before we both burst out laughing.

※※※

It was after midnight by the time I said goodbye to Sarah in front of her hotel in the first *arrondissement* close to the Louvre. I wanted to kiss her then. I moved closer, breathing in the citrusy scent of her perfume, but when I looked into those green eyes, any semblance of bravery fled with the wind whipping her brown hair about her face.

"Give me your phone," she demanded.

I had almost forgotten about it. I handed it over quite willingly and she tapped at the screen for a few seconds.

"Goodnight, Ambrose," she said as she pushed it back into my hands, before skipping up the steps and disappearing into the hotel. I looked down at the phone and felt a smile spread across my face. She'd given me her number.

I pointedly ignored the flashing blue light that showed that I still had unread messages and dropped the phone back into my jacket pocket. My head was filled with thoughts of Sarah; the way she had held my hand in the museum, her infectious laugh, her quick wit. I felt intoxicated.

I was so lost in thought that I hardly realised I had reached the Pont Neuf again on my way back to my own hotel. A thick fog lay across the bridge and it took me a few moments to notice the figure barring my path.

A chill ran down my spine, and it had nothing to do with the asrai's curse this time.

A ghostly woman hovered in front of me, mist eddying around her feet. Her hair floated around her head in the dead still air. It was so quiet I could hear my own ragged breathing.

I fumbled in my pocket for the silver whistle I always kept on my person now. I swore under my breath as I dropped it on the ground and quickly bent to retrieve it. When I looked up again, clutching the whistle in my white-knuckled fist as if it would protect me, the woman was gone.

I took a hesitant step forward, wondering if I'd had one too many glasses of wine and my imagination was playing tricks on me.

Then the mist swirled and parted.

The knot in my stomach untwisted itself and a sigh of relief escaped my lips. It was the girl from last night, the one I had danced with under the moonlight.

She beckoned me towards her.

I tucked the whistle back into my pocket and took a few tentative steps forward. She held an arm out to me. I took her hand in mine. She curtsied formally, and I returned an awkward bow. Silently, our bodies came together in the steps of a waltz.

I knew immediately that something was different tonight. Last night's jig had been fun, a frivolous, carefree dance with a pretty girl. Last night I had been oblivious, but tonight I knew better. There would be no excuse for a bruised toe or a misstep. Tonight, my life really did depend on how well I danced.

If only I had paid more attention when Cassie had made me watch all those hours of Strictly Come Dancing while we were still sharing a flat.

Palms slippery with sweat and a bottom lip chewed raw with concentration, it felt like endless nights passed while I was locked in this embrace, dancing to a silent tune that dictated the graceful movements of our bodies. The dance ended when I dipped her elegantly, her long platinum locks nearly touching the pavement.

I helped her up and she released me. I took a step backwards, gasping for breath as she studied me with pale, calculating eyes. Finally, she curtsied again and I bowed in kind. Then she nodded, and I stumbled past her and staggered across the bridge.

The Notre Dame towered above me before I came to my senses again. There was no doubt in my mind now. I had danced with the White Lady twice now, and I had passed the test both times. I had danced with death and escaped unscathed.

I glanced down at my white trainers. They really were lucky. I'd better drop in on Daniel when I was back in London and thank him again for making me buy them.

A shout suddenly rang through the air. A woman's voice. I heard the sounds of a scuffle and it seemed to be coming from inside the grounds next to the cathedral. I hardly hesitated, scaling the iron fence enclosing the Notre Dame in one leap.

I hesitated on the other side, though. Mist swirled, casting creepy shadows along the foot of the Gothic structure. My skin crawled. I felt eyes on my back.

There! I raced towards the noise I had heard and stopped short, stunned by the scene that confronted me.

A woman was pinned against the wall of the cathedral. Her attacker, bathed in shadows, loomed over her. She opened her mouth to scream, but no sound came out. She seemed frozen in fear.

Adrenaline pumped through my veins, spurring me into action and I raced towards her, leaping at her attacker. Sharp pain shot through my shoulder as I crunched into solid rock. I looked up into the face of my adversary and my throat went dry.

It was not human.

A monster with long fangs and two horns protruding from the top of its skull growled at me. It straightened to its full height, standing up on clawed feet, and stretched out its wings. It was enormous.

"You've got to be kidding me," I said.

"Help me," the woman whimpered, still pressed up against the wall, trying to stay as far away as possible from the monster's talons.

Father's neat handwriting flashed before my eyes. *Gargoyle: guardian. A fearsome beast that will stop at nothing to protect its charge. Proceed with caution.*

The monster lunged at me and I scuttled backwards, just out of reach. Wind whipped past my face as its claws raked past me. There was no time to think. I ran. I was across the fence in one smooth jump. The monster bellowed, and I risked a glance behind me. It had turned back to the woman, ignoring my escape.

I halted my retreat. I had hoped she would make a run for it while its attention was focussed on me, but she seemed rooted to the sport, too afraid to move. I looked around for something I could use as a weapon.

My eyes were drawn to a white cat shimmering in the moonlight. It sat on a fencepost, watching me with pale grey eyes.

Weird.

I renewed my search, scanning the souvenir shops lining the buildings across the road. Maybe a commemorative letter opener?

Then a light from a window display in a tiny shop hemmed in between a café and a postcard stand caught my attention. Luck was on my side, this time. It was the new Solar Simulator I had read about in the newspaper this morning. Perfect.

I sprinted across the street and rammed my already bruised shoulder into the window. Glass shattered around me as I tumbled head over heels into the shop. An alarm went off.

Shit.

No time to waste. I grabbed the light and ran back to the cathedral, leaping across the fence and tumbling back into the shadows.

I was too late. The monster held the woman aloft in one of its stone claws. Her feet dangled as she struggled in vain to loosen its grasp around her neck.

"Hey, ugly!" I shouted. The gargoyle turned its grotesque head my way and, just as its eyes met mine, I turned the Solar Simulator on.

A sharp beam of simulated sunlight hit the creature square in the chest. It bellowed, shattering the surrounding silence. Its claws opened and the woman fell to the ground. She scrambled away from the creature, gasping for breath.

I watched, fascinated, as its body stiffened and congealed into solid stone. The bellow ended abruptly as its face hardened, revealing large fangs in its gaping mouth.

The woman climbed to her feet.

"Are you alright?" I asked.

She stepped into the light and I finally had the opportunity to see what she looked like. Her long black hair was tied back in a ponytail and she was dressed all in black: leather trousers, leather jacket, a tight-fitting top. She bent to pick something up and my mouth fell open as she tucked the Cross of

Calais into her trousers.

"You men," she said in a thick French accent, a half-grin twisting one corner of her mouth upwards. "You always need to save the damsel in distress." She pulled a gun from behind her back and levelled it at me. "Who's in distress now?"

The white cat suddenly sprinted past between us and we both jumped as a terrifying shriek broke the silence. The hair on the back of my neck stood up. If that wasn't a banshee's wail, then I was a pixie's pet.

What I *was*, I suddenly realised, was a dead man.

I tossed the Solar Simulator at the woman and dived to the ground. A shot rang out and I flattened myself against the ground. Then, the splintering sounds of the light crashing to the ground and footsteps running away.

I looked up, amazed that I was still alive. The woman was gone and the world had once again been plunged into darkness. It was just me and the stone gargoyle. Did its talon just twitch?

I pushed myself to my feet again and pulled the silver whistle out of my jacket pocket. It was still strange not to hear anything when I blew on it.

There! Its wing definitely moved that time.

"Couldn't this have waited until morning, Ambrose?"

I turned to see Amari, the current Keeper of Exotic Animals, stepping out of the shadows. She was barefoot and wearing a leopard-print kimono. Her hair looked tousled, as if she'd been sleeping.

Amari stopped short when she saw the gargoyle, her lips forming a silent oh.

"I think it's waking up," I said, nervously watching for any movement.

"Well." Amari grinned. "This is quite a prize.

An actual gargoyle? Not just a stone carving?"

"As real as this bruise on my shoulder," I replied, wincing as I moved my arm around.

Amari's dark eyes lit up like a kid's in a candy store. She took a step towards the creature, but paused as I placed a hand on her arm.

"It was trying to protect the cathedral, Amari. I thought I was helping someone, but it turns out I was helping her steal a relic."

Amari frowned as she considered my words. Then she shrugged and pulled away from me. She laid a hand on the creature and said: "Our need is greater." A beam of white light enveloped her and I closed my eyes against the brightness. When I looked again, they were both gone.

"Arrêtez!"

Shit.

I turned around to see two police officers pointing guns at me. Slowly, I lifted my hands into the air. The last thing I needed was more bullets whizzing past my head.

I grimaced as a police officer pulled my arms down and wrenched them behind my back, sending a stab of pain up my injured shoulder. He slapped handcuffs around my wrists and then prodded me towards his companion, who grabbed me by the arm and pushed me towards the open gate in the cathedral's fence.

A handful of cop cars were parked outside, lights flashing. People were milling about the cathedral doors, their faces drawn and clouds of cigarette smoking hovering above them. I guess they knew the Cross had been stolen.

This was going to be tricky to explain.

⁂

Well, I supposed things could be worse.

I wasn't sure how, though.

The sole extent of my French language skills was limited to asking how much a croissant cost, where the loo was, and whether you could speak English. Apparently, the French police chief's English wasn't much better. In fact, there had been so much miscommunication during that interrogation session that I was fairly certain they now think I stole the Cross of Calais. And probably everything else gone missing in the last century or so, from the Kruger millions to Amelia Earhart's plane.

I shuffled around on the cold cement bench in my tiny cell, unable to get comfortable. I folded my arms across my knees and laid my head down. Might as well try to get some sleep at this ungodly hour. I might be here for some time. I'd used up my one phone call to contact Sarah, but she hadn't been able to reassure me much. No jurisdiction in Paris, apparently.

To be honest, things looked rather bleak at the moment.

At least they had confiscated my phone. I could finally get some peace and quiet from all the incessant text messages pestering me. I wondered what Rachel would say if she knew I was locked up in a containment cell right now. Probably run so fast a lightning bird couldn't keep up.

The lock of my cell door clicked and I looked up, surprised to see an officer wave me out. I stumbled to my feet and hurried through the door. Sarah stood just outside. Her smile was like a Solar Simulator for my heart.

"Ambrose!"

She gave me a quick hug before hustling me through the corridors of the police station. She handled all the paperwork, talking non-stop in fluent French to the police officer on duty, while I retrieved my belongings. I tucked my mobile into my jacket pocket again, pulled the silver whistle's chord around my neck and wrapped my scarf over it, and then we were out the door before I could say *so long and thanks for all the fish*.

"Sarah!" I said, laughing uncertainly as we hurried away. "What just happened? What did you do?"

"I asked them to check the CCTV footage," she answered as she pointed upwards. I looked up and saw for the first time that there were cameras mounted at regular intervals on the building walls. "There was a lot of static on the feed from the Notre Dame, and everything was in shadow," she said, steering me along. "We could hardly make anything out. But it was clear enough that there was a woman who shot at you and then ran away. I managed to convince the police chief that you were a victim and not an accomplice."

She stopped then and turned towards me, her eyes serious. "You *were* a victim, right?"

"Absolutely," I said. "Wrong place, wrong time."

She nodded and exhaled deeply, clearly relieved, as a smile returned to her lips. "I thought so. I'm a pretty good judge of character, usually." She took my arm and started walking briskly again. "But we need to get you out of the country as soon as possible, just until things have cooled down a bit. I don't know if you know what happened at the cathedral?"

I shook my head, feigning ignorance.

"The Cross of Calais was stolen," she explained. "It's a priceless artefact. Just the fact that you were on the grounds at that time would normally be enough to keep you detained indefinitely. I had to talk really fast to persuade the police chief that he didn't want an international incident on his hands on top of everything else too." A frown creased her forehead and she glanced sideways at me as we hurried onwards. "You must be the luckiest guy I know to walk away unharmed from that. The feed was blurry, but I recognised the woman's face, and she's bad news. Her name is Monique Tesserier and she's wanted by Interpol. Antiques smuggler."

I stumbled, but caught myself before I tripped and fell. Lucky indeed! But whether that luck was good or bad was certainly up for debate.

"Misty tonight, isn't it?" Sarah said.

We had reached the Pont Neuf and a white fog was suddenly billowing around us. I groaned. Not again.

"Not tonight," I called politely as the White Lady stepped out of the haze. "I have company."

I felt Sarah's eyes on me, but I kept my gaze on the woman blocking our path across the bridge. She said something in French that I didn't understand.

"She says she has a message for you," Sarah translated. "Ambrose, who's this? Is she a prostitute?" She sounded scandalised.

"No, no, nothing like that," I hastily reassured her. I reached for the whistle around my neck and saw the white woman's eyes widen. She held a hand out to me, half placating, half demanding. Her words were urgent.

"She says she saved your life tonight," Sarah whispered.

I remembered the banshee's shriek that had startled the woman in black, making her miss her target. I nodded my thanks, letting my hand drop away from the whistle.

"But she says you're cursed," Sarah continued. The woman said something and Sarah gasped. She repeated the words in French, a questioning tone at the end. The woman nodded and Sarah turned to me, apprehension in her voice. "A dead man walking."

I placed a hand on my heart, shooting a questioning look at the white woman. She nodded again.

"Ask her if she knows of a cure," I said.

The woman nodded, and Sarah translated: "Touch of frost, breath of fire. What does that mean, Ambrose?"

"Thank you," I said to the white woman. She smiled sadly and lifted her hand in farewell. The mist swirled again and she disappeared into it.

"What is going on, Ambrose?" Sarah demanded. "You're a dead man walking? Are you in over your head? What have you gotten me into?" She looked furious, her green eyes blazing behind her black-rimmed glasses.

There was no sane way to explain the truth to Sarah. She was a detective. She needed cold hard facts and I didn't have any. I said the first thing that came to mind. "It's a game."

"A game?"

"Yes, um…" I grasped at straws. "Role-playing. LARP'ing. Have you heard of that?"

"Live action role-playing?" she asked, incredulously. "You're one of those nerds that dress up as elves and stuff and pretend you live in Middle-Earth?"

"Geeks," I replied. "Nerds do math. Geeks do fan things."

Judging by the look on Sarah's face, I might have done better telling her the truth.

She suddenly burst out laughing. "Is that what happened earlier tonight? A game gone wrong?"

I nodded sheepishly, feeling heat rise to my cheeks. The last thing I wanted right now was for Sarah to think me a fool, but telling her the truth was out of the question. At least this way, she didn't think I was some sort of criminal.

She tucked her arm into mine. "Come on, let's get your things and get you back home."

※※※

It felt good waking up in my own apartment again. I'd taken the first Eurostar out of Paris early this morning, jumped on a Tube home and stumbled into bed just as the sun started rising. I glanced at my mobile phone to see what time it was. Almost noon. The little blue light was still flashing.

I ignored it. I would deal with that after I'd showered.

When I emerged from the steaming bathroom half an hour later, I felt like a new man, and one that was warm for a change. It was best not to think about the fact that I might not be welcome in France anymore, or that a harbinger of death thought my days were numbered, or that the only reason I wasn't shivering was because the central heating was set to boiling point, or that I still had a persistent ex-girlfriend to deal with.

Speaking of…

"Hello, Ambrose," Rachel said as I stepped into my living room.

She was immaculately dressed as always: a plaid-printed mini skirt, white blouse, high heels. Rose-scented perfume hung so thickly in the air it surprised me I hadn't choked on it earlier.

And here I was, bare-chested and wrapped only in a damp towel that covered the bare minimum required of decency. I hadn't exactly expected company. She stared openly at my exposed chest and I regretted not buying the extra-large bath sheets instead. I crossed my arms over my chest and tried to act nonchalant.

"You haven't even read any of my messages. I'm hurt." Her cherry-red lips pouted in a way that I used to find adorable. For some reason, it just seemed juvenile now.

Embarrassment faded away and was replaced by anger as I noticed she was scrolling through the text messages on my phone.

"How did you get in?" I asked, taking the mobile from her. Tact had never been my strong point.

She dangled the key I had given her months ago between two fingers. I held out my hand and she placed it in my palm, a tightness about her eyes betraying her annoyance.

"You know, Am, just because we had a little misunderstanding doesn't mean we can't make it work again."

"You dumped me when I lost my job, Rachel. When I was at my lowest, you left me without so much as a backwards glance." And you took my signed first edition of The Silmarillion with you. That really was unforgivable.

Rachel twirled a finger through her blonde ringlets. "But you're working again, right?" she said.

"That's not the -" I sighed and took a step backwards, putting some distance between us. I pulled my fingers through my wet hair, taking a deep breath. I'd thought I knew what I wanted. I'd thought I wanted the suit and tie, the corner office and the dream girl. But as it turns out, I don't want any of those things now. Not anymore, not after all I'd seen.

Not after Paris.

Maybe I'd been lucky to get fired. And maybe Paris had been a good idea after all.

She took a step towards me.

"There's someone else."

Rachel stopped as if she'd been turned into a pillar of salt. I guess it had never occurred to her that I might not actually want to get back together again. She'd never been good at hiding her emotions, and I could see her thoughts playing out across her face now. There was confusion, followed by disbelief, culminating in red-hot anger.

"Well," she said finally. She picked her handbag up from where she'd left it on the couch. "Probably for the best." She turned away from me and walked towards the door, her heels clacking on the parquet flooring. "I wouldn't want to be associated with a drug addict, anyway."

"Wait, what?" I'd thought she might invent an excuse to save face, but this was not what I'd had in mind.

She pointed at my chest. "Just look at you," Rachel said, her anger turning into what might actually be genuine regret. "I'm sorry that you needed to get shot up to get over us, Ambrose, but it just won't do. You need help. Goodbye." A freezing wind blew through the door as she slammed it behind herself.

Confused, I returned to the bathroom and wiped the steam from the mirror over the sink. My mouth fell open in disbelief. A dark blue shadow, like a brand-new bruise, covered my chest across the heart and from it streaked angry ice-blue veins, like lightning bolts criss-crossing a stormy sky. I touched it tentatively and quickly pulled my finger back again - my skin was freezing and the indigo patch across my heart was hard as ice.

A spasm shook my body.

I stumbled over to the shower and turned the hot water back on. Remembering the phone in my other hand, I dialled Cassie's number. It went over to voicemail.

Shivers shot uncontrollably through me. My knees gave in and I fell to the ground, dropping the phone just as my sister's perky voice asked me to leave a message after the beep.

The last thing I saw was steam fogging up the mirror again, and then the world faded into darkness.

Part 3

Asrai's Curse

"Ambrose? Oh, gods, Ambrose!"

I opened my eyes. The world was hazy and wet.

It took me a moment to realise I was lying on my back in the shower. The last thing I remembered was the sneer on my ex-girlfriend's face as she slammed the door behind her. And my body covered in blue veins.

Hot water splashed across my face and into my mouth, rudely reminding me of my present predicament. I spluttered, coughing up warm liquid that did nothing to still the uncontrollable shivers that wracked my body.

A warm hand gripped my arm and helped me to a sitting position. Wide green eyes filled my vision. Cassie was here, and she was blowing frantically on a silver whistle, her face red with the effort.

I wanted to tell her that it was no use. That whistle wasn't going to make any noise, no matter how hard she blew on it.

Another shiver spasmed through my body. I rolled onto my side, glad I was still wrapped in the tiny towel that provided some measure of modesty, for my sister's sake, and proceeded to try to cough my lungs out. My whole body ached as ice ran through my veins and, although the scalding hot water raining down on me burned my skin, I was so cold I couldn't stop my teeth from chattering.

"Ambrose!" Cassie yelled, giving up on the whistle. "What the hell?"

Cassie's head whipped to the side as a bright light illuminated the steam-filled room. The startled look on my sister's face as Amari stepped into view would have had me in stitches if I weren't currently dying.

"Who are you?" Cassie demanded, standing up to confront the newcomer.

The Keeper's dark-skinned face paled visibly when she saw me, blue as a frost giant and curled up in the foetal position.

"No time to waste," Amari said, pushing Cassie out of the way. She knelt down by my side and placed a scorching hand on my forehead. Her brown eyes looked worried. "It's going to be alright, Ambrose," she said. I didn't catch her next words as wind rushed through my ears and a white light seared my eyes.

Then all was dark again.

✕✕✕

I woke up in a large four-poster bed, snuggled under a warm comforter and wearing soft flannel pyjamas. The walls of my windowless room had been carved from stone and were decorated with faded tapestries depicting scenes I recognised from old myths that Father used to tell us at bedtime when Cassie and I were still little. A fire crackled in the hearth on the other side of the plush Persian carpet that covered most of the stone floor.

I could only be in the Repository, the hidden mountain fortress in which the Elder Council housed the last remnants of the world's mythical creatures.

Cassie was asleep in a chair by my side, her hand clutching one of my own. Her eyes were puffy and worry lines seemed permanently etched into her forehead. She must have had one hell of a rough night.

My hand twitched and she woke up. Her eyes met mine and, instead of the relieved smile I had expected, her mouth turned down into a scowl.

"I can't believe you didn't tell me," she accused as she straightened in her chair.

"I wanted to," I replied.

"Oh please, Ambrose! I find you half-dead in your shower, covered in blue veins like you're some kind of junkie who'd overdosed, and now we're here. Here!" She threw her arms into the air, her eyes sparkling with wonderment. "You've seen them, these creatures, and you never told me. Everything we've always dreamed about, all true! And you kept it to yourself. I'm not sure I'll ever forgive you."

"It wasn't up to him to tell you." Amari stood in the doorway with a tray in her hands. She entered and placed it on the side table next to me. My stomach rumbled as the smell wafting from the bowl of soup reached my nostrils and I eagerly accepted Cassie's help into a sitting position.

"How do you feel, Ambrose?" Amari asked as I loudly slurped my soup, manners be damned.

"Surprisingly good," I replied between mouthfuls.

"Mind if I have a look?" the Keeper asked, pointing at my chest.

I placed the empty bowl down and unbuttoned the shirt I was wearing. My jaw dropped as I looked at my chest. The bruise across my heart was gone, and so were the angry veins. My skin was still cold to the touch, but it looked normal and the asrai's curse seemed to have subsided.

Cassie exhaled loudly. "What did you do?" she asked, leaning in for a closer look.

Amari brushed her fingers across my chest,

leaving goose bumps behind, before she nodded, satisfied, and buttoned up the shirt again. "It's the magic of the Repository," she replied. "The whole fortress is steeped in protective spells to keep the creatures safe. The curse is still strong, Ambrose," she said, her dark eyes holding my own. "But as long as you're here, you should be safe enough."

A heavy feeling settled in the pit of my stomach. "You're saying I'm trapped here? In the mountain? Forever?" If my room had had a window, I might have made a dash for it now.

"It's not as bad as you may think," Amari said, smiling.

"But…" I didn't know how to respond. Cooped up here, for the rest of my life… The thought sent shivers of an entirely different kind through me. I'd never see the sun again. I'd never get to do the million things I still needed to do. What about all the places I haven't been to yet? All the things I haven't seen?

What about Sarah?

"Think about it," Amari said as she withdrew. "I could use another pair of hands around here. There's always something that needs to be done." She nodded at Cassie and left the room.

"Ambrose…" Cassie said, chewing on her fingernails. I reached over and pulled her hand away from her mouth. She stuck her tongue out at me, as if we were both children again.

"Did you see the unicorn?" I asked.

"Yes!" she squealed, gripping my arm excitedly. "Amari took me right into Una's enclosure. I ran my hand through her mane!" Cassie's eyes sparkled, but sadness tinged her words. "I can't believe she's the last of her kind. No wonder she needs to stay here, to be protected."

"What else did she show you?"

"The griffons! They'd just had a litter, so there

were three tiny little babies - so cute with their little wings and their little paws. And the minotaur – magnificent! I didn't care much for the harpies. They looked like grumpy old hags, sitting around gossiping and judging everyone. Ugh, and the smell coming from the yeti's enclosure was just… abominable." We laughed and for a moment, everything was fine.

"Father was right all along," Cassie said and we both sobered up. "I wish he could have seen this."

"Do you think I should stay?" I asked her.

"What choice do you have?" she asked. "I'd never been so scared in my life, Ambrose. When I saw you lying there, looking like that… I thought you were going to die."

"I'm sorry." I took her hand in my mine, squeezing it tightly.

"If you stay, you could carry on his research, you know," Cassie said, her eyes lighting up again. "And you'd have access to everything. Think how much you'd learn!"

"But who would believe me? No," I said, coming to a decision. "I can't stay here. I can't be trapped inside a mountain for the rest of my life. I need to find a cure."

"I thought there was no cure. Amari said -"

"Amari doesn't know everything. But there is someone who would know, and she's right here. I think it's time I go pay her a visit."

※※※

If I hadn't known better, I would never have believed I was standing in an enclosure confined within a cavern inside a mountain fortress. A soft mist rose from a waterfall cascading down a series of rocks into a pond enveloped by leafy trees. Crickets chirped and the scent of holly hung in the air. The little pond glistened as if bathed in moonlight.

It looked like a dream come true, someone's happy place brought to life.

It gave me the creeps.

The surface rippled and a head appeared from the deep. A beautiful woman emerged from the water, Victorian dress clinging to her limbs, rivulets running down her perfect figure, blonde hair spilling down her back.

I released a breath I hadn't even known I was holding. Clenching my fists, I took a step backwards. I'd have felt better if there had been something between us. Like a pit of vipers. Or a suit of armour, at least. Instead, I stood there barefoot in someone else's flannel pyjamas, feeling like an idiot.

The asrai's lips lifted in a cruel smile. "Still alive, I see," she said, her voice sultry and full of unspoken promises. She sat down on a rock and started running her hands through her long hair.

"Barely," I croaked, my throat suddenly dry as a djinn's backyard. I worked some moisture back into my mouth and tried again. "That's why I'm here."

An incredulous laugh burst from her lips. "Surely you don't expect me to help you."

"Why not?" I asked. "You tried to drown me first, remember? I think you got the better end of the bargain, all things considered."

"You think being locked up for an eternity is the better end of the bargain?"

I swallowed guiltily. I could hardly blame her for not being overly fond of me. After all, I did sentence her to a lifetime behind bars. A paradise compared to a real prison, of course, but a prison nonetheless. But she was a killer. She deserved this. Hell, she deserved much worse, if you asked me.

"I know there's a cure." I took a few reluctant steps closer and the asrai surged to her feet, ready to dive back into the water. "Will you tell me how to lift the curse?"

Her eyes narrowed and a frown creased her brow. "There is no cure."

"Touch of frost, breath of fire," I said, slowly closing the distance between us.

Her pale blue eyes narrowed. "Who told you that?" she demanded.

"What does it mean?" I countered.

She was so close I could touch her now. The asrai placed a hand on my chest and I winced instinctively, but nothing happened. My cold heart was immune to her charms. She lifted her face up towards me, her innocent eyes as big as the moon. When she spoke, her voice was seductive, although any hold it had had on me in the past was now long gone.

"If you help me escape, I will tell you."

For a minute, I was tempted.

It would only be fair, after all. Her freedom for my life. We could both escape the mountain. I could live my life and she could find a nice lake somewhere where no one would bother her again. After all, everything she had done had been in self-preservation.

And then I remembered what Sarah had said. Multiple drownings. I couldn't have that on my conscience.

"I can't do that," I said softly, somewhere between genuine regret and dismay.

The asrai laid her head on my chest. Her voice was barely a whisper. "Please."

"I'm sorry."

She shoved me away and I stumbled backwards, catching my balance just in time to prevent a fall. Turning her back to me, she strode into the pond.

"Then you have doomed me. Ask your precious Keeper how safe she thinks we really are in here. Ask her what the bruises on the unicorn's neck mean."

Her head disappeared under the water, leaving me flummoxed and no closer to finding a cure.

✖✖✖

"Come in, Ambrose."

Amari's office always gave me a warm sense of belonging. I wanted to kick my shoes off and sit by the fire while reading one of the ancient tomes stacked on the shelves lining the wood-panelled walls. Instead, I slumped down in a chair facing her large mahogany desk.

She lifted an inquisitive eyebrow. "That's not the face of a man who's found a cure."

"No," I agreed, shaking my head. "I didn't really expect any help from her, but it was worth a try."

"What will you do now? My offer still stands: you'll be safe here in the Repository. And if you're not interested in working with the animals, I'm sure we could find something else for you to do. The Council could use a man of your background."

I took a deep breath, considering my options. A portrait hanging on the wall behind her desk drew my eyes. A stern-eyed woman gazed back at me, her blonde hair piled on top of her head in a style that had been fashionable a century ago.

"Who was she?" I asked.

Amari glanced at the portrait behind her and sighed as she turned back towards me. "As if being the Keeper isn't pressure enough, I have to have Diana look over my shoulder all the time."

"Diana?"

"A legend I can never live up to," Amari admitted ruefully. "Diana was Keeper about a hundred years ago. She's responsible for most of the creatures I have in my care now. She single-handedly liberated them from a smuggling ring that operated in Europe around the turn of the century. And," Amari waved a hand to indicate the impressive library surrounding her, "most of these books were hers too. She knew more Words of Wonder than anyone alive now does."

"Words of Wonder?" I asked.

"Spells, I guess you'd call them," Amari said. "The world is pretty much devoid of magic nowadays, which is why the preservation of magical creatures is so important. But we do still remember some words from the first language, from the dawn of time, and these Words have a magic all of their own. I only know a few, and I've spent years poring through these books in search of more."

The scholarly interest I had inherited from my father was intrigued and, for a moment, Amari's offer tempted me. I could see myself delving into these old tomes, searching for remnants of a nearly forgotten language. Magic. I exhaled loudly. The world was stranger than I had thought, and I'd seen some pretty strange things lately.

But I still couldn't face the thought of being trapped here forever.

"Something tells me you've made your decision," Amari noted perceptively.

"I need to find a cure," I said, nodding. "I wouldn't want to stay here knowing I had no other option, that the curse was still running through my veins. There has to be a way to get rid of it."

"Any ideas?"

"Only one," I said, trying to sound more

confident than I felt. "But I'll need time."

"I can give you some," Amari said. She stood up from behind her desk and walked towards me. I jumped to my feet and flinched as she placed an icy hand on my arm. "Sorry," she said, smiling sheepishly. She leaned in and whispered a Word in my ear.

A shooting pain stabbed through my brain and my knees turned to jelly. Amari's firm grip was the only thing preventing me from falling flat on my face.

"I'm sorry, Ambrose," she said, a concerned frown creasing her forehead. "The pain should go away soon."

I grimaced. It was already fading away, leaving a burning taste behind in my mouth, like I'd licked a jalapeno.

"You have to hurry," Amari said as I pulled myself together. "The Word is potent, but temporary. Blow the whistle to call me and I'll come speak it for you, but only if you have no other choice. I'm sure it can't be good for you."

I nodded, my tongue too numb to speak.

"Hurry Ambrose," Amari said again. She spoke another Word then, and the world faded into white.

⁕⁕⁕

When I could see again, I was standing in my living room. I glanced at the clock on the mantelpiece. Eight o'clock. It was still dark outside.

I turned a light and the TV on, letting Sky News blare in the background while I changed out of my borrowed sleepwear and into jeans, a brown tweed jacket and my lucky white trainers. I could certainly use some luck now. The clock was ticking and I didn't know what to do. My one idea was a slim chance at best, and I did not know where to start. Where would I even find the mystery woman from Paris? And would she still have the relic that was my only hope now?

As if in answer to my thoughts, I heard the word "relic" mentioned on the TV and hurried back into the living room. Images of a hall filled with ancient vases, shining icons, and other antiques filled the screen. I turned the sound up.

"This exhibition is one of a kind and showcases some of the world's most important relics," the reporter said as the camera panned across a collection of priceless artefacts. The scene changed, showing a ring of standing stones in front of a stately white building. Golden daffodils swayed in the breeze. "It will be on display at the National Museum of Cardiff until the end of the week."

I muted the TV and stared, dumbstruck, as images of the Welsh capital flashed across the screen. "Luck," I said out loud. You'd think I'd be used to it by now, but I hardly believed it. For once, the luck might just work in my favour.

I was in the bathroom retrieving my phone and the silver whistle that Cassie had dropped when Amari had whisked us away when I heard the front door opening. I pocketed the phone and hung the whistle around my neck before going to investigate. My sister frowned at me as she stepped into my apartment.

"I thought you'd be here. I hoped you weren't."

"Nice to see you too," I said.

"You know what I mean." Her nose wrinkled as the frown turned into a smile. "I came to bring you this." She held up a small glass bottle.

"What is it?" I asked, taking it from her for a closer look. It was plain, unmarked, and sealed with a cork stopper. Inside was a thick red liquid that had a purple shine to it when it caught the light.

"I honestly don't know," Cassie admitted. "Or rather, the shopkeeper wouldn't say. I got it from that Wicca store near my apartment. You know, the one that plays those awful whale-song noises at all hours. I asked if they had anything that could cure ice running through your veins. The guy didn't even blink. Just walked to the back office and came back five minutes later with this."

I shook my head in disbelief. "You went to a magic shop?"

"It was the best I could think of!" she said, a little defensively. "I knew you wouldn't do the sensible thing and stay in the Repository, where it's safe. We have to find a cure, so I thought maybe someone in the magical community would know something. I hope it's genuine," she added. "It did *not* come cheaply."

"How much?" I asked, hoping she hadn't just spent half her student loan on a hoax.

"Oh, just the soul of my firstborn child," she quipped.

"What?!"

Cassie punched me playfully on the arm. "I'm joking, Am, of course. Sheesh, lighten up, will you."

I exhaled loudly, feeling like I'd just dodged a bullet. "How much?"

"Two thousand."

"Quid?!" So this was what a heart attack felt like.

"I figured you're worth it, if it works."

"If it works!" I grabbed her shoulders and stared into her eyes, willing some sense into her. "Cassie, you need to take this back, now."

She didn't even flinch. "Sorry Ambrose, but I won't," she replied calmly. "Try it out first. Then we'll go and knock that guy's teeth in if we find out it's just tomato juice or something. But if it works, it'll be worth every penny."

I blinked at her wordlessly for a heartbeat, and then I wrapped her in my arms. "Thank you," I whispered into her hair.

"Don't thank me yet," she replied as she squeezed me back. Then she extracted herself from my arms. "I have to go. Early class. Let me know if it works."

"I will," I promised as she waved goodbye and closed the door behind her. I held the bottle up again, suddenly realising just how fragile this expensive little object was. Would it work? What *was* in it? To be honest, at this point I didn't really care what it was, as long as it would keep me alive long enough to find a true cure. I tucked the bottle into my shirt's breast pocket just as my phone rang.

"Hey, mate," Daniel's Irish lilt greeted me. "How was Paris?"

Paris! Paris almost felt like a lifetime ago. "I'll tell you all about it on the train," I promised.

"What train?"

"The one we're taking in about an hour, give or take."

"Alright," Daniel said easily. "I wouldn't mind a break from all these shoes staring at me. Where are we going?"

"Cardiff."

※※※

People always looked twice at Daniel Brady. His bonfire hair drew eyes like a distress signal in the sky. I was watching him now while we were sitting across from each other in a four-seater booth on a train clattering past the outskirts of London. Daniel was staring out the window as if he'd escaped from confinement and was savouring his freedom. Perhaps he was, in a way.

A frown creased his freckled face and I gazed past him to see what he was looking at. A rainbow hovered in the sky above us. I grinned, knowing exactly how much that thing irritated my friend. It's hard for a creature of myth to hide in plain sight when a rainbow followed you around all the time.

"So... Wales..." Daniel drawled, turning towards me. "Land of sheep and dragons. What's up with that?"

I placed a hand on the table between us and pulled up my sleeve. I was startled to see just how blue the veins in my arm were. I hadn't expected it to be this bad so soon again.

Daniel gasped. "The asrai's curse?" he asked astutely.

I nodded. In a hushed voice low enough to ensure that the people in the neighbouring booth didn't overhear us, I told him about the shower incident and how I had ended up in the Repository. "I had a chat with the asrai while I was there and she wasn't too happy to see me, as you can imagine," I continued. "Unreasonably bitter, even," I joked.

"Understandably." Daniel nodded. "It still doesn't explain your sudden urge to drag me halfway across the country."

"This brings us to Paris. I had a *pas de deux* with the local White Lady -"

"A Dame Blanche?" Daniel chuckled in disbelief. "You sure know how to attract trouble, my friend."

"You don't know the half of it," I agreed. "She shrieked at me."

"Shit..." Daniel's eyes were wide as saucers.

"But she said she knew of a cure for the

curse."

"Only you would take the time to chat to a harbinger of death after she'd called out your name." Daniel looked slightly impressed. "And?"

"She said: 'Touch of frost, breath of fire.' A little vague, I'll admit."

Daniel snorted.

"I have no idea what it means," I confessed. "But I also met another woman in Paris. A normal one. Well, normal is relative, I suppose. She's a wanted thief. Now, before you say anything -" I interrupted his protests. "She stole an artefact. The Cross of Calais. It's known for its healing powers. If I can get my hands on that, it could be the answer to my problem."

I pushed the newspaper I had bought at Paddington station before boarding the train towards him, tapping on an article about the special exhibition at the Cardiff museum. "She wouldn't miss this for the world."

Daniel scanned the article before looking at me, frowning. "I don't know, Ambrose," he said. "Very few items have any intrinsic magical properties. Their power mostly lies in belief. I don't think that relic is going to be of much use to you."

I pushed the sinking feeling away with a brave smile. "It's my only hope."

"No," Daniel disagreed. "We need to figure out the White Lady's clue. Luckily, I happen to have some friends in Cardiff who might know more."

"Who?"

"I'd rather not say." He shrugged at me. "Sorry Ambrose, but you're too involved with the Council, and they'd rather remain anonymous. I'm sure you understand."

"Fine," I huffed, sitting back in my chair. You'd

think your best friend could cut you some slack. "I still want to check out the museum, though." I couldn't give up on the Cross, not yet. It seemed like my only chance, much more real than a cryptic riddle.

"If it would make you feel better." Daniel also leaned back in his chair. His blue eyes suddenly sparkled. "What did you decide about Rachel? You two lovebirds back together again?"

I scowled. Rachel was out of my life for good now. And good riddance. My face softened when I thought of Sarah instead.

Daniel misinterpreted my goofy grin. "You're kidding me, right?" he asked incredulously. "You took her back? After everything she put you through?"

"Hell, no," I replied. "But I met someone else in Paris. Actually, we'd met earlier, when all this started. Her name's Sarah."

The mischievous twinkle was back in Daniel's eyes. "Do tell."

※ ※ ※

I shivered as I stepped off the train at Cardiff Central station. The wind was bitingly cold and the sky was that dull shade of grey that promised sleet. A chill ran down my spine. Uh oh. Trouble was coming, and the inclement weather was the least of it. I needed to hurry.

A dog howled in the distance as Daniel led the way through the Welsh capital's streets while I gawked like a wide-eyed tourist at the fairy lights hanging from trees, the carol singers filling the air with Christmas songs, and the imposing castle walls dominating a large thoroughfare. The nation's emblematic red dragon winked at me everywhere I looked: from the flag on the castle's turrets flapping in the chilly breeze, to plush toys in shop windows and street signs on the corners of old buildings.

Since we'd missed lunch while on the train, Daniel and I stopped at a street vendor's stall and each bought a packet of Welsh cakes to nibble on while we walked. The sweet flatbread, dotted with raisins, was surprisingly delicious and I couldn't resist buying more to munch on later.

We soon passed out of the shopping district and entered a large park where a winter wonderland had been set up for the holidays. A tall swing ride lifted giggling children high above the dragon glowering down from the top of City Hall, while families with rosy cheeks held hands on the outdoor ice rink, laughing and calling to each other as they swirled around in circles. We passed them all and followed the footpath through a pretty garden that led towards the striking white façade of the National Museum of Cardiff.

Daniel paused in front of a circle of standing stones and tossed a Welsh cake into the grass between them. He grinned at my astonishment.

"For luck," he said, winking.

I shrugged. I could always use a little more luck. I threw a piece of cake in too, pocketing the last one for later, before following my friend up the stairs and in through the doors of the museum.

The foyer was packed. Daniel went to buy tickets for the special exhibit while I scanned the crowd. Monique had to be here. She was my only hope. A cold spasm ripped through my body and I grabbed the arm of a nearby statue for support. A security guard frowned at me and I quickly let go again, pursing my lips to prevent a nonchalant whistle from escaping.

"You alright, mate?" Daniel asked when he

returned. "You look a little pale."

"Fine," I lied, wrapping my jacket tighter about myself. The press of so many people around me was starting to work on my nerves and I felt lightheaded. I wanted to find who we were looking for and get the hell out of here.

We jostled past the scowling security guard and into the gallery containing the special exhibition.

I spotted her immediately. The woman in black, the one who had tried to kill me right after I had saved her life in Paris, was actually here, examining the relics on display. She was dressed in blue jeans and a leather jacket, her long black hair tied up and hidden underneath a baseball cap. She looked like the girl next door. If I hadn't known better, I would never have guessed she was a wanted criminal.

She looked up from the golden chalice she was inspecting and caught my gaze. Her eyes narrowed, as if she was trying to remember where she knew me from, and then she casually looked away. Apparently, I hadn't quite made the same impression upon her she had on me.

"Who are we looking for again?" Daniel asked, his eyes roving across the crowd.

"She's over there," I said, but when I glanced in her direction again, Monique was gone.

A cold stab of frost suddenly shot through my heart and I stumbled, seizing someone's steadying hand. I gasped for air, clutching at my chest. It felt like shards of ice were scraping through my lungs.

"Ambrose!" Daniel's eyes were wide with concern. "Help me ease him to the floor," he said.

As they lowered me to the ground, I reached into my shirt pocket. My fingers were nearly frozen solid, but I managed to pull the vial of red liquid out. It slipped through my clumsy digits and fell.

"Got it!" Daniel said as he caught the little bottle moments before it would have shattered on the tiled floor. He quickly unstoppered the vial and held it to my lips. The viscous liquid burned like lava going down my throat. Heat ran through my body, down my arms and legs, and into my fingers and toes. I coughed and sat up. Spots danced before my eyes, but adrenaline surged through my veins. I felt like I could run the London Marathon right then.

"What is this stuff?" Daniel asked, looking at the vial. Half the liquid was gone, the remaining fluid glinting a purplish-red in the museum's harsh light. Daniel scowled. "Ambrose, where did you get this? Do you know what this is?"

I coughed again as he and the woman by my side helped me back to my feet.

"Who cares?" I replied. "It's working."

Daniel's tone was urgent this time. "Ambrose," he hissed. "This is unicorn blood."

A circle of concerned onlookers had formed around us. I smiled, embarrassed, and said loudly: "I'm fine folks, just a little dizzy. Local brew is potent." The crowd parted, some grinning knowingly and others shaking their heads. The security guard settled back onto his stool, his beady eyes lingering on us before continuing his vigilant watch over the artefacts on display.

I turned back to Daniel and shrugged. "The stuff works, that's all I care about. Do you know where I can get more?"

Daniel gaped at me as if he had just stared into the face of a gorgon. "You're not serious," he said.

I shrugged again, squishing any feelings of guilt down, and turned to the woman by my side. It took me a moment to realise it was Monique.

"Is this true?" she whispered in her heavy French accent. "Unicorn blood?"

"Hey, are you -?" Daniel asked, noticing her for the first time.

"She is," I confirmed. "I need the Cross of Calais," I said to her, my fingers digging into her arm urgently.

The look she levelled at me made me drop her arm like a hot coal.

"That is long gone," she said. "But this…" Her eyes were big as she stared at the vial of blood. "This is worth much more than these dusty old artefacts." She reached for the vial and Daniel quickly shoved it into the pocket of his jeans.

"Sorry, lady," he said, all traces of his usual good humour gone. "This should not be out in the world."

"Hey, I need that," I said, reaching for his pocket. Without the relic, this was my only hope. The unicorn was safe in the Repository. She could afford to lose a little blood if that meant keeping me alive another day.

Daniel took a step back, glaring at me. "No, you don't. We'll find a cure, Ambrose. This isn't it."

Monique sidled up to Daniel, running a finger suggestively down his arm. "Just let me have a look at it," she said, batting her eyelashes charmingly.

"No," Daniel said.

"Fine," Monique pouted, tucking her hands into her jeans' pockets. "Gentlemen," she said and left the two of us staring after her as she disappeared into the crowd.

Daniel turned towards me. "Ambrose, you need to tell me where you found this. I -" he paused, his eyes suddenly wide. "It's gone."

"Monique." I scanned the crowd frantically for the thief, but she was nowhere to be seen. "Come on," I said to Daniel. "We can still catch up with her."

We pushed past everyone, ignoring the annoyed

glances thrown our way, and hesitated outside in the foyer.

"There!" I pointed as she dashed up the stairs.

"Go!" Daniel shouted. "I'll take the other side."

I sprinted past an elderly couple and took the stairs up three at a time, marvelling at the energy that coursed through me. I'd never felt so alive before!

The first set of doors banged together just as I reached the second level. I surged through them into an empty hall containing classical paintings. Rodin's two lovers embraced passionately in the centre of the room. Sarah would have loved this place.

With no time to stop and appreciate the art, I ran into the next room. Empty too, but the doors to the next gallery swung shut just as I entered. I burst through them to see Monique running down the hallway. She halted when she saw Daniel coming from the other side.

She turned back to see me blocking her way. A lopsided grin pulled a corner of her mouth upwards. Before I could do anything, she sprinted towards the railing looking out over the ground floor and vaulted into the air.

Daniel gasped and we both sped towards the spot where she had jumped over. Monique smiled up at us as she was rappelling down from a cable speared into the railing. She dropped the last few meters from the ground, ignoring the security guard's astonished splutters and was out the door before we had a chance to react.

"Quickly," I said to myself, but Daniel grunted in response and we dashed for the stairs again, opting to take the regular way down instead.

The guard barred our way as we ran towards the entrance. "Here now," he exclaimed, holding a hand out to stop us. "What's the meaning of this?"

We tore past him without answering and spilled out onto the front steps. It was almost dark outside. The sky had turned the colour of charcoal and shadows threatened to overwhelm the fairy lights and the revellers still partying outside.

"We lost her," I said, my heart plummeting while at the same time hammering like Hephaestus on his best day. I needed that potion. I dreaded the chill returning to my bones.

"She can't have gone far," Daniel said. "You keep looking for her, Ambrose. You need to find that vial."

"Where are you going?"

"To go see my friends. Perhaps they'll know more about the White Lady's hint. That's our only hope right now."

I nodded. "Right. Phone me when you have an answer."

I didn't think it was possible for Daniel's freckled face to turn any redder, but somehow it did. "Let me guess," I groaned. "No mobile?"

"Sorry," he said sheepishly. "You know me and technology..."

"Sure," I said, running a hand through my hair and scanning the crowd again. Dogs barked in the distance and I wondered idly if I could borrow someone's pooch to help me track Monique down. "So how will I find you?"

"Meet me at the *Dragon's Roar*. It's a pub close to St John's. Tell them I sent you." He clasped my shoulder reassuringly. "We'll find the cure, Ambrose. Trust the luck." Then he was off.

Trust the luck. Of course a leprechaun would say that.

I'd need luck to find Monique in this throng of people. She was probably long gone with that vial by now. What would she do with it? She was an antiques smuggler, so she probably had her fair share of shady connections, but would she know what to do with unicorn blood?

A cold shiver ran down my spine. Shit. I needed that vial.

I searched the crowd again, but it was near impossible to find anyone in it. I needed to be up high. A child's delighted squeal pierced the cold air and I looked across the green to see a mother strapping her daughter into the swing ride, an anxious frown marring her face.

A smile crept over mine. Perfect.

✕✕✕

My ears were freezing by the time the ride reached the top of its ascent and I berated myself for not planning ahead and bringing a hat. The ride twirled at a dizzying speed and I gasped as I swung past the dragon's maw at the top of City Hall. Icy icy wind whipped my face, making my eyes water. This had better work, or I might risk turning to ice for no reason.

The people below crawled like ants across the park. I scanned the crowd for a woman in a baseball cap, but to no avail. I slumped back in my seat. What a fool I was to waste time on a joyride.

As the swing ride started its descent, I cast my sights further than the immediate playground below me. There was a quiet patch of park on the edge of the fairground, back towards the castle. A statue lorded over a small garden and there, sitting on a bench, was a lone woman with long black hair, staring at something that glinted red in the headlights of passing cars.

The ride couldn't finish fast enough. I wanted to unbuckle myself and jump off, but adding a broken ankle to my list of ailments probably wasn't the best idea. My swing had barely come to a stop before I was off and running towards the park.

I stormed into the garden like a stampeding centaur. Monique swore loudly in French and was on her feet and out of the park before I had regained my breath.

I set off after her, vowing to renew my gym membership if I made it through this. Somehow, I kept her in sight, although she stayed ahead of me. She dodged passersby and ran across the street, risking life and limb in the face of oncoming traffic, and slipped into a dark alleyway just off the main road.

I hesitated. I wasn't overly fond of dark alleys, especially one I knew had a desperate woman who had tried to kill me less than a week ago hidden in it.

A dog barked again, closer this time. Its eerie howl echoed through the night. The hair on the back of my neck stood erect.

I stepped into the alley. Tall buildings loomed over me. A starless sky above ensured a darkness so complete I could barely make out my hands in front of me.

The silence shattered as dogs barked behind me. I spun about, but there was nothing to see. The entrance to the alley was empty.

When I turned around again, Monique was standing right beside me. My heart lurched into my throat. She placed a hand against my chest and shoved me so hard I fell to the ground. The sound of her boots on the cobblestones echoed through the night. A cold spasm shook through my body while I struggled onto my knees. I wouldn't say no to another sip from that vial right now.

I lifted my head and stared straight into the growling jaws of a hound.

I scrambled backwards and found my feet just as my back slammed into a wall.

There were two hounds, ghostly white with red-tipped ears, advancing on me. Their teeth were bared and slobber dripped from their fangs. The ground sizzled where their saliva fell. I had a feeling these two had been on my scent, hunting me, ever since I had arrived in Cardiff.

"Nice doggies," I said, holding a hand towards them. The hound closest to me snapped at it and I flinched back. I glanced around. There was nowhere to go. I was trapped.

Another icy shiver shot through my body and I shoved my hands into my jacket pockets for warmth. The brown paper bag containing my lunch crinkled, reminding me I still had one Welsh cake left over.

"Luck," I mumbled and tossed the piece of cake at the hounds. The dogs yapped and dived at it, gulping the pieces down greedily. I inched past them and scampered out of the alley.

✺✺✺

My teeth were chattering by the time I found the *Dragon's Roar* and, to make matters worse, it had started snowing. Normally I welcomed the tiny flakes of frost with childlike joy, but tonight they filled me with dread. I didn't have to pull up my sleeves to know that my arms were the colour of new bruises.

A stocky man stood next to the door of the pub, casually reading a newspaper and seemingly unaffected by the cold. I tried to step past him to open the door, but his arm shot out and blocked my way.

"Members only," he growled without looking up.

I looked closer at the bouncer, and suddenly wasn't sure that he was, in fact, a man. At first glance, he looked like your average muscle for hire: arms the size of tree trunks, neck larger than my thigh, eyes not overly burdened with intelligence. But there was just something strange about him that had me wondering if looks were deceiving me again.

"I'm meeting a friend here. Daniel Brady," I said.

The bouncer finally looked up from his paper and glared at me. His beady black eyes inspected me, before he grunted and opened the heavy oak door. I nodded my thanks and stepped through it, relaxing a little as warmth from the fire in the hearth welcomed me.

The door slammed shut behind me and I jumped. The noise inside had died down as soon as I entered and every eye in the establishment was on me. I stood there awkwardly for a moment, before everyone turned back to their conversations and the music resumed. I found an unoccupied booth near the front and tried to fade into the shadows.

The more I looked at the surrounding patrons, the faster my heart raced. It was clear this was no ordinary pub.

A woman sat at the bar, sipping a martini. Her long green hair floated in a non-existent breeze. The man next to her leaned in a little closer and suddenly her hair was erect, squirming and hissing at him. Snakes. Her head was covered in green, writhing snakes. My skin crawled.

A couple of tables across from me, two men were deep in conversation. One had tusk-like teeth protruding from his lower lip, while the other had shaggy legs and cloven hooves sticking out from his trench-coat. He saw me looking and I quickly averted my eyes.

I inhaled slowly, trying to steady my breathing. Was I safe here? What would these creatures do to me if they knew I worked for the Council? My hand crept towards the whistle I always kept about my neck. It was gone! Monique's sticky fingers must have struck again. I would have a few choice words for that bloody woman if I ever ran into her again.

The pub's door swung open, sending a shooting blast of cold air my way, but I hardly noticed. My gaze had fallen on the woman on the stage, singing seductively into the microphone. A silver dress clung to her lithe figure and she moved with such fluid grace I couldn't take my eyes off her.

"Careful now, Ambrose," Daniel said as he sat down across from me. "Don't listen to that siren too closely, or we'll never get you out of here to go get the cure."

I wrenched my gaze away and focussed on my friend. He was smiling from ear to ear.

"You found it?"

"I know where to go," he answered.

A dry cough wracked through my body and I clutched onto the table to keep from falling to the floor. I glanced at my hands. They were a pale blue.

"Not a moment too soon, either," Daniel said. "Come on, let's get out of here."

✳✳✳

I was shivering so violently Daniel had to hold me up as we walked through the snow-covered streets of Cardiff. The cold had driven most people indoors, and there was hardly anyone around.

"Where are we going?" I asked through clenched

teeth.

"Not far," Daniel said, his breath frosting in the air in front of him.

We both hesitated as a dog's howl ripped through the silence. Daniel's eyes widened.

"Oh yes," I said, wincing as my lower lip split. "There's a pair of red-eared hounds after me."

Daniel's face paled visibly. "The Cŵn Annwn are hunting you? We don't have any time to lose. Come on." He hastened our steps.

The stone walls of Cardiff Castle loomed ahead of us. Its dragon pennants hung listlessly in the frosty night air and the main gate was closed. Visiting hours were over.

"In there?" I asked.

Daniel nodded. "This way."

We veered left and stumbled towards the parkland next to the castle. Daniel steered me down a little side street. We scaled the fence that kept casual passersby out and walked beside the castle walls.

Suddenly, the barking of dogs was right behind us.

"Run!" Daniel shouted.

Summoning my last reserves of strength, I sped after my friend. I risked a glance backwards and saw the ghostly hounds leaping across the fence. I collided with Daniel, who had stopped at a little wicket gate in the castle walls. He fumbled with a key, trying to get it into the rusty lock.

"Come on, come on," I urged him. The dogs were almost upon us, their barking strangely soft now that they were this close to their prey.

With a creak, the key turned and we fell through the gate. Daniel pushed the door closed behind us just as the beasts barrelled into it. I leaned against the door for a moment, catching my breath and listening to the dogs' claws scraping against the wood.

Daniel placed a hand on my shoulder. He looked worried. "The Cŵn Annwn will hunt you until you can no longer run. If a Wild Hunt was called for you, Ambrose, then you've done something seriously wrong. They will chase you until the day you die, or redeem yourself. We will never be rid of them."

"The unicorn blood?" I asked.

Daniel nodded grimly.

"Alright," I wheezed. I would have to deal with that later. "How much further?"

"Not far." He pointed at the old stone keep set upon a high mound within the castle grounds.

I nodded. Even after all that exertion, my body was freezing and I'd lost all feeling in my hands. But I'd made it this far. I could go on a little further. Gratefully, I accepted my friend's extended arm and he helped me shuffle towards the keep.

We crossed the dry moat, overgrown with bushes, and climbed the many steps towards the keep. By the time we passed through its archway and entered its empty walls, I was gulping for air. I paused with my hands on my knees, my head lolling towards the ground. I gasped. Frost spread out from my feet, tracing delicate patterns across the ground.

"Wait here," Daniel said.

He walked towards the centre of the keep, where a thin layer of snow covered the ground. He said a Word and the mound trembled. A hole opened up in the earth, revealing steps descending into darkness.

I had a bad feeling about this, but with nothing left to lose and little time to lose it in, I trusted to luck and followed my friend into the depths of the earth.

※ ※ ※

It was pitch black inside the tunnel. With trembling fingers, I took my mobile out and turned the flashlight on. I saw Daniel grinning at me.

"Technology does come in handy sometimes," he admitted. "But we won't need it for long. Come on. Angharad probably knows we're here already. Let's not keep her waiting."

His lips pursed as he put a supporting arm around my waist. I could see goose bumps on his hands. He felt feverishly warm to me. Together, the two of us shuffled down the dark tunnel.

It didn't take long before the darkness receded and I put my phone away. An orange glow illuminated the end of the tunnel. I crinkled my nose as a sulphurous smell assaulted it. It must be very warm too, because I could see a drop of sweat running down Daniel's temple. I was as cold as ever.

The tunnel opened up into an enormous cavern bathed in orange light. Heat rose from a river of lava that flowed off towards one side. My eyes were inexorably drawn towards the glitter of a mound of treasure. My heart stilled as the hoard shifted and an enormous red dragon emerged. The creature turned its reptilian eye towards us. If I weren't on the brink of collapse, I would have been on the other side of Wales by now.

"Stay here," Daniel whispered.

I nodded wordlessly, frozen to the spot, quite literally, as my friend stepped up to confront the beast.

"Angharad! *Noswaith dda*," Daniel greeted the dragon in Welsh.

The dragon's response shook the walls of the cavern, bouncing off sparkling jewels and setting the lava to boil. I shuffled as far away from the beast as possible, squeezing up against the cavern wall and wishing I had a magic ring to make myself invisible.

Daniel glanced at me and said something. The dragon roared and reared onto its feet, towering above us. Angry steam spurted from flaring nostrils.

Daniel lifted both hands in a placating gesture and said something soothing. The dragon listened, cocking its head in a strangely human gesture. Its large slitted eye stared at me until I knew it could see right into my soul. It held me, trapped, until my eyes watered and I had to blink. More words I didn't understand rumbled through the cavern.

"She wants to know why she should help an ally of the Council," Daniel translated.

The dragon snorted angrily. "You brought an Englishman into my home?"

I sighed. Some enmities ran deep.

"Please…" I rasped.

"I offer you my pot of gold," Daniel said.

The cave shook as the dragon sat back on her haunches and laughed.

"What kind of fool do you think I am?" she asked when the floor finally stopped shaking. She turned to me again and I had to steel myself to meet her unblinking eye. "The leprechaun tells me you are nymph-cursed and that you drink the blood of a unicorn to stay alive." I glared at Daniel, whose flushed face looked alarmed. "You imprison mythical creatures."

"For their protection," I managed, before a wracking cough silenced me.

The dragon's gaze was implacable. "And you've led this one here."

I turned to see Monique step out of the tunnel and into the cave. Her eyes were wide, and all the blood had drained from her face, but the hand pointing the gun at the dragon was steady. I had to give it to her - she had nerve.

She winked at me as she walked closer. "All these riches," the French thief said, "… but I think the biggest prize is standing before me. How much would a dragon be worth to this… Council… of yours?"

"Come now, lass, you don't know what you're talking about," Daniel said, taking a step towards her.

A shot rang out and Daniel slumped to the floor, cursing in Gaelic. He grimaced as he pulled himself into a sitting position. "She shot me in the leg!"

"You'll live," Monique said. Her eyes were still locked on the dragon.

The dragon chuckled. "Foolish girl. You think your little firing device scares me? You think you can threaten me?"

Monique slowly lowered the gun and tucked it into her pants behind her back. A cunning smile crept across her face as she pulled my silver whistle out from a pocket.

The dragon roared.

I moved like lightning.

Ignoring my frozen digits and the pain that shot through my chest, I lunged for the whistle. Monique spun towards me, the gun suddenly in her hand again. She took a step backwards and slipped on the sheet of slippery ice spreading from my feet. She tumbled to the ground. I winced as her head hit the ice with a loud crunch. Her eyes rolled into the back of her head and her grip slackened around the whistle. It dropped to the floor, where I picked it up.

I held it out to Angharad, who was eyeing me wearily. "Dragon!" I wheezed. "This is your freedom. I trade you this for my life!" With my last bit of remaining strength, I tossed the whistle into the river of lava. I sagged to the frozen floor.

The dragon's unblinking gaze was upon me for centuries. Okay, hours. Probably seconds. And in that time, I knew for the first time that I was, without a doubt, all out of options and that I was going to die. What a fool I'd been, thinking my life was worth more than a unicorn's. Hell, who was I to decide whether that asrai should spend eternity in a cage? I knew I'd rather die than be locked up forever. And judging by the implacable reptilian stare that now weighed me and obviously found me wanting, I'd been a fool to think a creature of myth would help someone like me.

Defeated, I lay down on the warm floor, surrendering to the inevitable. My teeth chattered and my jaw ached from trying to clench it. I knew without looking that my entire body was criss-crossed in blue, aching veins. My blood was turning to ice. There was nothing left to do but give up and give in.

I'd always heard that your life flashed before your eyes in your last moments, but not mine. Instead, I was haunted by the pale eyes of the asrai who had cursed me. Her face, floating before me as if in a vision, was grave. And sad. And stubborn. She would survive, I knew in that instant. She would not have let something as small as a death curse stop her. She was strong.

And so was I.

Coughing, I pushed myself up into a sitting position. It was all I could manage as the blood drained from my face and the world started spinning.

I looked up at the dragon, and my heart froze. She towered over me and her jaws were open wide. Fangs as long as my arms glinted as a red-hot fire spewed from her throat.

The flames enveloped me. It was agony. It was bliss.

"Well, are you just going to sit there, mate?" Daniel's voice, rich with laughter, interrupted my reverie.

I opened one eye, and felt heat rise to my cheeks. The leprechaun and the dragon were both watching me with unconcealed humour on their faces.

I leapt to my feet. "What the..?" I spluttered, looking at my hands. They were no longer blue. In fact, they were impressively tanned, as if I'd just spent two weeks on a fishing trip in the Caribbean. And I felt warm. Not scorched, just-been-set-ablaze-by-a-dragon warm. Normal. I felt normal.

I couldn't stop the grin creeping across my face. I did a little jig on the spot, ignoring the deep chuckle that rumbled from the dragon's belly.

"You have passed the test," Angharad said. "Now go," she added, "before I decide to make a meal of you."

※※※

It felt surreal, sitting in the snow on the curb of the street that ran past Cardiff Castle, waiting for the ambulance to show up. A sparkling rainbow hovered in the air above us.

This time, it had been me helping Daniel along as we had lugged Monique's comatose body out of the dragon's lair and back up the steps to the keep. It had been Daniel's idea to leave her behind inside the castle, tied up inside the Clock Tower, where she would be protected from the elements during the time it took for the authorities to respond to our anonymous tip-off.

A snowflake landed in the palm of my hand,

and I marvelled at its delicate beauty. I was enormously pleased to see it melt against my body heat. I still couldn't believe I was cured.

"You know what just occurred to me, Ambrose?"

"What?" I asked distractedly, tracing the melted snow against the palm of my hand.

"That I still owe you two wishes."

I froze. I closed my eyes and exhaled slowly. "You mean to say -"

"Aye. That might have been easier."

I opened my eyes again and stared at my friend. My shoulders started shaking with laughter, and I shook my head in disbelief. I had no words.

Daniel's own chuckle stopped abruptly and he nudged me urgently. I looked up at his worried face. He seemed ready to run, bullet-ridden leg or not. I followed the direction of his gaze.

The two white hounds stepped out of the mist, their red-tipped ears alert. I held my breath as they padded closer, tensing myself for an attack. Beside me, I sensed Daniel doing the same.

The animals walked slowly towards me and stopped inches from my face, sniffing. I lifted a hand, intending to ward away a lunge for my throat, but instead, one of the hounds placed its head under my hand and I found myself scratching its crimson ears. Its tail wagged happily as I shot an incredulous glance at my companion.

A horn called somewhere in the distance and, even though I have never gone hunting in my life, I knew this sound signalled the end of the hunt. The dogs barked happily and sped off into the distance.

Beside me, Daniel exhaled loudly. "Now I've seen everything," he said, grinning.

❊❊❊

The door swung open and Cassie leapt straight into my arms, squealing. Behind her, the fire crackled invitingly and a warm yellow glow filled with the promise of wine and a hearty meal beckoned.

With a fond smile hovering across my lips, I extricated myself from my sister's embrace and turned towards the woman standing beside me. Her eyes were twinkling with humour behind their black-rimmed hipster glasses.

"My sister, Cassie," I said.

"And you must be Sarah!" Cassie squealed again, grabbing Sarah's hands and pulling her into the apartment. "Don't mind his scruffy appearance," she said as she led Sarah into the living room. "He's quite a catch, really."

Sarah smiled, amused, as I stood there, mortified. "I think so too."

"And this," Cassie said as she let go of Sarah and slipped her hand into the coffee-skinned palm of a young woman waiting by the fireside. "This is Pavithra."

"Hi," Pavithra said, lifting her other hand in greeting. She had the flawless looks of a Bollywood goddess, her black hair cascading down her back and her lips painted a subtle shade of red.

For a moment, I was speechless. What had happened to Sir Galahad? And then I saw the way my sister's face lit up as she looked at the woman next to her and explained: "We met in Art class. Pavithra was one of the models." She was happy, and that was all that mattered.

"Hi Pavithra," I said, walking closer. Her grip was firm in mine as we shook hands. Her dark eyes were ringed with heavy eyeliner, enhancing her exotic appearance, and a small hollow circle with a thin vertical black line through it was tattooed between her brows. A hint of cloves scented the air around her.

When she turned to greet Sarah, I cast an enquiring glance at my sister. The look Cassie flashed me while the two women introduced themselves warmed my heart and I suddenly realised she had been very nervous, not knowing how I would react. I smiled at her and nodded, and Cassie's face beamed like sunshine after a cloudy day.

The doorbell rang and I groaned. "Please tell me you didn't invite Mother too?"

"Of course not," Cassie replied, looking shocked at the idea. A timer buzzed from the kitchen. "That would be the roast. Can you get the door please, Am?"

She hastened out of the room as I went to let the mystery guest in.

The second surprise of the evening looked at me with unconcealed humour in her dark brown eyes. "This is for your sister," Amari said as she pushed a potted plant into my hands. I stood aside to let her in and she immediately went to introduce herself to the other two women sipping mulled wine by the fire.

A delicious smell wafted from the kitchen and in its wake, Cassie bustled into the room, carrying an enormous tray of roast lamb. I placed Amari's gift on a side table and took my seat at the dining table beside Sarah. She held my hand as we waited for the others to get seated as well.

Cassie, at the head of the table, clinked a spoon against her wineglass and said: "We don't usually do big speeches. Well, not since Father left, anyway." For a moment, it looked like she might tear up, but she took a deep breath and continued brightly. "But tonight I want to say thank you to you all. Amari, you helped my brother out when he was really down on his luck. I know he wouldn't be sitting here tonight if it weren't for you."

I saw the questions in Sarah's eyes and I shrugged, hoping she wouldn't make too much of it.

"Sarah, you came into Ambrose's life at just the right time. I haven't seen him this happy in years. You are all he's been talking about since he came back from Cardiff."

"Cardiff?" Sarah whispered beside me. "When were you in Cardiff?"

I pressed a finger to my lips and shook my head. A frown furrowed Sarah's brow, but I turned my attention back to my sister.

"Pavi, you are my sunshine. You chase every dark day away, and there have been a few lately. Thank you for being my beacon." Pavithra nodded, her face solemn enough that I wondered what my sister had been keeping from me and if I hadn't been paying enough attention to her lately.

"And Ambrose," Cassie's voice had taken on a stern tone. "Don't you ever frighten me like that again. Promise me you'll come to me if you need help again. I mean it," she said over my feeble protests. And then her eyes softened. "And thank you for finding your way back."

"Always," I said, trying not to choke up. Must be something in the wine.

"Okay," Cassie said, blinking back a tear. "Let's dig in."

Dinner was delicious, and the conversation around the table was scintillating, although Pavithra was quiet and seemed to prefer listening over talking. Cassie more than made up for her friend's reserve and told one hilarious story after another, drink in hand and face glowing with pleasure. Amari, not to be outdone, regaled everyone with tales from her travels around the world. I sat back, feeling warm and fuzzy and happy, listening to their banter.

"Tell me how you know Ambrose, Amari," Sarah asked at one point and I paused with my fork lifted halfway to my mouth. It was an innocent question, but I couldn't help but worry that the detective might learn something best kept secret.

The Keeper didn't hesitate. "He sometimes does some freelance work for me."

"Gets him into some pretty weird situations," Cassie piped in, ignoring the warning look I shot her. Her cheeks were a rosy pink as she took another sip of wine. "You know what happened in Paris, don't you?"

"Yes…" Sarah said, confused. "I didn't realise he was there for work."

"Not for work," I confirmed quickly.

"You don't call the White Lady work?" Cassie asked, giggling.

"Ambrose was not officially on assignment in Paris," Amari said smoothly. "But he did deliver, nonetheless."

"So…" Sarah looked from Amari to me. "The White Lady is the one who gave you that warning? While you were playing that game?"

Cassie snorted. "Some game that was!"

"Yes," I nodded at Sarah. "And yes," I said, shooting another warning glance at Cassie. "The role playing thing didn't go quite as expected, as you know, Sarah. But Amari accepted the article I delivered in any case." Which was technically true, just not in the way Sarah understood it.

I could see she had more questions, so I quickly changed the subject. "Pavithra, have you ever been to Paris?"

"Oh yes," she replied. Her words carried a hint of an unusual accent. "I was there last summer on assignment. I think I spent the entire month just wandering through the Louvre."

I thanked my lucky stars as I saw Sarah's interest sparked. While the two of them discussed the merits of art education, and Cassie weighed in on why comic books should have their own special section in the Tate as well, I slowly exhaled in relief. Amari's face was unreadable, but she nodded at me. Our secret was still safe.

After dinner, I cleared the table while Sarah stepped into the hallway to answer a call and Pavithra helped my somewhat tipsy sister to a couch.

"That was a close call," Amari said as we found ourselves alone in the kitchen. "Are you sure you can keep such a big secret from your girlfriend?"

"I have to," I replied. "Do you honestly think she'd believe me if I told her?"

Amari didn't respond as she stacked some plates in the sink.

"I've been meaning to talk to you, Amari," I said. "I lost my whistle."

"I figured as much. Are you going to tell me what happened? You're obviously not cursed anymore." She lifted an enquiring eyebrow at me.

"Maybe someday," I said evasively. "But there's something more urgent we need to discuss. I'd almost forgotten about it, but it's been on my mind ever since I..." I paused. I wasn't about to tell her about Angharad and how the dragon had accused me of using mythical creatures for my own benefit. "Since I returned from Cardiff. When I went to see the asrai, she told me to ask you how safe you really think the creatures in the Repository are."

That made Amari pause.

"She said to ask you what the bruises on the unicorn's neck are."

"What?" Amari asked, her face wrinkling with

worry.

"And when I got home from the Repository, Cassie had bought a vial of liquid from the local Wicca store. It worked, Amari. It stopped the curse for a few hours."

Amari's eyes widened. "That's not possible," she said.

I held the little vial I had retrieved from Monique's comatose body out towards her. She took it with trembling fingers, holding it up to the light where it shone a telltale purplish-red.

"I have it on good authority that the bottle contains unicorn blood."

"No," Amari said, lifting a hand to her mouth in shock. "That can't be."

"Ambrose." Sarah strode into the kitchen like a thundercloud about to explode. "Amari, if you would give us a minute, please." It was not a request.

Amari's face was pale as she complied, shooting me one last anxious glance as she stepped out of the room.

"What's this?" Sarah thrust her mobile phone at my face.

I took a step backwards, gently taking the phone from her so I could get a better look. A ball of lead dropped into my stomach. It was a picture taken at the Cardiff museum, inside the room containing the relic display. My face was clearly recognisable, and so was the woman's standing next to me, her one hand on my arm. It was Monique.

"Ambrose Davids," Sarah said in a dangerously official tone of voice. "You're under arrest for aiding and abetting a known criminal."

I gulped audibly and slowly lifted my hands into the air...

PART 3.5

TRICKSTER'S DECEIT

A mari, the Keeper of Exotic Animals, yawned as she locked the enclosure gate. She peered through the barred door at the creature inside. It glared back at her, its eyes shining dimly in the darkness of the small cell. A low growl emanated from deep within the creature's stone belly.

"You'll be quite safe here," she assured it. "You might not believe me now, but this really is for the best."

The gargoyle wrapped its wings about itself and purposely turned its broad back to her.

Amari sighed. Few of her charges were happy to find themselves inside the Repository when they first arrived, but given time, they soon realised that the mountain fortress set aside by the Elder Council for their protection was a sanctuary rather than a prison. The world outside no longer cared for magic, and creatures of myth would be hunted, killed out of fear or scavenged for bits and pieces that would form part of love potions or aphrodisiac concoctions. This was the only way to keep them safe.

She just wished she didn't have to feel like a jailer every time a new resident arrived.

She yawned again and pulled her leopard-print kimono about herself. As enormously pleased as she was at this recent addition to the menagerie, she wished Ambrose had delivered it at a more sensible hour. Her bare footsteps echoed through the stone-carved hallway as she hurried away from the temporary cells towards her living quarters. Time enough tomorrow to move the gargoyle to a more comfortable enclosure in the Repository's central cavern. Her bed was calling her now.

She slipped out of her kimono and was just about to dive back under the warm comforter when her mobile phone beeped. Rubbing at her eyes, she dipped a hand into the kimono's pocket and retrieved her phone. She looked at the message scrolling across the display and then at the clock on the home screen.

"Busy night," she muttered as she slung the garment back on again and slid her feet into the slippers tucked under her bed. Her cold toes would not do well in the snow outside. She cast a quick glance into the gilded mirror hanging over her nightstand – her brown skin seemed a little washed out, the consequence of too many sleepless nights, and her black curls were dishevelled, but would have to do at this late hour – before suppressing another yawn and heading for the East Wing.

The helicopter hovered like a hunting harpy by the time she arrived at the helipad. Its rotors cut through the crisp mountain air and blasted an icy wind towards Amari as she stepped through the heavy oak doorway that sealed the mountain fortress against the outside world. Her eyes widened when she recognised her visitor.

"Councilmember Bottenfeldt," she shouted over the noise. "What an unexpected surprise."

The blonde woman scowled as she climbed out of the helicopter, one gloved hand clutching onto the door handle as her designer boots slipped on the icy landing pad. She huffed angrily as she regained her balance. The cold had turned her cheeks rosy and she wrapped her faux ermine coat about herself.

At least, Amari hoped it was faux.

"I won't be staying," the woman said in the

thick German accent that so grated on Amari's ears. "I just came to deliver this."

She held a carrier case out at Amari.

"What is it?" the Keeper asked as she took the container. It wasn't very heavy. Whatever was inside couldn't be much bigger than a lapdog.

"No idea. It was a gift. I'm sure you'll know what to do with it." Without further ado, the Councilmember climbed back into the helicopter and shut the door against the icy wind.

Amari retreated as the helicopter lifted off. She waited until she was back inside, with the gate firmly closed behind her, before cautiously opening the case. Her breath caught in wonder. A small two-tailed fox lay curled up on a roughspun blanket. It opened one sleepy eye and blinked at Amari.

A kitsune!

"Welcome, little one," the Keeper said, her hands trembling with excitement as she slowly reached into the cage and stroked the kitsune's soft, red fur. It smelled faintly of green tea – the good kind; fresh, soothing and slightly chestnutty. She vaguely remembered mention of kitsunes in one of Diana's old books, but she'd paid little attention at the time. She would never have imagined having one of the little Asian creatures under her care one day. "You're a long way from home."

The kitsune yawned, baring tiny razor-sharp teeth, and closed its eye again.

"I know the feeling," Amari agreed. She shut the case's door again and returned to the temporary cages, where she could hear the scrape of stone on stone as the gargoyle paced the small confines of its cell next door. She really needed to move it to a more suitable enclosure soon. The noise stopped when Amari turned a tap on to pour water into a bowl, before extracting the still-sleeping kitsune and the blanket it rested on from the case and carefully placing it inside the cage. She tiptoed out and locked the door behind her.

She glanced into the gargoyle's cell. The creature had retreated into the farthest recess, hunched up in a corner, its wings wrapped about itself like a cloak.

"Tomorrow," Amari promised it in a whisper.

A menacing growl was all response she received.

Shaking her head, Amari returned to her room. She sighed blissfully as she lowered herself into bed, pulling the cosy blanket up to her chin. Her eyes remained open, however, her body tingling with excitement. There would be little sleep tonight, she knew, as she started planning the perfect enclosures for her two new charges.

※※※

"It's going to be alright, Artemis," Amari comforted the griffon. She dribbled some water into the animal's beak while placing a reassuring hand on her paw, softly stroking the warm fur. The griffon screeched, pain contorting her avian face.

Amari felt a nudge and she turned to see Artemis' mate standing next to her. The leonine creature's fear pressed down on her like a thundercloud heavy with storm. His wings were folded back against his feline body and his tail whisked nervously from side to side.

"I won't let anything happen to her, Apollo," she assured the male griffon. "Perhaps you should go hunt while we wait. The little ones will be hungry when they arrive."

The griffon nuzzled her shoulder, threw one last worried glance at his mate, and bounded into the air.

Amari returned her attention to the sweat-soaked mother-to-be. Births inside the Repository were rare and she was always filled with both anticipation and trepidation when a new litter was on its way; excited to see a species thrive and yet fearful for a safe delivery. This particular birth was incredibly important. These little cubs would be the first of their kind to be born inside the Repository. Amari held some hope that there were still other griffons out in the wild, but she had seen no evidence of it so far. The survival of their species could depend on what happened here this morning.

Artemis screeched again and strained, her breathing short and sharp. She exhaled raggedly and pushed. Amari moved just in time to catch the little cub as it entered the world. For a few seconds, she stared at it, entranced. It looked like a little kitten with soft golden-brown fur, but it had a tiny bird-like beak, two small wings on its back, and a splash of red feathers on its forehead. It was perfect!

"Hello, Calliope," she crooned as the cub mewed for the first time, melting her heart instantly.

She put the little animal down next to her mother, watching as the griffon bit the umbilical cord off and started licking the little one clean. When Artemis yelped again, Amari quickly took Calliope and placed her on a pillow to one side.

The second cub came soon afterwards. "Clio," Amari named her; mahogany fur and a tuft of white feathers on top, just like her father.

By now, Artemis was exhausted and wailed in pain, her powerful body trembling like a leaf in the wind. Amari stroked her back and whispered soothing words. The griffon's breathing was shallow and she had little energy left for the third cub.

"Let me help you," Amari said, squishing down her own rising panic. She couldn't lose Artemis now.

The griffon nodded once, and Amari drew a deep breath. Gently, she took hold of the little padded foot that appeared and pulled the cub free.

Her hands shook as she wiped him clean. He was white with a blue crest, even smaller than his older sisters. His little tail curled around her fingers and Amari's lower lip quivered with relief.

"Caerus," she welcomed him.

She placed the last cub beside his siblings on the pillow and moved them all next to their weary mother. Artemis snuggled closer to her litter, her tired face somehow conveying both wonder and contentment as she closed her eyes and fell asleep.

Flapping wings announced the return of the male griffon, carrying the body of a squirrel in his beak. He cast a curious glance over the newborn litter as he nuzzled his dozing mate. The feathers on his chest puffed out and he strutted beside his family, announcing their arrival to the world with proud squawks.

Amari wiped the sweat from her brow as she rested on the ground, watching as Apollo shredded the meat and started feeding tiny bites to the little ones. A smile crept over her face. It was days like these that made being the Keeper worthwhile.

※※※

Amari stared at the shelves housing the Asian tomes in her vast collection of ancient books. Somewhere between these leather-bound volumes was the information she needed to care for the kitsune, who had still been sleeping the last time she had looked in on him. Without knowing what the creature was capable of, or even where it came from, she had no idea how best to design the little kitsune's paddock.

The gargoyle's enclosure had been straightforward enough. The beast had clambered up the wall of the faux Gothic cathedral with practised ease, glaring down at her and mumbling the word *trompeur* repeatedly until it had lifted its head towards the moonlight spilling onto its perch and turned to stone.

Trompeur. Deceiver.

Clearly, it would take some time to win the creature's trust.

Her mobile phone pinged and she glanced at the message popping up. Ambrose was summoning her again so soon? He must be having quite the adventure in Paris. She wondered what surprise he had for her this time.

She said a Word of Wonder and blinked as she stepped out of the white light and into a steamy bathroom.

"Who are you?" a young woman demanded, her face pale with fright. She was kneeling on the floor next to a half-naked man lying on his side in the shower. The man's skin was tinged blue and angry veins streaked across his chest from a dark bruise over his heart.

Amari felt the blood drain from her face.

Ambrose!

"No time to waste," she said, pushing the girl out of the way and kneeling by Ambrose's side. She placed a hand on his forehead. He was as cold as ice. A frown creased her forehead.

"It's going to be alright, Ambrose," she said. She spoke another Word and bathed the world in white.

"He'll probably sleep for a few hours until the magic has had a chance to heal his body," Amari said as she led the young woman out of the room in which Ambrose was recovering. "It might be best if we let him rest for a while."

The woman frowned as she looked at the corridor carved into the mountain. "Where are we? And who are you?" Her green eyes narrowed as she looked at Amari. "And what do you mean, magic?"

"You must be Cassandra," Amari said, holding her hand out towards the woman. "Ambrose's sister?"

"Cassie." Her hand was soft but firm in the Keeper's grip. A confident young woman, Amari decided. A good ally.

"My name is Amari Kerubo, and you are inside the Repository." She smiled at the blank stare Cassie directed at her. At least she knew for sure now that Ambrose could be trusted with a secret. "Follow me and I'll show you."

They walked through the stark corridors in silence. Amari glanced at Cassie once or twice. The woman was alert, her eyes taking in every detail they passed. Amari wouldn't be surprised if Cassie was counting doorways, trying to formulate an escape plan, or dropping breadcrumbs.

The Keeper paused in front of the iron gate that led to the central cave and turned towards Cassie.

"What I'm about to show you is a secret. You can't talk to anyone other than Ambrose about this. Do I have your word?"

"How can I make a promise like that?" Cassie exclaimed, heat suddenly colouring her cheeks. "My brother's on the brink of death and I don't know what happened! Or where we are." *Or who you are*. The unspoken words lingered between them.

"You'll understand when we go through this door," Amari said soothingly. "I promise, everything will make sense once you see this." She smiled reassuringly. "Your brother was sceptical at first too."

Cassie's eyes widened. "Wait. Is this some secret government facility?" she asked, half mocking, half serious. "Is Ambrose in trouble? You know, apart from nearly dying, that is."

Amari laughed. "Come and see."

Amari paused as she felt Cassie's hand on her arm. The Keeper looked up into the woman's green eyes, wide and pleading.

"Am I going to be in trouble if I see what's in there?" Cassie asked.

"Not if you can keep a secret."

Cassie took a step back from Amari and the door. She hesitated. Then she squared her shoulders and nodded. "Show me."

Amari opened the gate. She stepped onto the platform that overlooked the enormous cavern sprawling out below them. Beside her, Cassie gasped.

Amari turned to see the woman gaping at the enclosures visible below. "How is this possible?"

"The Repository collects and takes care of mythical creatures," Amari explained. "Your brother finds them for us and we protect them here, safe from anyone outside who might wish them harm."

"This can't be real," Cassie said, breathless.

Amari didn't respond. Instead, she started descending the steel stairway and smiled as she heard Cassie's eager footsteps following her. From the ground level, the Repository looked like a zoo filled with dozens of unmarked pens. After so many years of living inside the mountain, Amari knew what each of them contained without needing to peer through the bars for confirmation. Most creatures usually chose to remain out of sight, anyway. In fact, she kept their need for privacy foremost in mind when she designed their new homes.

She led Cassie to one of the larger enclosures. She whispered the Word that unlocked the gate and heard Cassie inhale sharply as they stepped into the enclosed space.

They were on a small footpath on the edge of a craggy cliff. An indigo sky faded into the distance and far, far below them, rolling green meadows undulated in a soft breeze. Amari led the way along the rocky path. She heard pebbles cascading downwards and looked back to see Cassie pressing herself up against the mountain as much as she could, her face pale and her hands shaking. Amari reached out and Cassie clasped her hand gratefully, her mouth drawn in a tight line. Slowly, Amari led her a few steps further along the cliff towards the mouth of a cave.

As they stepped away from the edge, she let go of Cassie's hand and watched as the woman's fear faded into amazement.

"Griffons…" she whispered.

"She's just had a litter, so she might be a bit cranky. Let me introduce you first."

Amari walked towards the female griffon who lay snuggled up in a straw nest, her three cubs dozing closely against her body. She looked up as the Keeper approached.

"How are you doing, Artemis?" Amari asked as she knelt down by the new mother and gently stroked the fur on her back.

The griffon clucked contently.

Amari beckoned for Cassie to come closer. The young woman knelt beside her and hesitantly stretched a hand out to stroke one of the little cubs. A warning rumbled from the griffon mother and Cassie snatched her hand back.

"I'll just look then, shall I?" she said, blushing.

"This is Calliope and her sister Clio," Amari said, pointing at the two larger cubs. "And their little brother, Caerus."

"I just want to cuddle them," Cassie crooned.

"Best not to," Amari warned quickly. "They're cute, but they're still predators. No telling how strong those beaks are yet, but they devoured a squirrel minutes after they were born, so I wouldn't risk it if I were you. And I'm fairly sure mommy here will not allow it." She smiled fondly at Artemis.

"Noted," Cassie replied. "Not pets, are they?"

The Keeper shook her head. "Definitely not pets."

She stood up and helped Cassie to her feet. "It looks like they're all doing fine. Let's leave them to their rest."

She grinned at Cassie as they exited the cave. "She's not a pet either, but I think you'll enjoy meeting Una."

※※※

Later that evening, Amari closed the door to Ambrose's bedroom behind her, giving him and his sister some privacy to discuss his options. The look on his face when she'd told him he would have to stay in the Repository, where the mountain's protective magic would prevent the asrai's curse from killing him, was telling. She had a feeling he wouldn't take that lying down, although she quite liked the idea of having him stay.

She loved her job as Keeper and the creatures she took care of, but she'd been on her own ever since she took up her post in the Repository, and the place was sorely lacking in human companionship. The odd times one of the Council's pool of Freelance Procurement Specialists made a delivery hardly allowed her to make any true friends.

Homesickness suddenly assailed her and she wrapped her arms about herself, swallowing a sudden lump in her throat down. She missed her family. She missed the noise of many people together in a room, talking and laughing and arguing. And she'd seen enough snow to last her a lifetime.

Perhaps it was time for a holiday?

She snorted dismissively. Who would take care of her creatures if she left? She was needed here.

The Keeper's footsteps echoed through the empty hallway as she made her way to the kitchen before heading towards the temporary cells. She realised she still knew nothing about the kitsune or how to house it yet. It certainly couldn't stay cooped up in its little cell for much longer.

"That's odd," she mumbled as she reached the kitsune's cage. The door was slightly ajar.

She opened it all the way and peered inside, breathing a sigh of relief as she saw the red-furred kitsune sitting demurely on its pillow, slowly licking one of its two tails clean. It paused when it noticed her, looking up with eyes that seemed much more intelligent than Amari had expected.

"Hello, little one," she said as she stepped into the cell. "I hope you're alright in here. I'll be moving you somewhere much more comfortable soon, I promise."

The kitsune cocked its head towards one side,

its tufted ears twitching slightly, a telltale sign of sentience that Amari immediately recognised.

"Did you enjoy the chicken?" she asked as she cleared the remnants of its previous meal and filled the bowl with fresh water. The kitsune didn't respond, but watched her with interest. "Not a big talker, hey?" She put the meat she had brought from the kitchen down and turned to the creature. "Anything you need, let me know, little fellow. I want you to be happy here."

She expected a response, but the kitsune remained silent. Amari fleetingly wondered if English was the barrier here and if she should learn some Mandarin or Japanese phrases instead. She closed her eyes and inhaled deeply as the pleasant scent of green tea wafted towards her.

When she opened them again, the kitsune was still watching her with wide eyes, the tail it had been cleaning still lifted in the air but forgotten for the moment.

Amari smiled. "Goodnight, little one."

She stepped out of the cage, checking to make sure that the door was firmly closed behind her, before going in search of her own bed.

※※※

The basilisk was unusually reclusive when Amari entered its enclosure the next morning. Normally, the large reptile enjoyed laying on a rocky outcrop next to its lair, basking in the warm sunshine and catching dragonflies that hovered over the murky pond it liked to cool off in. But today it only peeked its monstrous head out of its hole and flicked a tongue out, tasting the air nervously.

Amari wrapped a scarf across her face so that the opaque cloth would prevent accidental eye contact with the creature. She really couldn't risk being turned to stone again. The last time it had taken days before someone from the Council had come looking for her.

Something crunched underfoot and she bent to pick it up. The obsidian scale filled her palm, cold and strangely brittle. She quickly did the math in her head and frowned. It wasn't time for the beast to shed yet.

"Everything alright, Hector?"

The basilisk snorted through its nostrils, shooting a viscous spray of yellow bile all around the entrance to its lair. Then it receded back into the hole, leaving only the tip of its beak visible from outside.

Amari wrinkled her nose at the sulphurous stench assailing her senses. Everything was definitely not alright, it seemed.

She was still worrying about the basilisk when she plopped into the chair behind her desk. Her fingers played with the scale while she considered its implications. Hector wasn't normally this temperamental, and he had made it abundantly clear that he wanted to be left alone. Could he be sick? The basilisk was half serpent and half rooster and would be susceptible to any number of avian or reptilian diseases, but since it was safely ensconced in its own enclosure, the chance of him catching anything was highly unlikely. And whatever was wrong was making him lose his scales, which was the most worrisome of all.

A knock on her office door startled her and she dropped the scale on the thick Persian carpet underfoot. She bent to pick it up, but paused as she noticed a clot of blue powder on the floor under her desk.

She frowned.

Another knock, more insistent this time, drew

her back to the present. She retrieved the scale and shoved it into a drawer. Straightening the scarf around her neck, she took a took a deep breath to regain her composure.

She had sent Cassie home the previous evening, so there could only be one person waiting to gain entrance to her study.

"Come in, Ambrose."

※※※

"Welcome to your new home, little one," Amari said as she opened the carrier case's door. She had expected the kitsune to dart outside and go scampering through the underbrush, relishing its newfound freedom, but the animal didn't stir from the cage.

The Keeper peered inside. The kitsune was backed up against the far wall, its ears laid flat against its head and its sharp little teeth bared in a snarl.

Odd. She wondered if she'd scared it somehow, but it had been quite willing to get back into the case. Apparently its fear of the unknown overpowered its will for freedom.

"I'm going to pick you up," Amari said, careful to keep her voice as soothing as possible. She carefully extended one arm into the case. "Please don't bite me."

Anticipating tiny fangs nipping at her arm, Amari cautiously wrapped her hand around the kitsune's soft, red fur. It hissed at her, but didn't attack. Amari was sure she recognised a look of dismay in its eyes as she pulled it out of the case.

"What do you think?" she asked, still holding the creature in her hand, her other arm sweeping across the expanse of her latest enclosure. She bit her lower lip nervously as she watched the kitsune survey its new territory.

Tufted ears perked up as it considered the woodland meadow before them. A copse of trees encircled a grassy hill dotted with burrows, wildflowers swaying in a pleasant breeze. The buzz of insects filled the honeysuckle air, and a small bird called out of sight.

The little body quivered in her hand.

Amari gently placed the kitsune on the ground. As soon as its paws touched the grass, it shot off like a pebble from a slingshot, yipping enthusiastically. Amari sat down, a warm happiness creeping into her heart, as she watched the kitsune frolic; pouncing on butterflies, startling a group of pheasants into flight and darting in and out of rabbit holes.

Finally, after it had worn itself out, it loped towards her and sat down on its haunches in front of her, its tongue lolling out in what Amari could only assume to be a smile. She stretched her hand out towards it, and the little two-tailed kitsune nuzzled her fingers.

"Seems like I got it right after all," she said. The kitsune gazed up at her with big, round eyes. "I don't even know what your name is, little one... Can I call you Kit?"

The kitsune's ears twitched and she saw laughter in its expressive eyes.

Amari nodded to herself, convinced now that the kitsune was intelligent enough to answer, but chose not to. That was fine with her, for now. She was patient and she'd made some progress today. Time enough to gain its trust. The Repository was home to both of them now.

"Can you tell me where you came from? Do you have a family?"

The kitsune snapped back from her hand as if it contained a snare. It jumped to its feet and glared at her before it dashed off into the forest.

"Kit!" Amari called after it, surging to her feet. It was too late. The kitsune had already disappeared into the undergrowth.

Perplexed, Amari shook her head. There was more to this new acquisition than met the eye, and the highly unusual way the kitsune had arrived at the Repository suddenly filled Amari with suspicion. Procurement Specialists delivered new animals, not Councilmembers.

She now recalled that Councilmember Bottenfeldt had said Kit had been a gift. A gift from whom? And why? Who dealt in the exchange of mythical creatures without her knowledge?

She needed to find out more. If Kit had been wrenched from his family, then Amari wanted to know where they were and why he had been taken from them.

※※※

Goosebumps on her arm warned her even before the fire in the hearth of her study turned blue. Amari put the book she had been unsuccessfully perusing for more information about kitsunes down. The spectral head that appeared before her belonged to the blonde woman Amari had been trying to phone all evening.

"Councilmember Bottenfeldt -" Amari greeted her superior.

"I need you to intercept a new Freelance Procurement Specialist, Miss Kerubo," the woman interrupted her. "I'll text you the coordinates. She's in somewhat of a predicament. Hurry. And be discreet."

The head disappeared before Amari had a chance to respond. She frowned as her mobile phone beeped. This was highly irregular. She wasn't aware of any new operatives... And why was the Councilmember contacting her through mystic fire instead of her mobile phone?

She glanced at the GPS coordinates that had been texted to her and said the Word.

When the white light faded, Amari felt her eyebrows lift into her hairline. She stood in the centre of a small wood-panelled room, opulently decorated with gilt furniture and stained-glass windows.

A woman in blue jeans and a leather jacket was leaning against one wall, staring at her with intense, dark eyes. Her long black hair was threaded into a ponytail through the gap in a baseball cap. A red welt against the side of her head promised an ugly bruise in the morning.

"About time," the woman said, her French accent unmistakable.

"I don't think we've met," Amari said. She held a hand out in greeting. "Amari Kerubo. And you are?"

The woman lifted one eyebrow, her arms remaining folded across her chest. Amari dropped her hand and clenched her jaw irritably.

"My name is not important," the stranger said. "I was told you can get me out of this bloody tower."

The woman rubbed her wrists, and Amari saw red welts chafed on her skin. A quick glance around the room revealed a pile of discarded rope lying off to one side.

Amari's brows furrowed. This just didn't feel right. Why was this woman locked in a medieval tower? And why did Amari need to rescue her? Discreetly.

"Well? Can you?" the woman snapped. She shifted her weight slightly forward, and Amari noticed the tension in the woman's seemingly casual stance. She was ready to act at a moment's notice. And she looked like someone who wouldn't hesitate to use violence to get her way.

"Yes," Amari replied through gritted teeth. She would follow orders, this time, but Councilmember Bottenfeldt would have some explaining to do the next time they talked. "Where do you want me to take you?"

One corner of the woman's mouth pulled up into a half-grin.

Why did Amari have the feeling that she was going to regret this?

✕✕✕

Medieval clock towers and mysterious women were far from her thoughts the next morning. She chuckled as the male baby griffon nibbled softly on her finger.

"Don't tell the others, but you're my favourite, Caerus," she whispered, tickling the downy feathers underneath one of his tiny white wings. The cub purred at her touch as she softly stroked the blue crest of feathers poking out at the top of his head. Amari wanted to take him home with her and snuggle him on her lap while she read by the fireside.

Instead, she handed him to his waiting mother, who picked the cub up by the scruff of his neck and started bathing him. Amari turned towards Apollo, watching the majestic male play a game of peekaboo with his two tiny daughters. They squealed in delight whenever his proud face peaked out from behind his wing feathers.

Suddenly, it was all she could do to keep the sting of hot tears from spilling onto her cheeks. A heavy weight settled in her chest. This family was protected in the Repository, but were they the last of their kind? How many mythical creatures could she save before it was too late? Were all her efforts in vain if most of these cages were filled with single creatures, without the promise of companions or offspring? What would happen to the world if all hope of saving them were lost?

She wished she could show everyone what was hidden inside the mountain fortress. If only people could see the unicorn's pure soul, or the basilisk's steadfast resolve, or the cyclops' single-minded focus. Surely then, they could be trusted to take care of these creatures instead of abusing them for their own ends.

She wished she could believe that.

She sniffed loudly and wiped her eyes with the back of her hands, pulling herself back together again. If wishes were unicorns, she'd not be worrying about any of this right now...

Her mobile phone pinged, startling her back to the present. She swiped the screen to check her messages. There was a text from Cassie.

--Ambrose cured! Celebratory pre-Christmas dinner at my place tonight. Please come.--

Her heart skipped a beat. So, Ambrose had found a cure for the asrai's curse. She had never heard of anyone surviving before. She itched to know how he'd managed it.

--Love to. See you tonight.--

She put her phone away and said her goodbyes to the griffons. As much as she may have liked to, she couldn't stay here all morning. She had other duties.

⁂

Amari knew something was wrong the moment she stepped into the next enclosure.

Normally she would have been splashed with water by now as the nymphs who lived in this meadow cavorted in the babbling brook running through the verdant countryside. They would have grabbed her hand and pulled her into the fray, or they would all have been sitting on a grassy knoll, drinking ouzo and gossiping about long-gone gods and goddesses. Once or twice she had even been party to an immense debate, the flighty creatures talking over each other in a great cacophony, invoking the memories of Plato and Aristotle as they each tried to win their listeners to their cause.

Today, a silent forest greeted her.

"Melia? Dryope? Lotis!" she called out.

The trees remained mute.

Tension hung thick in the air. Amari wanted to brush it from her face like a spider's web. A leaf crackled underfoot, sending her heart pounding, war drums in her ears.

She placed a hand on the coarse trunk of the nearest tree and recoiled as something stung her. She looked at her finger. A spot of blood bubbled where she had been pricked by a thorn.

"Talk to me," she begged.

Leaves rustled overhead, but the trees remained stubbornly reticent.

"I can't fix it if I don't know what's wrong."

A word floated on the air.

Deceiver.

A chill ran down Amari's spine.

The trees loomed over her, eerie and ominous. The sky had turned dark. A faint scent wafted her way, oddly familiar, but one she couldn't quite place.

Suddenly, the wind howled around her, filling

her ears with noise and pelting her body with leaves and twigs and pebbles.

Deceiver. Deceiver. Deceiver!

Amari ran for the gate and didn't stop to catch her breath until the enclosure was sealed behind her. She released a breath as she leaned against the stone wall.

What the hell was going on?

✴✴✴

Pushing her worries aside, Amari rang the doorbell and watched her breath frost in the cold air as she waited. She had the rare opportunity tonight of spending an evening away from the Repository and in the company of humans. Whatever drama the wood nymphs were embroiled in, it could wait until tomorrow morning.

Ambrose opened the door. His cheeks were flushed and his eyes showed surprise, but she couldn't see any blue veins stretching beyond the sleeves of his tweed jacket, nor any sign of the shivering that had wracked his body before. Beyond all expectations, he seemed remarkably healthy.

"This is for your sister," Amari said, handing him the potted plant she had brought from the Repository's greenhouse. He stepped aside, a wordless welcome, and she pressed past him into a festively decorated apartment. Music playing softly from someone's mobile phone wished her a white Christmas as she made her way to the fireplace crackling invitingly in the lounge, where two other women were already gathered.

"Hello. I'm Amari," she introduced herself as she joined them.

"Sarah," the woman wearing dark-rimmed

hipster glasses replied, her grip firm as they shook hands. Her keen eyes met Amari's, scrutinising her in a practised manner. She had the sudden urge to fix her scarf and stand up straighter. "And this is Pavithra," the brunette added.

"Nice to meet you," the young Indian woman said as she shook Amari's hand.

"Likewise," the Keeper replied, distracted by the symbol that had been tattooed between the woman's brows. A thin vertical line slashing through the middle of a small hollow circle. Now where had she seen that before?

She was about to comment on it when Cassie bustled into the room, carrying an enormous tray of roast lamb. Amari's stomach rumbled as the smell wafting from it reached her nostrils. She took her place at the table as everyone gathered around for dinner.

She studied the other guests as Cassie spoke a few words of welcome. Ambrose sat opposite her, with Sarah next to him, their shoulders touching, their hands probably clasped together underneath the table. Ambrose must feel like a hare finally outwitting the tortoise, what with the curse lifted, a full bank balance and a new girlfriend by his side. She wondered how much Sarah knew.

Her attention shifted to the woman sitting next to her. She was sure there was more to Pavithra than met the eye. The woman's accent was English, although a faint trace of somewhere more exotic still lingered in some of her words. Was she an expat like herself? The dark-haired woman was listening attentively to Cassie's speech, but a quick glance in Amari's direction revealed that she was not unaware of Amari's scrutiny.

"Okay," Ambrose's sister said, interrupting Amari's thoughts. "Let's dig in."

※※※

She found Ambrose alone in the kitchen after dinner.

"That was a close call," she said, remembering how Cassie had nearly revealed too much to Sarah before Ambrose had deftly evaded the truth and steered the conversation in another direction. "Are you sure you can keep such a big secret from your girlfriend?"

"I have to," he replied. "Do you honestly think she'd believe me if I told her?"

Amari didn't respond as she stacked plates in the sink. Ambrose was in a difficult position, lying to a woman who was not only his girlfriend but also a police detective. She wished she could let him come clean, but the risk was too great. The Repository must remain safe. The fewer people who knew of its existence, the better. She was already regretting showing Cassie as much as she had. If a little wine was all it took to set the woman's tongue wagging, then she might prove a problem in future.

"I've been meaning to talk to you, Amari," Ambrose continued. "I lost my whistle."

"I figured as much," she said, suppressing the flash of annoyance stabbing through her. Those whistles were her only contact with the Specialists. She couldn't keep track of Ambrose if he didn't have his anymore. "Are you going to tell me what happened? You're obviously not cursed anymore."

"Maybe someday," he replied evasively. "But there's something more urgent we need to discuss. I'd almost forgotten about it, but it's been on my mind ever since I…" He hesitated, clearly considering how much he was going to tell her. Amari pursed her lips, but continued tidying up, saying nothing. "Since I returned from Cardiff.

137

When I went to see the asrai, she told me to ask you how safe you really think the creatures in the Repository are."

Amari paused, a chill running down her spine. She turned towards Ambrose, wondering if he was serious or playing the fool with her.

There was no hint of a smile on his face. "She said to ask you what the bruises on the unicorn's neck are?"

"What?" Amari asked, frowning. A cold lump was settling in her stomach.

"And when I got home from the Repository, Cassie had bought a vial of liquid from the local Wicca store. It worked, Amari. It stopped the curse for a few hours."

Amari's eyes widened. "That's not possible," she said, shaking her head.

Her hands trembled as she took the half-full vial Ambrose held out to her. Its contents gleamed purplish-red in the harsh kitchen light.

"I have it on good authority that the bottle contains unicorn blood."

"No," Amari said, lifting a hand to her mouth. It felt as if the world had stopped spinning for a second, the universe zooming in on this moment, the two of them in this kitchen, the vial in her hand. "That can't be."

"Ambrose." Sarah strode into the kitchen as Amari steadied herself against the granite countertop. Her knees had lost all ability to keep her upright. "Amari, if you would give us a minute, please."

Amari's head reeled. She cast a last anxious glance at Ambrose as she exited the kitchen. His face was grim. He was telling the truth.

She walked into the living room in a daze. It felt unbearably hot. She couldn't breathe. Her hand fumbled with the scarf wrapped around her neck.

"I have to go," Amari said, hearing her own voice as if from afar. She vaguely registered that Cassie was asleep on the couch and that Pavithra sat on the floor next to her.

She didn't wait for a response, but somehow remembered to step into the hallway before saying the Word that sucked her into oblivion.

※※※

The fireplace surged as she stepped into her study in the Repository, casting strange shadows across her book-lined walls. Amari stumbled to the chair beside the hearth and dropped into it.

She looked at the little vial of blood she was still clutching in one hand. A sob escaped her lips.

Her fingers clenched around the vial. She jumped to her feet and strode out of her office, biting her bottom lip all the way to the unicorn's enclosure. Her breath caught as she realised the gate was unlocked.

"Una!" she called as she ran into the grove. Stars twinkled above, mimicked by fireflies sparkling all around her. Any other night, Amari would have stopped to appreciate how magical the unicorn's enclosure was, but tonight she barely noticed. "Una!" she called again, a note of panic entering her voice.

A whinny sounded and Amari placed a hand on her pounding heart as the pure white unicorn stepped out from behind the trees. She ran over to the animal and threw her hands around the unicorn's neck. Una whickered softly, nuzzling her cheek.

Holding her breath, Amari ran her hand across the unicorn's neck, underneath the glossy mane. She gasped. A closer look revealed the truth she didn't want to believe. A fine prick had scabbed over on the unicorn's neck. There was no denying that someone had drawn blood.

"Who did this?" Amari whispered, barely able to hold back her tears. The Repository was supposed to be a sanctuary. Una was supposed to be safe here.

The unicorn whinnied quietly. Amari's shoulders drooped as the animal's sadness nearly overwhelmed her. This beautiful, magical creature trusted her with her life, and she had failed her. Her hands balled into fists as her resolve turned to steel. She wiped the tears from her eyes.

"I'll find the one who did this, Una," she promised, a hint of steel creeping into her voice. "I'll find them and make sure they can never hurt you again."

※※※

Amari's nose wrinkled as she pushed past the flowering shrubs that encircled the asrai's enclosure. Something smelled rotten. The air was stagnant, close. A bead of sweat dripped down her temple as she stopped two arm-lengths away from the asrai's pond, dismayed by the green layer of algae that coated the water's surface.

"Show yourself," she said, retreating another step as a ripple spread out from the centre of the pond.

The asrai's head broke the surface and Amari gasped. The woman's pale hair clung in ragged tufts to her head. Her eyes held the heat of a desert sun.

"So the Keeper has finally deigned to visit her prisoner," the asrai jeered.

"You are not my prisoner," Amari replied sadly. "You're my guest, and your safety is my responsibility."

The asrai's laugh sent chills through Amari's bones.

"Clearly you've shirked your responsibilities." She tilted her ravaged head sideways, waves of anger radiating from her lithe body.

"What happened?"

A shudder ran through the nymph's body and her pale face turned even whiter. "I was attacked. A creature -" she paused, wrapping her arms around herself, as if cold in the torpid heat. "A creature of pure darkness." Her eyes met Amari's appalled gaze, fiery as a steaming geyser. "I was promised safety! The only reason I tolerate this imprisonment was the hope that I would be safe here. Now even that is denied me. Release me!"

"I can't," Amari said simply. Her heart ached as she saw the asrai's feistiness fade, her shoulders slumping. "I can't let you go," she repeated. "But I can make you safe again. Help me find this creature. Is there anything you can tell me that will lead me to it?"

The asrai's sensuous mouth contorted into a sneer. "Do you have any creatures of darkness in your keep?"

Amari shook her head. "No..."

"Then I think your answer should be obvious."

"A shifter? You think Reese is responsible?"

"Who else can come and go as they please in here? Who else can disguise themselves so that no one would know it was them?"

Amari scowled. "No, I can't believe Reese would do such a thing..."

The asrai pouted. "Believe what you will. I've told you what I know. But perhaps you'll listen when it's too late. The next time it may not just be my hair they're after." She turned her back towards Amari and stepped into the water again.

"Wait!" Amari called. "Is there anything else? Anything? Even something that seems silly to you?"

The asrai hesitated. Without looking back, she said: "There was a strange smell. Not unpleasant. Almost herbal." Then she disappeared into the deep.

Amari frowned. It wasn't much to go by, but it was better than nothing.

※※※

Amari yawned as she watched her phone's display ringing. She'd barely slept last night, tossing and turning into the early hours of the morning until worry had finally given in to fatigue. A few short hours later, she'd been up again, quickly popping into each of the enclosures to check up on her creatures. Most of them had still been asleep. All had seemed fine.

But she knew everything was far from fine.

She tapped a fingernail impatiently on her desk as she looked at her phone again. Perhaps it was a little too early to hope for anyone from the Council to be available, but she couldn't wait. She needed to inform her superiors of the state of affairs. She wanted someone else to know what was going on. And, if she were honest with herself, she wanted someone to tell her how to make things better.

Finally losing her patience, she ended the call. She turned around in her armchair and looked at the picture hanging on the wall. The stern-eyed woman stared wordlessly back at her.

"What would you do, Diana?" Amari asked. Unsurprisingly, she received no answer.

Amari turned back to her phone and dialled another number. She left it ringing while she dropped her head into her hands, staring sightlessly at the blinking icon on the screen's display.

She nearly fell off her chair when the ringing stopped and a face popped into view.

"Yes?" Councilmember Bottenfeldt's tone mirrored the annoyance on her face.

"Oh," Amari stammered, caught by surprise. She hadn't really expected an answer.

"Miss Kerubo, I have no time for idle chit-chat this morning," the blonde woman scolded. Her hair was still in curlers and only one of her eyes had makeup applied, a shade of green that did nothing for her pale complexion.

Amari took a deep breath, suppressing her own exasperation. As if she frequently phoned the woman for idle chit-chat.

"I apologise for disturbing you, Councilmember, but this is urgent. Someone, or something, has been attacking creatures in the Repository. I have it on good authority that unicorn blood is for sale in the outside world." She was proud to hear that her voice was steady, as if she wasn't howling on the inside.

"Are the creatures in any immediate danger? Have we suffered any losses?"

Amari hesitated. "We've had no casualties…"

"Then this can wait."

Amari's mouth fell open. "With all due respect, Councilmember -"

"Keeper," the woman cut her off. "This is your responsibility. These creatures are in your care. So take care of it. I know you are cloistered up there in the mountain, but out here it is Christmas morning and I am about to spend the day with my family. We will discuss your failings tomorrow."

The phone's screen blacked out as the woman ended the call. Amari stared at it, unable to believe the Councilmember's callous attitude toward what could be one of the biggest crises since the Repository had been founded. It might be her personal failure, but the Council was just as responsible for the creatures in her care as she was.

Disappointment tasted bitter on her tongue. A headache flared into life, pulsing against her temple.

Suddenly, it was all just too much. She couldn't do this on her own anymore. It felt like the walls were pressing in on her, the weight of the mountain heavy on her shoulders. She needed to get out of there.

She jumped to her feet, thrusting her phone into her pocket, and closed her eyes against the blinding white light that overwhelmed her.

When she opened them again, the glare of an African sun was burning down on her. Unwrapping the scarf from about her neck, Amari looked up at the Johannesburg skyline visible behind the tall wall that wrapped around the house in front of her. She nearly jumped out of her skin as a hadeda bird called out behind her, just before launching its ungainly body into the air and flying off toward the Hillbrow Tower.

"Amari?"

The Keeper wrenched her gaze from the cloudless sky. Her mother stood in the open doorway, dressed in a long skirt and a head wrap embroidered with traditional patterns, her Sunday-best for this special day.

Amari closed the distance between them in seconds. Her mother's ebony arms wrapped around her, warm as a hand-woven blanket.

"You made it," her mother whispered against her ear.

"Of course, Mama," Amari replied. "It's been too long."

Her mother released her and placed both hands on either side of her face. "Look at you!" she said. "My beautiful girl. Come, the whole family is here." She ushered her into the house.

A loud cry went up when Amari entered the living room. The entire family really was there, all crowded into the open-plan living area. Uncles and aunts, nieces, nephews, even a few people she didn't recognise. Amari hugged her little sister and steadied herself as her three older brothers tackled her in a tight embrace. Her father nearly dropped the enormous tray of meat he was carrying in his haste to kiss her cheek.

"What's wrong, my daughter?" her father asked, his face wrinkled with worry.

"Nothing, Baba," Amari said, wiping the tears from her eyes. "I'm happy to be home."

His hand was warm around hers, and for the first time in a long time, Amari felt like she belonged.

※※※

Much later, when the noise of constant conversation had turned into a dull buzz in her ears and the straining buttons of her jeans attested to the magnificence of the barbequed feast, Amari staggered out into the garden. Her eyes softened when she saw her grandmother sitting underneath the shade of a white stinkwood tree, her face lifted towards the breeze fluttering around Amari's scarf.

"May I join you, Gogo?" Amari asked.

"Come," her grandmother said, patting the grass beside her.

Amari kicked off her shoes and sat down beside the ancient woman. When Amari was a little girl, her Gogo had been a *sangoma*, a traditional healer; in her own way, a keeper of their culture's traditions and beliefs. Now, her sightless eyes looked upon memories only, but she still loved to tell stories to anyone who would listen. Amari had always liked the tales of clever animals outwitting human hunters best. They were probably what had set her feet upon the path that eventually led to the Repository.

Her shoulders slumped as she thought about the mountain fortress again. Her creatures would not be safe until she had found the shifter who had attacked Una and the asrai.

"I sense you are worried, little Amari," her grandmother's gravelly voice interrupted her thoughts.

"Yes, Gogo," Amari admitted.

"There is something threatening the animals you are caring for."

Amari couldn't help but smile at her grandmother's astuteness. No one in her family knew the truth about what she did for a living. They were all under the impression that she was still a zoologist at the London Zoo, a position she had landed straight after completing her studies at Oxford. Her brothers loved teasing her about leaving Africa behind to work with animals in a faraway city. If they only knew the truth, they would understand why she chose to remain so far from home.

"Gogo, what do the stories say about shapeshifters?"

Her grandmother chuckled. "That they are clever and wily and not to be trusted."

"But, how does one find something that can change into anything else?"

"Oh, there are ways," the old woman replied. "There is always something of their true self that they cannot change. Have I ever told you about the lion-men of the Ovambo tribe?"

Of course she had. "No, Gogo."

"Then listen closely, child."

Amari wrapped one arm around her grandmother's frail shoulders and listened patiently as the old woman's hoarse voice filled the quiet afternoon with the stories of her youth. As the shadows lengthened, Amari knew there was only one way to learn the truth.

She needed to confront Reese.

※※※

The winged monkey was perched in a sunny spot, high above the ground, his tail draped around the branch of an enormous tree. His head lolled on his chest, his breathing regular, a soft snore escaping his lips every now and then.

Amari clung precariously to a branch across from his, while two tiny monkeys scrambled across her body, leaping over each other and popping into brightly coloured birds as they vaulted into the air and flew even higher. Leaves rustled overhead, betraying more of the little rapscallions hiding from their siblings.

Amari shrieked as a monkey darted out of a hole in the tree, nearly colliding with her. It stopped as she gripped the branch with white knuckles and exhaled loudly. It cocked its head and cheekily stuck its tongue out at her before darting away again.

The Keeper couldn't help but laugh. No shortage of offspring here, at least. She took a deep breath to regain her composure and looked across at their grandfather. The ancient shapeshifter was still fast asleep.

"Reese," she called across to him.

He stirred, scratching his stomach, before settling down again.

"Reese!"

The winged monkey harrumphed and opened a sleepy eye. He saw her, lifted a paw in greeting, and closed his eye again.

"I need your help, Reese," Amari said.

With his eyes still closed, the monkey finally responded in a wheezy voice: "Let these old bones rest, Keeper. Find a young one to help you."

"Una was attacked."

The shapeshifter's eyes snapped open. They were no longer the dazzling sapphire blue they had been when Amari had first come to the Repository. Old age had weakened them and watered them down, but they were still striking enough to attract notice.

"Who would do that?" Reese asked.

"A creature of pure darkness, someone called it," Amari replied. She paused for a second, wondering how best to phrase her question. "There are no such creatures in the Repository."

"So you suspect a shapeshifter," the old monkey said, grimacing. "I'm too old to go around attacking others, Amari. And why would I? I worked tirelessly with Diana to bring them here to safety. Why would I do that just to turn on them in my dotage?"

"Not you, Reese, never you," Amari said. She hesitated.

"You think one of my children did it?"

Amari rubbed the back of her neck, shame flushing her cheeks, but she didn't answer. The question hung heavy between them.

"Look around you, Amari," Reese said. "What do all the little ones have in common?"

Amari let her gaze travel around the tree swarming with little winged monkeys. She found it endearing that they had taken their elder's preferred shape as their own, although most had incorporated their own youthful changes. One of them had pink fur, another the beautiful plumage of a peacock's tail, a third a long green elephant trunk. They were all different, but all had one thing in common. Sapphire blue eyes.

"Look into your shifter's eyes, Keeper, and if it mirrors my own, then you'll know where to come searching for the culprit," Reese said. He closed his own eyes again, and almost immediately resumed snoring.

"Thank you, Reese," Amari whispered.

"Oh, and Amari..." the old shapeshifter added as she was about to start her descent.

"Yes, Reese?"

The winged monkey opened his eyes again, and this time they were as clear and as electrifying as she remembered them. "Although she could never prove it, Diana wondered if the Repository was never meant to be the refuge we thought it was. Look to the Council. I believe you'll find your answer there."

Amari stiffened. A cold lump settled in her stomach as she considered the implications. Diana was a legend. With Reese assisting her, she had been responsible for bringing the vast majority of the animals now in Amari's care to the Repository. She had dedicated her life to rescuing mythical creatures from black markets and private collectors. If she had had doubts...

Amari lost her grip on the tree as the world started spinning. The monkey's tail wrapped around her wrist just as she felt herself slipping from her perch, steadying her.

Sapphire eyes gazed into her own.

"Do what Diana never could, Keeper. Make this sanctuary safe again."

Amari's stomach muscles clenched into a tight knot, and she felt a vein in her temple throb. She took a deep breath.

Then, the Keeper nodded.

✖✖✖

When Amari stepped out of Reese's enclosure, she immediately knew something was wrong. Cage doors rattled and yells, hoots and growls bellowed from the pens. All the creatures were in an uproar.

A high-pitched screech rent the air. Fear spiked through her heart. She knew that sound. She had named it only a few days ago.

She looked up just in time to see a dark shape slip through the steel door at the top of the stairs leading to the administrative wing. The door clanged shut behind it.

Heart racing, Amari took the steps up two at a time. She yanked the steel door open and saw the dark shape disappear behind the corner at the end of the corridor. Her feet pounded on the stone floor as she sped after it. A strange scent permeated the passage, almost like roasted chestnuts.

She shot around the corner just as the door to her office slammed shut. She reached the solid oak door in time to hear the lock being turned.

Amari yanked on the handle, grunting. It wouldn't budge. She banged her arms against the wood, shouting threats that sounded horrible in her own ears, and yet she knew she would carry them out if she had to.

She swore as it occurred to her to use the Word that unlocked the enclosure gates. It tore from her lips like a lightning strike on the savanna, rending the barred door in two. She stormed into her office.

Her heart heaved into her throat as she lurched to a halt.

The thing that confronted her must have been ripped from someone's deepest nightmares. Darkness roiled across its immense frame like a thundercloud, nebulous and menacing. Amari's throat went dry as the creature's burning eyes focused on her.

Red eyes, she realised. Not blue.

She took a step back as the monster loomed over her. It seemed to grow taller until its presence filled the entire room. Behind it, blue flames rose in the fireplace.

Amari gasped.

The youngest of the griffon babies squirmed in the creature's grasp. Before she could react, it tossed the little cub into the fire.

"Caerus!" Amari shouted as he disappeared into the flames, a heart-wrenching wail echoing in the small space. "No!" Amari sprinted toward the hearth, but it was too late. The baby was gone.

Her vision turned crimson. She spun towards the creature, too angry to be afraid anymore. "Where did you send him?" she shouted.

The blackness wavered as the monster retreated before her fury. A Word toppled from her mouth just as that strange scent washed over her again. It smelled of green tea.

The darkness exploded.

Amari closed her eyes and braced herself as the blast threatened to sweep her into the fireplace. Wind roared through her study. Amari curled in upon herself as books whipped around her, pummelling into her. Her eardrums throbbed with the noise.

When quiet finally fell, Amari opened her eyes, dreading what she knew she'd see. A sob escaped her lips as she extracted herself from a pile of old tomes and slowly walked towards the centre of the room.

Where the monstrous shadow had stood before, the kitsune now lay crumpled.

"Kit," Amari said, falling to her knees by the little two-tailed creature's side. Tears streamed down her face. Gently, she placed a hand on the soft fur of the animal's chest. She bit her lip when she felt the flutter of a heartbeat.

"My name… is Riku," the kitsune whispered.

"Why, Riku?" she asked softly. "Why did you do this?"

"To protect… my mate," Riku wheezed. He tried to sit up, but Amari gently restrained him.

"Take it easy," she said. "You're hurt."

"Keeper?"

Amari looked up to see the winged monkey entering her study. He frowned as his gaze flitted around the room, noticing the blue fire in the hearth, the books tossed across the floor. Reese's sapphire eyes widened as he saw the kitsune.

"You found the shifter."

Amari nodded as he flew over and landed on the ground beside her. His clever fingers lightly explored the kitsune's body. His mouth drew into a thin line.

"Well, I think he'll live. Shapeshifters are quite resilient, you know," Reese said. He lifted a shaggy eyebrow. "Although a Word that potent would have killed most other things. Are you sure you wanted him to survive?"

Amari exhaled loudly as relief washed over her. She turned to the kitsune again. "What happened to your mate?" she asked.

The creature whimpered. "Taken. Exchange… others, for her."

Amari straightened, her fists clenched. "That will no longer be necessary. Reese, please take Riku back with you and ask your family to look after him until I return."

"Of course, Keeper," the old shapeshifter replied. The winged monkey shimmered and coalesced into the shape of a silverback gorilla. Reese gently picked the kitsune up and cradled him in his powerful arms. "And what will you do?"

"I'm going to confront the Council."

✳ ✳ ✳

"What's the meaning of this?" a Councilmember demanded.

Amari examined the members of the Elder Council assembled before her. She had broken protocol by bypassing her superior and invoking the summons that had plucked them from their lives and gathered them together in the main boardroom of the CPPCC's corporate headquarters. She grimaced as she remembered it was still Christmas day. The man who had spoken wore festive reindeer antlers and had one half of a Christmas cracker in his hand. Another woman placed a half-eaten turkey leg on the boardroom table while glaring at the Keeper.

"Miss Kerubo." Amari turned towards the German woman striding towards her. Councilmember Bottenfeldt's face was a thundercloud. "Didn't I say this could wait?"

Amari said a Word that stopped the woman in her tracks. She ignored the blonde woman's outraged splutters. "I charge Councilmember Bottenfeldt with the illicit trafficking of mythical creatures."

Gasps filled the room. She watched in satisfaction as angry glares turned from her to the captive Councilmember.

The woman snorted. "That is absurd. Release me immediately. How dare you use magic on a member of the Elder Council?"

Amari made no move to comply. "I contacted Councilmember Bottenfeldt this morning to tell her that creatures inside the Repository have been attacked and harvested," she said, her voice rising in anger.

"Impossible," someone said.

"But true," Amari countered. She pulled the vial of purplish liquid Ambrose had given her from her pocket and held it aloft for everyone to see. "Unicorn blood. Purchased at a magic shop in London."

Everywhere she looked, faces paled as the Councilmembers considered her words. Two women reached for each other, as if seeking support. The antlered man slumped into a chair, his face grim.

"Not only that," Amari continued, "but the culprit kidnapped a creature right before my eyes. A baby griffon born a few days ago. The first of its kind to be born in the Repository, plucked from its family to satisfy this woman's greed." She pointed an accusing finger at her captive.

"Lies," the blonde woman spat.

"There is only one way of knowing for sure," a deep voice said. All eyes turned to the man who stepped forward to confront the Councilmember. He was impeccably dressed in an expensive Italian suit. The lines around his eyes deepened as he frowned at the Councilmember. Amari had never met the man before, but she recognised him immediately as the Chief Chairman of the Council.

The Chairman pulled a mobile phone from his pocket and started scrolling through his list of contacts. "I'll just give our Asian colleagues a quick call," he said, his British accent as refined as his choice of clothes. "They recently acquired a sin-you which I think would serve our purposes quite well right now."

The blood drained from Councilmember Bottenfeldt's face. "You wouldn't do that to me," she said, a hint of panic creeping into her voice.

"Now, Ingrid," the Chairman said. "You have nothing to fear if you're telling the truth."

Amari looked at the approving nods from the other members of the Council. She wished she'd paid more attention to Diana's foreign collection.

"Excuse me, sir," she said, heat rising to her cheeks as the Chairman fixed his piercing gaze on her. "I'm not very familiar with Asian creatures," she admitted, feeling like a fool. She was the Keeper of Exotic Animals, after all. She should be more informed. "What is a sin-you?"

"A noble creature from the Far East," the Chairman explained. "It has a single horn, much like our dear Una, and, more importantly, also an uncanny sense for the truth. If a lie is told in its presence, the sin-you will impale the deceiver on its horn, which unfortunately often turns out to be quite fatal for the liar."

Amari gulped.

"Ah, here it is," the Chairman said. He turned his mobile's speakerphone on and the sound of the call ringing on the other end reverberated through the boardroom.

"Konnichiwa," a female voice answered.

"Stop! Stop, I confess," Councilmember Bottenfeldt exclaimed, her lower lip trembling.

The Chairman smiled coldly. "Apologies, Masuyo-san. I'll call you back later." He ended the call. His smile faded and his face turned stony. "Tell us," he said to the German woman.

A tear leaked down the blonde woman's face. "My family is in debt," she began. "Do you know how expensive it is to keep up appearances while my departed father's funds dwindled off into all sorts of causes? Save the rhino, and ban single-use plastics, and conserve the rainforest, and, and, and!" she sneered. "The money went out faster than interest could accumulate. And then one day, while wading through a stack of unpaid bills, I came across a message. Unmarked and unsigned, it offered me a chance. All I had to do was provide samples of mythical creatures. Not the creatures themselves, I made sure of that. I know their worth. But a feather or a scale or a vial of blood. And in return, I would be compensated." She glared at the accusing faces around her. "What would you have done? I accepted, and the next day that little two-tailed fox was delivered to my door. It would get what I needed, and I would pass it on."

Amari's jaw clenched and her fingers balled into fists. "Did you pass the baby griffon on too?"

"Yes," the disgraced woman admitted, her shoulders slumping. "I hadn't expected that, but what else could I do?"

"Who did you pass it on to?" the Chairman asked, his face red with fury.

"I don't know," Councilmember Bottenfeldt admitted. "The fox would send me the item via mystic fire and then I would blow this." She pulled a silver whistle out from around her neck. It looked like the ones Amari gave to the Procurement Specialists to contact her with. "I'd leave the item in the fireplace and when I'd come back an hour later, it would be gone."

"You don't know who you've been supplying animal parts to?" the Chairman demanded, his eyes blazing. "You never tried to catch a glimpse of whoever came to pick them up?"

"No!" she sobbed. "I didn't want to know. I swear, I never wanted it to go this far. I just needed the money."

Amari saw her own disgust mirrored in the Chairman's sneer. "You should have come to me, Ingrid. We could have worked something out. Now, look what you've done. All our efforts, wasted."

The blonde woman sagged, tears streaming down her face. Amari wanted to feel sorry for her, but she couldn't. She held out her hand and the woman deposited the silver whistle into her palm.

"Do you have any clue that could lead us to this mysterious buyer?" she asked.

Councilmember Bottenfeldt sniffed and wiped her nose on the back of her hand. She nodded slowly. "The courier company that delivered the fox made me sign a receipt. The destination of origin was on it. It came from Rome."

The Chairman turned towards Amari. "Keeper-"

"I know just the man for the job," she said.

The Chairman nodded, and Amari's world blazed white.

PART 4

HUNTER'S RESOLVE

For a city so steeped in myth and legend, Rome had been utterly disappointing so far.

Three months walking the cobbled streets of the Eternal City and I had yet to encounter any fantastical creatures. Everywhere I looked, buildings, fountains, museums and curio shops bombarded me with images of the gods and goddesses of this ancient civilisation. Hell, my somewhat seedy apartment in Trastevere was graced with a mural of a crazy-eyed Zeus casting lightning bolts from between billowing clouds on the bathroom wall. I couldn't even brush my teeth without being confronted by that other world most believed were stories, but that I now knew to be true.

And yet, for someone who had nearly had their veins frozen to ice, danced with a harbinger of death, been hunted by hounds from beyond the grave, and been breathed on by a real honest-to-Zeus dragon, I have managed to completely evade any nymph, satyr or tea-loving faun that might call this city home.

It was a dead zone, mythologically speaking.

The statue of Oceanos leered down at me from its vantage point at the centre of the Trevi Fountain. Its mocking gaze reminded me just how much I hated being near water these days. It was as if the marbled Titan knew I hadn't gotten around to swimming lessons yet and was daring me to take the plunge.

If I'd had a can of paint, I'd spray graffiti all over that smug smirk.

Instead, I fingered the coin I'd been meaning to throw into the fountain, and then thrust it back into the pocket of my tweed jacket.

I doubt I'd ever want to return to Rome, anyway. Nothing but regrets here.

I pulled the collar of my jacket up as the wind ruffled through my hair and glanced up at the clear blue sky. Rome was between seasons, on the cusp of spring, an in-between time when the winter tourists had left and the summer throngs hadn't yet arrived. It would have been a wonderful time to explore the Italian capital, if I hadn't been so frustrated.

At least I could look forward to a sweltering summer if I stayed in the city a while longer. It would be nice to feel truly warm again, after so long.

I turned my back on the famous fountain, for once not covered in scaffolding, and ambled towards the ice cream shop at the corner of the empty piazza.

"Un gelato al cioccolato, per favore."

The downside of failing a mission was the frustration of feeling trapped in a Sisyphean purgatory, showing no progress and doomed to stay in one place until you had redeemed yourself. The upside was that you got to eat chocolate ice cream. Lots and lots of it.

While I waited for the lanky teenager behind the counter to serve my scoop, I glanced back at the piazza. It wasn't empty anymore. A dark-haired girl with black-rimmed glasses was admiring the fountain. A smile crept over my face as I watched her snapping selfies while pretending to toss a coin over her shoulder.

She reminded me of another woman I had left behind in London, so many months ago.

※ ※ ※

Things hadn't ended well with Sarah.

"How can I trust you?" she'd asked, her green eyes blazing, as we stood in Cassie's kitchen on Christmas Eve, looking at a picture of me and Monique inside the Cardiff Museum. "You didn't tell me you'd been to Cardiff and here you are practically holding hands with the woman you claimed had attacked you in Paris."

"She *did* attack me," I said. "You saw the CCTV footage – she tried to shoot me!"

"Tried, or deliberately missed?" Sarah countered. "You could have staged it for the cameras. Or it could have been a double-cross between two thieves, and you were the one drawing the short straw."

"You can't really believe that."

"I don't know what to believe, Ambrose. You haven't been completely honest with me from the day we first met."

"So that's it?" I asked, my temper flaring. Nothing like the truth to get a guy riled up. "You're going to arrest me?"

Her eyes bored into mine, as if she wanted to draw the truth from me by sheer force of will. Then her shoulders slumped and she wrapped her arms about herself. "No." I reached out to her, but she pulled away from me. "Look, I'd better go," she said. "Early shift tomorrow."

"It's Christmas Day!" I protested.

She shook her head, not looking at me, and left the kitchen. I wanted to follow her, but something kept me rooted to the spot. Pride. Anger. Guilt. Who knew? Probably all three.

By the time I realised what an idiot I was and returned to the living room, Sarah was gone.

I still hadn't heard from her by noon the next

day as Cassie and I trudged through the slush towards our family home, our breaths frosting in the cold air. I ignored the temptation to look at my phone again and thrust my gloved hands deeper into my jacket pockets as Cassie rang the doorbell of the three-storey house in Kensington.

"Ugh, I don't know if I can face her today," my sister muttered, pressing a finger against her temple as we listened to the doorbell chime Mozart's *Eine Kleine Nachtmusik* in analogue.

"You shouldn't have drunk so much last night," I said.

She glared at me with bloodshot eyes. "Don't start. Or I'll tell her what you really do for a living."

I lifted both hands in surrender just as the door opened. Jenna Davids was impeccably dressed, as always, her trim figure enveloped in the latest fashion, from Milan, no doubt. Black hair framed an ageless face marred only by a few lines around the corners of her down-turned lips.

She opened both arms in welcome and Cassie and I stepped reluctantly into her embrace.

"What's this?" Mother said, rubbing her hand across my cheeks as I extricated myself from her arms. "You couldn't bother to shave for Christmas? How will Rachel ever take you back if you refuse to make some effort?"

"We're not getting back together," I mumbled, but Mother had already moved on.

"Cassandra darling," she said, looking at my sister as if the cat had dragged her in. "This simply won't do. Surely the stipend I allot to you every month can provide for something better than charity shop castoffs?"

Cassie's face turned a shade of red that promised trouble, but Mother was already halfway down the hall before my sister's indignant splutters could become coherent.

"She means well," I said half-heartedly, taking my coat off and hanging my scarf on a hook.

A vein in her temple pulsed violently as Cassie shook out of her own jacket. She drew a deep breath and plastered a smile on her face that wouldn't have convinced me, even if I hadn't known her as well as I did. Then, arm in arm, we trudged towards the living room.

"Is there anything I can help you with, Mother?" I asked as she bustled in from the kitchen carrying a bowl of something steaming. My mouth watered as the scent hit my nostrils. The old Edwardian dining table was groaning under the weight of all the food Mother had already laid out, enough to feed an extended family, not just the three of us.

"Of course not, dear," she replied. "I have it all under control. Please, sit down. I'll just bring in the duck and then we can say grace."

"Duck?" Cassie grimaced as Mother disappeared into the kitchen. "How typical. We couldn't just have a turkey for Christmas dinner like the rest of the world?"

I shrugged as I settled into my chair. Mother had her faults, but cooking wasn't one of them. I lifted the lid on one of the dishes and nearly swooned as the aroma of roasted potatoes wafted my way. Jamie Oliver and Nigella Lawson combined couldn't compete with Mother's culinary skills.

"Et voila!" Mother said as she reappeared with the main course. She placed the duck in the centre of the table and took a step back to take it all in. Her dark eyes gleamed with pride.

"Everything looks delicious," I complimented her as she took her seat at the head of the table, and was rewarded with a rare smile that reminded me of days when the food had been simpler, but we had all been much happier around this table.

"That's Father's place," Cassie said, reaching for the roast vegetables.

"Your father isn't here, dear," Mother said, the smile slipping as she pursed her lips. "And please mind your manners until we've given thanks for the food."

"And whose fault is that?" Cassie mumbled, pulling her arm back and slumping in her chair, pouting like a teenager.

"Cassie, that's hardly fair..." I tried.

"No, Ambrose," Mother interrupted me. "Let her have her say. Your sister still thinks it's my fault that your father left us."

"He didn't leave us, you divorced him!" Cassie shrieked, jumping to her feet. "You couldn't handle his failure and you pushed him away. Well, I have news for you, Mother. Father was right!"

"Cassie..." I warned.

She glared at me, her bloodshot eyes wild with anger. Somehow, her hair had gotten all messed up with static electricity, wisps wafting in the air like snakes on Medusa's head. I held her gaze until she looked away, a blush colouring her cheeks, and turned her attention back to Mother.

"Your father was a delusional dreamer," Mother said calmly. Her jaw looked like it was chiselled from stone as she fixed my sister with a piercing stare. "He was so obsessed by those old stories that he couldn't see how ridiculous he sounded. I warned him he was going too far, but he wouldn't listen. And see what happened? He lost it all. We lost it all." She took a deep breath while her one hand tried to strangle a napkin. "But while he took the coward's route out and disappeared, I had to take care of two children," she continued. "Who made sure there was food on your plate, and money for university, Cassandra?

Me, not your father. I juggled jobs, I made it work. Your father is probably sleeping under a bush somewhere, looking for fairies or goblins or hobbits, or whatever nonsense he's dreamed up. Dreaming is nice, but reality is not so forgiving."

Mother's words struck a chord within me. I knew all about dreams versus reality. Dreaming had cost me my career and my girlfriend, after all. I looked at Mother with new eyes. For the first time since that fateful day when Father had disappeared, I suddenly saw things through her eyes. Her perfectionism, her pressure on us to perform – those were her ways of coping, of preparing us for the harsh world she'd been thrust into. She'd made the best of a difficult situation. We had just never realised how much it had cost her.

I glanced from one angry woman to the next. They were at a standoff, neither willing to budge. You could cut the tension in the room with one of Mother's silver butter knives.

"Mother's right, Cassie," I finally said. My heart ached as I saw the betrayal in my sister's eyes, but it was time she faced the truth. Time we both did. "Please sit down."

Cassie plopped into her chair and Mother shot me a grateful look. Her voice was strained as she said grace and we spent the rest of the evening in near silence, cutlery clinking loudly against china. I hardly tasted any of the food while I tried to think of ways to lift the mood, and although they were perfectly civil to each other through four courses and dessert, it was clear neither had forgiven the other by the time Cassie excused herself and went home.

"I'm sorry, Mother. We haven't been kind to you these last few years," I said as we both sat staring at the crackling fireplace, sipping an after-dinner drink.

"Thank you, Ambrose," she replied. The hard lines on her face had softened. She seemed uncharacteristically vulnerable in the dim firelight. "I've only ever wanted what's best for you."

"I know that. And deep down, Cassie knows it too."

"Your sister will learn soon enough that the world is not the fairy tale your father made you believe in when you were children. Sooner or later, we must all grow up. No matter how much we dislike the idea."

Mother's words echoed in my head as I walked home later that evening. I knew now that Father had been right, that the world was more than the black and white Mother believed it to be. But I had seen that other world for myself and been burned by it. What's more, I had let my selfishness bring harm to innocent creatures. When a unicorn's blood seemed the only thing that could keep me alive, I had only wanted to save myself, no matter the cost to a beautiful creature of myth. It had taken a dragon's gaze to show me the error of my ways.

I couldn't capture mythical creatures anymore.

Even if Amari's intentions were good and all she wanted was to keep them safe, that decision was not mine to make. It never had been. Who was I to decide over anyone else's freedom? I would let Amari know I could no longer work for the Council.

My heart lurched as I realised that I'd need a new source of income now. But so be it. Perhaps it was time to face up to my mistake and set the wrong I had done right again. Perhaps it was time to grow up and face my responsibilities. If I wanted to make things right with Sarah, I needed to get my life back on track again.

By the time I entered my apartment, I had resolved to distance myself from the mythical world and return to my career in finance, if possible. If not, I still had enough savings stored away to go back to university and retrain myself. I'd find a way.

I closed the door behind me.

"Ambrose, I need your help."

My hand shot to my chest where it felt like my heart wanted to make a break for it. I closed my eyes for a second and counted three Mississippis before I confronted my unexpected visitor.

"Amari, are you trying to give me a heart attack?"

The Keeper of Exotic Animals grimaced. "Sorry. I didn't know where else to look for you, so I thought I'd just wait until you got home."

"In the dark?" I asked as I turned the light on. "And how do you know where I live?"

"Never mind that now," Amari said. Her face was drawn as she pulled two silver whistles out of her handbag.

I held both hands up. "Woah, there. I know we haven't discussed everything that had happened to me in Cardiff yet, but I was going to let you know that I no longer want to hunt creatures for the Council."

"This is different," Amari replied. "You're not hunting, you're finding."

I frowned. "I uh... don't really see the difference," I replied awkwardly.

"I want you to find a creature that has been stolen from the Repository." My eyes widened. "A baby griffon, to be precise. I want you to find him and the person who took him. This," she held up the whistle dangling from a black cord, "is a replacement for the one you lost. This one," she held up the other, hanging from a red cord, "is the one that will lead you to the buyer. Blow on it, and he will come to you."

"How do you know? Have you tried it?" I asked as I took both whistles from her.

"No," she said, sounding resigned. "I can't risk letting the buyer into the Repository." She held up a hand as I was about to ask the obvious. "There was an unwilling accomplice. The griffon was kidnapped by a creature inside the Repository. I was a little overzealous when I captured him. He's still recovering."

I whistled in amazement. I'd always thought of the Keeper as a scholar, a specialised veterinarian even, but this was a different side of Amari I hadn't seen before. I should have known better. Her job was probably highly hazardous. I'd only had a few chance encounters with mythical creatures so far, and all of them had nearly cost me my life. I suddenly had a lot more respect for the young woman standing before me.

"Why don't you go after the buyer yourself?" I asked.

Amari sighed. "I can't leave the Repository unattended, otherwise I would. I'm aching to get my hands on the guy behind it all." At the sudden steel in her voice, I made a mental note never to cross her. "You were right," she continued. "It was unicorn blood in that vial you gave me. I can't leave Una, and everyone else, unprotected. I need to keep watch in case someone tries to infiltrate the mountain again."

A hint of desperation entered her voice. "The Council was involved, Ambrose. I don't know who to trust." Amari's agate eyes locked with my own. "But I trust you."

I considered her words. Just moments before, I had resolved to keep my distance from the mythological world, but Amari's concern was contagious. If the Council couldn't be trusted, then every creature inside the Repository was in danger. I couldn't stand idly by if there was a chance I could help protect them. I wouldn't add to their collection, but I'd sure as hell try my best to rescue a baby that had been kidnapped. And if finding the buyer meant protecting the creatures already in the Repository, then that was what I had to do.

I squared my shoulders, my decision made.

"Thank you, Ambrose," Amari said, her keen gaze almost reading my thoughts. "Ready to go?"

"Right now?" I asked, taken aback by her haste.

"No time like the present."

I did a mental check. I had my wallet on me, was wearing my lucky white sneakers, mobile phone in my pocket. Anything else I could get as I needed.

"Sure."

I closed my eyes against the bright light that painted the world white.

⁂⁂⁂

When I could see again, my mouth dropped open in surprise. I was standing in a pool of moonlight spilling into the middle of a circular room from a hole in the roof. I'd seen enough pictures of this place to know immediately where I was. The Pantheon in Rome.

Rome! I hadn't expected that. I didn't even have my passport with me. And I knew even less Italian than French. Not sure how much my childhood Latin would be worth here.

I was alone inside one of the world's most visited sites. If Amari's haste hadn't been so firmly imprinted on me, I might have stopped to savour the moment and explore its marbled interior. Instead, my footsteps echoed in the empty space until I reached the main door. I tried the handle. It opened! I stepped through into the bustling piazza, ignoring the startled glances from a few nearby bystanders.

I glanced at my watch. It was close to midnight, but it was Christmas Day and the Eternal City was celebrating. The square was filled with people in warm jackets and rosy cheeks, chatting animatedly and listening to the quartet singing carols beside the Pantheon.

I wrapped my tweed coat about myself and sat down on the steps leading up to a fountain. I pulled the whistle with the red cord out from underneath my scarf. This would be a good place to remain anonymous if the buyer did come looking.

I blew on the silent whistle, then sat back, watching and waiting.

I didn't know what to expect, but a gasp still escaped my lips when I saw a familiar face in the crowd. The woman's long black hair shone almost purple in the moonlight and her smile was lopsided when our eyes met. Monique placed two fingers on her brow and gave me a mock salute. I jumped to my feet, but she was gone, lost in the throng, before I could follow.

That was the last time I saw her, and the last time I tried to blow the whistle on the red cord.

✕✕✕

"Signore?"

I blinked and stared dumbly at the young man holding a *gelato* out at me, for a moment surprised by my surroundings. Then the scent of the chocolate ice cream brought me back to the present.

"Sorry," I said, scrounging in my pockets for change. I dropped a few euros in his outstretched palm in exchange for the cold treat.

I stepped out of the shop, licking the ice cream, and shivered. It had suddenly turned blustery. The sky was an ominous grey and the wind sliced through my thin jumper. I looked at the ice cream in my hand in dismay.

Just my luck.

When I looked up again, I was staring straight into the maw of a monster. A giant serpent reared up out of the Trevi Fountain, its shimmering olive coils looped tightly around Oceanos' marbled form. Somehow, the statue's expression didn't seem quite as smug anymore. The creature snorted and I gulped as my gaze was wrenched back to the razor-sharp teeth inches away from my face.

I tried to take a small step back, but wind buffeted me from behind, keeping me in place. Vaguely, I felt the wind whipping my hair and saw leaves twirl around my feet as if a storm raged about me, but my attention was entirely on the reptilian face in front of me.

The snake snorted again, almost as if it was sniffing the air, and its black tongue darted towards me.

I snatched my hand back in reflex. The snake hissed and turned its head sideways. Its lidded eyes blinked at me and it sniffed again.

A ridiculous thought crossed my mind. I held the *gelato* out at it. "You want my ice cream?"

The grotesque tongue flicked out again, and now the maw seemed less threatening and more like a macabre smile. The snake panted in excitement.

I tossed the *gelato* into its mouth and watched, incredulously, as it gulped my dessert down. It smacked its jaws together, almost like a child licking their lips, then uncoiled itself from the statue and dived into the fountain's pool. As its monstrous body disappeared from view, the wind settled and the sun poked out from behind the clouds again.

"Incredible," I said, shaking my head.

"Ambrose?"

I nearly jumped out of my skin. This was the last voice I had expected to hear while in Rome. I spun around to see Sarah standing before me. My heart quickened as our eyes met. I wanted to wrap my arms around her, but I stopped myself as a frown lined her face.

"I can explain..." I said, wondering how she could be so calm after witnessing a monstrous snake disappear into a fountain. Then again, she was a detective. She'd probably seen it all.

Or she hadn't seen anything.

"You'd better," she interrupted me, moss-green eyes flashing behind the black hipster glasses she favoured. "I don't hear from you for three months and now I find you here, in Rome, just when *she's* been seen here too."

"The stories are all –" I paused, realising what she had just accused me of. "Wait, what?"

"Don't you think it's just a little convenient that your thieving friend's been spotted in Rome, and here you are too?" She folded her arms across her chest. I hoped it was to warm her hands against the cool breeze, but I suspected it was more to place a barrier between us.

I frowned, trying to get my thoughts straight. "This is about Monique?"

"Who else?" she exclaimed. "The wanted antiques smuggler who, apparently, you're on a first-name basis with. What's the job this time, Ambrose? Have your eye on something in the

Vatican?"

"Is that why you're here?" I asked, ignoring her accusation. "Isn't this just a little bit outside of your jurisdiction?"

"Special assignment," she countered. "I've been seconded to Interpol. As soon as I'd heard she'd been spotted here, I volunteered to come track her down. I hadn't expected to find you too." Her jaw clenched. "I probably should have known better."

"Look, I can explain," I said again, thinking fast, because I really couldn't explain. Nothing she'd believe, in any case. But surely I could come up with something in between myth hunter and relic thief that would sound plausible. How hard could that be?

"Save it," Sarah spat. "I was wrong about you, Ambrose. I don't know what you're up to, but I swear I'm going to find out."

I grit my teeth, frustrated. How had we gone from Paris to this?

Plink-plink-plonk.

I stared at the small earthenware bowl that had come to a stop between us. It was slightly wonky, like it was someone's homemade pottery attempt; not quite as round as a ball, with an open end that had been covered with red chequered cloth. If I'd seen it on a table at a restaurant, I'd have expected to find jam in it.

"What the –"

"Watch out!" Sarah yelled. She charged into me, knocking me off my feet just as the bowl exploded. Shards shattered everywhere and I winced as a small slice nicked my cheek. Smoke billowed as a pungent mixture of herbs and rotten eggs filled my nostrils. I coughed as the stench stuck in my throat. My eyes started watering and the world spun when I tried to get up.

The last thing I saw was Sarah, unconscious on the ground, her long brown hair framing her waxy face. Then everything faded in the haze.

✕✕✕

My nose woke me.

The stench had changed to that of musty hay and manure, but it was still strong enough to make my eyes water. I shook my head to clear it, coughing the last remnants of the smoke I had inhaled earlier from my lungs.

My shoulders ached and I could hardly feel my fingers. The floor below me was swaying.

Pain flared through my upper body as my head wrenched upwards at the realisation of my predicament. My hands were tied together by a rope wrapped around a thick wooden rafter. I looked down again at my dangling feet.

Well, this was problematic.

Ignoring my screaming shoulder blades, I slowly twisted my body to take in my surroundings. I was in a barn, or a stable, judging by the amount of hay and manure scattered on the floor. The walls were made of stone, crumbling in places, and looked like they hailed from Julius Caesar's time, which was probably also the last time the floor had been swept.

Sarah was hanging beside me. Her face was still pale, but I could see her chest move in regular breathing, and I let out a relieved breath of my own.

She groaned and her nose scrunched up as the stink hit her, too. Her eyes blinked as she regained consciousness.

"Ugh," she said, subduing a gag reflex. "What is that smell?"

"That is what retribution smells like," a deep

voice answered.

I looked up just in time to see the owner of the voice silhouetted against the light spilling in through the open barn door. For a moment, I wondered if I were dreaming. Then I remembered the myths were all true, and that the creature trotting towards us was as real as Sarah and I were.

The upper half of its body was human, with the powerful build of a warrior who spent his days training and honing his physique. His broad chest was enclosed within a bronze breastplate, and a red-crested helmet protected his head. A sword was strapped to his waist, a plain unembellished weapon that was notched with use.

Below his waist... Powerful muscles rippled as his four legs came to a standstill in front of me. His brown horsehair hide looked sleek and shone in the rays of light filtering in through gaps in the roof.

A centaur!

Sarah inhaled sharply. "What was in that bomb?" she muttered, shaking her head as if trying to clear it.

The centaur glared at her, but she seemed undaunted, staring back at him with undisguised curiosity. Even through the discomfort of hanging suspended from the ceiling, her eyes sparkled in a way that made me think she was probably an equestrian at heart.

The creature turned its gaze on me. His face was classically handsome, with a strong nose and prominent cheekbones. A lock of black curls had escaped from underneath his helmet. When he spoke, his voice was tinted with a heavy Italian accent.

"Why did the Council send you?" he demanded. His breath smelled of apples, a strangely pleasant respite from the surrounding stench.

"I don't work for the Council anymore," I replied. His face was uncomfortably close to mine, his eyes the same height as my own while I hung from the ceiling. I tried moving away from him, but that only set me swinging back and forth like a pendulum.

He reached out and stopped my motion, harrumphing irritably.

"Do not take me for a fool," his deep voice rumbled. "We've been monitoring you for months now. Today you interacted with the bissabova, and yet you let it leave in peace. I ask again: why are you here?"

I glanced at Sarah. She was following the conversation so closely, she might as well be sitting there with a box of popcorn. This was not how I had wanted her to find out, but I guess the centaur was out of the bag now.

"I am here on behalf of the Keeper," I admitted. The centaur snorted and his tail whipped angrily from side to side. "But I'm not working for the Council," I added quickly.

"Explain yourself."

How much should I tell him? I glanced at Sarah again. Her gaze was inquisitive. That was a good sign. Perhaps it was time to come clean after all.

I returned my attention to the creature in front of me. "A thief managed to infiltrate the Repository. It supplied an unknown buyer with animal parts. A baby griffon was stolen before the Keeper could intervene."

Sarah gasped, but the centaur's face turned as red as a summer sunrise. I flinched as he reared onto his hind legs, screaming in anger.

"The Repository is a slaughterhouse!" he roared. "The Council claim they want to protect mythical creatures, but we centaurs know the truth! They have been hunting us for centuries."

I flinched as a drop of spittle settled on my cheek. My heart raced as the creature dropped onto his front hooves again. His nostrils flared and his breath was ragged.

"The Keeper has no part in that," I said carefully. "Her intentions are sincere. She sent me to Rome to rescue the griffon cub and confront the buyer."

"The Keeper!" the centaur snorted. "She's a jailer. A prison keeper. She's just as bad as the rest of them."

"No," I said firmly, shaking my head. "She's not. She wants to help. And so do I. If you don't believe me, Angharad will vouch for me."

The centaur froze. "Angharad?" he asked. "You've spoken to Angharad?" His ears twitched nervously.

"And lived to tell the tale," I replied, failing to keep the hint of pride from my voice. Mentioning the dragon was a gamble, but I figured the risk was worth it.

There was a moment of strained silence as I watched the centaur consider my words. Then steel rasped as he drew his sword and lunged towards my head.

I yelped, then tumbled to the ground as his swipe severed the rope that had held me aloft.

The centaur sheathed his weapon again and extended an arm, helping me to my feet. "What are you called, friend?" he asked, untying the knots that bound my wrists together.

"Ambrose Davids," I replied, stretching the ache from my shoulders.

"Well met! I am Gaius Aurelius Equustos, Commander of the Army of the Green Grove. Come, I will introduce you to my men. And then we will take some refreshments while we discuss your mission."

Beside me, Sarah cleared her throat loudly.

Gaius cocked an eye at her. "Your mate?"

Heat rushed to my cheeks as Sarah snorted. "This is Sarah Miller. A friend," I quickly explained.

The centaur's sword flashed again as he cut her ropes, too. Sarah landed much more gracefully than I had, like a cat rather than a sack of potatoes.

"Well met, Sarah Miller, friend of Ambrose Davids," Gaius said as they formally shook hands. "Come," he commanded, and headed for the door.

Sarah rubbed her wrists where the rope had burned red marks into her skin. The look she gave me was unreadable, but none of her previous animosity showed. Perhaps I could still salvage our broken relationship? She inclined her head and took my offered arm as we followed the centaur out of the stable.

We stepped out of the building and into a large clearing surrounded by dense woodland. Tents were pitched at precise intervals, topped by pennons emblazoned with a single oak tree flapping in the breeze. Members of the Army of the Green Grove were milling about, polishing swords or playing dice. They all surged to their feet as Gaius cantered past them, saluting smartly.

We followed in his wake, relieved to be free of the smell of the stable. The camp was spotless, and I wondered if they had imprisoned us in their latrine, or some sort of penance area.

Gaius led us to a large circular tent, holding the flap open so we could enter. The interior was sparsely furnished; there was a high-legged table on which stood various bottles of wine, a pile of hay to one side which I suspected served as the Commander's bed, a large wooden chest perhaps containing a blanket for cold nights, and a weapons rack holding a selection of swords and a crossbow with a quiver of steel-tipped arrows. A rough-woven rug under our feet was the only concession to luxury that I could see.

Gaius removed his helmet and stepped up to the table. While he poured an amber liquid from a crystal decanter into three silver goblets, I tried to gauge Sarah's mood. She was handling the situation better than I had expected, and much better than I had when I had met my first mythical creature. She was scanning the tent as if she found every object in it fascinating. When I finally caught her eye, she smiled back at me.

I opened my mouth to say something, but she put a finger to her lips and nodded towards the centaur. He had finished pouring the drinks and was turning towards us, holding a goblet out to each of us.

"Tell me about the buyer, friend Ambrose," Gaius said. "What have you learned so far?"

"Nothing," I admitted grudgingly, accepting the goblet. I took a small sip of the crimson liquid. It was wine, and an excellent vintage. My next sip was not so small. "I thought if I could find mythical creatures, I would eventually encounter the buyer, or someone who works for him. But it's been three months, and apart from that big snake thing this morning –"

"La bissabova," he corrected me.

I nodded, taking another sip to wet my throat. "That. Yes. Apart from the… bissabova… and you, of course, nothing. I thought the Keeper had made a mistake when she sent me here. The only reason I've stayed so long is because a woman I know, who I believe to be in league with the buyer, is here in the city." I glanced at Sarah. She mouthed Monique's name, and I nodded.

"The French woman. Yes, we know of her," Gaius confirmed.

"Do you know where I can find her?" Sarah interjected. "She's a wanted criminal. If I can interrogate her, we might find out more about this buyer Ambrose is looking for."

"She's clever. Hides her tracks well." Gaius rubbed two fingers over his chiselled chin as he contemplated the French thief. "She might just be the key that will unlock the mystery. We are fairly sure she will be at the next black market."

I nearly spat out my wine in surprise. "Black market?"

The centaur grimaced. "There is an illegal market that trades in creatures every blood moon. The location is secret, of course, one that we have not yet been able to determine."

"We need to find out where that market is!" I exclaimed, jumping to my feet. I teetered and felt Sarah's hand on my arm, steadying me. When had the room started spinning like this? "We'll find the buyer there, and the baby griffon."

"How much time do we have?" Sarah asked.

Gaius' mouth drew into a thin line. "The next blood moon is tomorrow night."

"Then we'd better act fast," she said.

"The Council must be brought to justice first," Gaius insisted. "Their prisoners must be released!"

I shook my head and wished I hadn't. I blinked my eyes a few times to get the room to come into focus again. "I disagree," I said, wondering which Gaius to focus on, because, for some reason, there were suddenly two centaurs facing me. "The creatures in the Repository are safe. For now," I quickly added as a low growl emanated from somewhere in the middle of them. "We can worry about them later. They will not come to any harm under the Keeper's care. The creatures to be sold at the market must be our priority. Who knows what will happen to them if we don't find them first."

Both Gaius' seemed to consider, then finally nodded, a double motion that didn't help my vertigo at all. "Agreed," he said. "Safety before freedom. The Army will assist you as much as possible. We will bend all our efforts into finding the location of the black market."

"How can we contact you if we need you?" Sarah asked, ever practical.

"You have heard of *Bocca della Verità*?"

Sarah nodded, and I noticed her grip on my arm tighten slightly. "The Mouth of Truth, yes of course."

"Just whisper into his lips, and we will find you."

"Ave," I blurted, standing to attention and giving the centaur my best salute. Wasn't this how the legionnaires always responded to their commanders in Asterix comics?

Beside me, Sarah giggled, and then slapped a hand across her mouth, eyes wide. She looked at her empty wine goblet and then placed it carefully down on the floor. "What was in this wine?" she asked, her speech a little slurred.

Gaius grinned. "A brew worthy of Bacchus!" he exclaimed. "I should have warned you. We make it ourselves, strong enough to knock a horse from its feet. You humans may not have the constitution for it."

He opened the tent flap for us and, arm in arm, Sarah and I stumbled out into the camp again.

"Follow the path," the centaur said, pointing out a trampled footpath that led from the clearing into the trees beyond. "It leads into the Borghese Gardens. I trust you'll find your way home from there again. And worry not, the way to the Green

Grove will be open should you need us. And here..." He ducked back into the tent and returned with the two whistles Amari had given me, as well as our mobile phones. "I took this from you when you were captured, but you may have it back now."

"Thank you," I said, pulling the whistles' cords over my head and tucking my phone in my back pocket. "We will keep the Army's location safe from the Council."

Gaius nodded his thanks, his face grave. Then he held out a hand, and Sarah and I each shook it in turn. Together, we set out on the path away from the camp, giggling and holding on to each other for support.

Somewhere along the way, the woods turned into parkland, the muddy trail became a paved road, and before we knew it, we had reached a lookout point.

"Wow," Sarah exclaimed, and I followed her gaze out across Rome. The city was truly spectacular. Red-tiled roofs and marble palaces stood beside crumbling stone ruins, and not far off in the distance, the rounded domes of the Vatican sprawled across the horizon. The sun was at its zenith and the Eternal City sparkled beneath the azure sky.

Perhaps there was something magical about Rome, after all.

"I need coffee," Sarah declared. She grabbed my hand and we hastened down the road that led past Villa Medici towards the Spanish Steps and back into the city centre. We descended the famous steps and, risking the *Carabinieri*'s ire, I sat down somewhere in the middle to watch the flow of people pass, completely oblivious of the army of centaurs encamped only a short walk away, while Sarah ducked into a corner shop to grab some espressos.

"Thanks," I said as she returned with a small takeaway cup and sat down beside me. The hot liquid burned down my throat, but it worked miracles to clear my head.

"So," Sarah finally said, putting her cup down and turning her keen green-eyed gaze on me. "You want to tell me what that was all about?"

I ran a hand through my hair. "I should have told you from the start, but..."

"You didn't think I'd believe you?"

"No, but that's no excuse," I admitted. "I should have come clean in Paris."

Sarah took my hand in hers. "You should have. Amari wouldn't have been happy with you, but you should have."

"She'd have been livid. It's supposed to be a secret." I paused, letting her words sink in. "Hey, how did you –"

Sarah rolled her eyes at me. "I'm a detective, Ambrose. I'll admit I didn't see the centaurs coming, but it's not rocket science to deduce that Amari is the Keeper you've been referring to. And this... Repository?"

"A secret fortress, somewhere in the Alps, as far as I can tell. You should see the things I've seen, Sarah. It's... unbelievable."

"You'll show me," Sarah said, her eyes sparkling. "And you'll tell me all about the White Lady and what really happened in Cardiff. And who Angharad is. But first we'll capture Monique and rescue the baby griffon. Two birds, one stone."

I laughed, unable to believe my luck. If I'd known she'd take it so well, I would have told her the truth ages ago. I could have saved myself months of agony.

I pulled the whistles from around my neck and

blew on one of them. At Sarah's inquisitive gaze, I said: "This will summon Amari. I need to tell her about Gaius and the centaurs."

Sarah nodded. "And what does the one on the black cord do?"

A sharp spike of ice shot through my spine. I looked at the whistle in my hand. It was dangling from a red cord.

I jumped to my feet just as a flash of blue fire reared up before me. When the flames subsided, I was staring into the barrel of a gun. Monique's lopsided grin taunted me from its other end.

"You've been very good at hiding from me, Ambrose," she said in her thick French accent. Her eyes flicked over to Sarah, dismissing her, before returning her attention to me. "Didn't think you'd be stupid enough to blow this whistle again."

"You always seem to underestimate me," I quipped. I eyed Sarah, wondering when she was going to pull her own gun, and then realised that if she'd had one at all, the centaurs had probably taken it when they captured us. It was up to me to get us out of the situation. I knew from experience Monique wouldn't hesitate to shoot at the slightest provocation.

"Look, I'm the one you want," I said. "Let my friend go and we can talk this through."

"Ever the hero," Monique sneered. She swung her arm and aimed the gun at Sarah.

Sarah reacted so fast, her movements almost blurred. Her hand shot out in some sort of martial arts move, slapping Monique's wrist and sending the gun flying. Sarah dropped to the floor, her one leg sweeping Monique off her feet. The French thief fell to the ground with a grunt. She was back on her feet just as a premature whoop escaped my lips. One arm flashed behind her back. Sunlight glinted on steel as a wickedly edged knife slashed towards Sarah.

Sarah stumbled backwards with a sharp cry. She slapped a hand across her upper arm. Blood seeped from between her fingers.

"Sarah!" I shouted, finally spurred into action, even though my stomach churned at the sight of her blood. I lunged forward, throwing myself between the two women.

Monique's sarcastic grin pulled at one corner of her mouth as she faced me, knife in hand, Sarah's blood dripping from the blade.

"Ambrose, wait," Sarah warned, but testosterone spurred me on. I lunged for the thief. My lucky white sneaker tripped on a step and I fell flat on my face.

"Damn it!" I said through gritted teeth. "Damn this bloody luck."

Monique grabbed me and pulled me to my feet. She yanked one arm behind my back and I grunted as I felt the cold press of her blade against my neck. I looked up to see Sarah, eyes wide, standing in front of us. Blood dripped from the slice in her shirt, but her fists were bunched, her stance martial.

"I didn't come here to kill you," Monique said, her mouth close to my ear. There was a hint of alcohol on her breath. Something fruity. "I came to make you an offer."

"Ambrose!" Sarah's shrill scream was suddenly cut off as blue fire flared again.

✖✖✖

I wasn't so much seasick as scared silly.

Monique and I were standing on a yacht and the turquoise waters of what I assumed must be the Mediterranean Sea sparkled all around us. The thought of the cold depths below me sent a shiver down my spine. I swallowed loudly.

Monique removed the knife from my throat and tucked it into the back of her pants.

"Come," she said, releasing my arm.

I only noticed the men then, two thugs that looked like they spent way too much time staring at themselves in the mirror at the gym. Muscles bulged under their silk suits. Both glared at me like I had just said something offensive about their mothers. They fell into step behind me as I followed Monique to the bow of the boat, where two deck chairs stood side by side, facing out towards the ocean.

A bronzed man lounged on one of the chairs, sipping on a yellow drink that could possibly explain my captor's citrusy breath. The man was wearing the tiniest Speedo I had ever seen and looked about as oily as the *focaccia* I'd had for breakfast that morning.

A cage stood on top of a deck table beside the man's chair. Inside it was a tiny blue-furred fox. The animal was curled up into a small ball and looked utterly miserable.

"Sit," Monique instructed, and I plopped down on the empty recliner. She retreated a few steps and leaned with her back against the boat's railing. The thief pulled her knife out and started cleaning her fingernails with it.

"You must be Ambrose Davids," the man said, sitting up to face me. He extended a hand and I shook it warily. His grip was slack and sweaty. "You can call me Marco. Can I offer you a drink? Limoncello? Beer? Perhaps a cup of tea?" His English was impeccable, with only a hint of an Italian accent to betray his background.

I shook my head.

"Alright, let's get straight to the point then," Marco said. "Monique has told me much about you."

"All good things, I hope," I replied uneasily.

Marco laughed, a deep belly rumble. "Of course. In fact, so good that I want to make you an offer."

I narrowed my eyes. "What kind of offer?"

"The lucrative kind. I will pay you double to deliver what you find for the Council to me."

"I don't work for the Council anymore," I said, almost in reflex by now.

"All the more reason for you to take up my offer. Living in London can be very expensive, and a young man of your reputation could probably use all the help he can get."

I cleared my throat nervously. He did have a point. But no, I was done with that. "I'm sorry, I can't help you," I said stubbornly. And what did he know about my reputation, anyway?

Marco's greasy smile faltered, and a hint of menace entered his voice. "You know, Ambrose, you remind me of your father. Just as noble, and just as stupid."

It felt like someone had dumped a bucket of cold water over my head. I jumped to my feet. "What do you know about my father?" I demanded.

Marco pursed his lips. Then he shrugged. "If you won't help me, you're of no use to me," he said.

I lunged for him, but Monique was quicker. She grabbed my arm and yanked me away from her employer, pushing me up against the side of the boat. Her breath was hot on my face when she smiled and said: "*Au revoir*, Ambrose. It's been fun."

Then she shoved me.

My feet lifted off the deck, and I tumbled overboard. I gulped water, my heart racing as the ocean closed in over me. My feet kicked spasmodically and I somehow managed to get my head above water just in time to see the yacht speeding away, leaving churning water in its wake.

"Shit," I swore, and then something grabbed my leg and pulled me under again.

I gasped bubbles before I had the sense to close my mouth and save my breath. I looked down to see a woman pulling me towards her. She was clearly not human. Maybe it was the fishy tale that glinted silvery white in the clear blue water that gave it away. Maybe it was the translucent fins that flapped where her ears should have been. Or perhaps it was the fact that her eyes were entirely black, like the depths of the ocean down below.

A mermaid or, knowing my luck, a siren.

Either way, I was in trouble.

She pressed her clammy lips against mine. It felt like kissing a fish. Revulsion rolled over me and I tried to pull back, but one of her webbed hands gripped the back of my head and held it in place. I spluttered in vain, but when she removed her lips, I realised my lungs were no longer straining for air. She'd been blowing oxygen into my mouth.

She wasn't trying to kill me.

Well, that was a first.

Her fathomless eyes stared into my own for a few seconds while I tried to reconcile the thought of being underwater with not drowning. I failed miserably and felt panic bubbling in my chest again. Just as I was about to kick for the surface, the woman spoke, her words slurred underneath the water. Her dialect was strange to my ears, but the words were familiar.

"Toccato dal gelo," she said, touching the fingers of one hand lightly to my chest. She bared her lips in a snarl, revealing pointed teeth. I repressed a

shudder.

Then her hand moved to my forehead and the snarl turned into a smile as she touched me lightly between the eyes. *"Segnato dal fuoco."*

Touched by frost. Marked by fire.

Apparently, my history was plain to see for those who knew how to look.

My heart thumped in my chest as the woman grabbed my arm and started pulling me. I said my goodbyes to the sun and everyone who knew me, with a sudden pang at the thought of Sarah, who I'd left behind. She'd never know what had happened to me. She'd never find my body. I was going to be food for the fishes.

The woman swam at a speed that would have Michael Phelps in jealous tears, her powerful tail propelling us through the water like a torpedo shooting towards its target. I gulped air gratefully when we broke the surface. Relief washed through me as I realised she had brought me to shore. I nearly sobbed when I felt firm sand underneath my feet.

I pranced out of the ocean and fell to my knees on the deserted beach, kissing the sand, and then wishing I hadn't. I barely noticed the woman speaking to me until a strange tug pulled me towards her where she lingered just inside the water's edge.

Definitely a siren then.

Spitting out sand, I shook my head to clear it. Her melodious voice was different outside the water and it had the strange effect of making me want to kiss her, fish lips notwithstanding. I clapped my hands over my ears and tried to read her lips, but hey, I wasn't a trained lip reader. I couldn't make anything out.

The siren frowned and pressed her lips together in a seductive pout. She beckoned me closer, but I hesitated. Just because she hadn't tried to drown me, didn't mean I trusted her.

She grunted, clearly frustrated, and pulled herself out of the water and onto the sand. I watched, fascinated by her scaly tale glimmering in the setting sun, as she drew an image in the sand.

It was an oval with small, concentric rings along the outside.

Was this the location of the black market?

"Grazie," I thanked her, excitement rising deep within my belly. There was still a chance to save the baby griffon.

The siren nodded. Then she flipped her body and rolled back into the ocean. Her tail breached in a final farewell, and then she was gone.

I licked my salty lips, remembering her fishy kiss and the lure of her voice. And the depths of the ocean from which she'd saved me.

I was lucky to be alive.

✕✕✕

It took me the rest of the evening to get back to Rome.

I might have survived my plunge into the Mediterranean Sea, but my phone hadn't. I was desperate to call Sarah, or at least an Uber, but my mobile bravely played a welcome tune when I tried to turn it on, just enough to give me hope, before dying completely and resisting any further attempts to revive it.

Of course, the siren had to dump me on a deserted beach next to the only stretch of road on the Italian coast that saw no cars passing by. Not while I needed a lift, at least.

The walk into the nearest seaside village, in soggy clothes under darkening skies, was unpleasant enough, but then an annoying scratch developed in my throat, warning of a cold that might come from it.

And, as luck would have it, the only time an inspector had ever done the rounds on the evening train was when I didn't have a single euro on me. He didn't take kindly to my rumpled appearance or stammering explanation of a lost wallet and no passport, but issued me with a fine that was probably specifically reserved for stupid tourists wanting free rides. I blew my nose on the offending piece of paper as soon as the man exited my compartment and would have felt much better about the whole thing if I hadn't felt so lousy.

I was standing dead on my feet and feeling thoroughly miserable in front of my apartment door in Trastevere when I finally realised that my keys were no longer in my pockets either.

There was only one thing left to do. I blew one of Amari's whistles, making sure this time that it was the one dangling from a black cord.

"Bless you," Amari said as she stepped out of the shaft of light that appeared out of nowhere. Even though it was late, the Keeper was still dressed in jeans and a jumper. A long brown feather was stuck in her black curls. I might have caught her in the middle of something.

"Thank you," I said. I accepted the tissue she offered and blew my nose loudly.

Amari raised an eyebrow. "I hope you didn't call me here just to spread your germs, Ambrose. There are several creatures inside the Repository that are susceptible to human viruses, so I really don't want to catch what you have."

"It's nothing," I said, shoving the soggy tissue as deep into my pocket as I could. "Just a minor cold. And yes, I have some news to share."

Amari's eyes lit up. "You found Caerus?"

"Who?" I asked, and sneezed again.

"Bless you," Amari repeated. "You're a mess, Ambrose. Let's go inside before you catch your death."

I sighed. "I lost my key, I'm afraid. You think you can...?" I wiggled my fingers in the general direction of the lock. Another sneeze echoed through the alley.

Amari shook her head. "Come on," she said. "I need you to be in top shape. Chicken soup isn't going to cut it." She touched my arm and said the Word that turned the world white.

⚹ ⚹ ⚹

The dark wood furnishings and roaring fire of Amari's study were immediately welcoming.

I walked towards the hearth and held my hands out at it. It wasn't too long ago that this fire was the only thing that had kept my body from freezing to death. I let the heat spread through me. My head felt clearer already, the healing magic of the Repository making quick work of my common cold.

"Sit down, Ambrose," Amari said, gesturing at the chair in front of her large mahogany desk. She plucked the wayward feather from her hair as she took her place opposite me. "Harpies," she said, and shrugged as she threw the feather into the dustbin by her desk. "Now, what did you want to tell me? Or did you just call me for my lock picking skills?"

"Two things," I said, ignoring her quip. "First: I may have found the buyer. He offered me alternative employment. Needless to say, I declined, and paid the price for it. They left me to drown."

"Hence the cold," Amari said, nodding. "Where is he now?"

I shook my head. "I don't know, but I'll find him. I've made... contacts in Rome. Finally."

"Contacts? I'm not sure getting involved with the Italian mafia is a good thing, Ambrose."

A laugh escaped my lips. "Ha! No, nothing like that. The Army of the Green Grove may be just as dangerous in their own way, but I think I can trust them in this situation."

Amari jumped to her feet. "The centaurs!" she exclaimed. "They're alive?"

I nodded. "But there's no love lost between them and the Council. They're willing to help me, but not if the Council is involved. And that includes you, I'm afraid."

Amari sat back down again, a frown creasing her brow. "Did they say why?"

"Gaius – that's their leader – said the Council has been hunting them for centuries." Amari's frown deepened. "And they have no interest in being locked up in the Repository either."

"It's for their own safety!" Amari said, exasperated.

"Is it?" I asked.

One of Amari's eyebrows shot upward as she pursed her lips.

"Be that as it may," I quickly continued. "The centaurs keep a close eye on Rome. Now that I know who to look for, I'm sure they can find the buyer. His name is Marco."

"Marco? Marco Mazzoni?" Amari's face paled visibly.

"He didn't share his last name. Why? Who is he?"

"A former member of the Council. He was booted from it four or five years ago, along with the Procurement Specialist he had recruited." Both of Amari's fists clenched on the table before me. "Marco liked to keep pets," she explained.

"The Specialist would deliver the creatures he found straight to Marco instead of bringing them to me. I recovered what I could, but I always wondered if he had more hidden somewhere else where I couldn't find them. Someone was supposed to keep an eye on them, to make sure they didn't continue with their illegal acquisitions."

"Well, that someone's been slacking," I said. "If this Marco is the same guy, he's definitely still stuck in his habits. He had a little blue fox in a cage when I met him."

Amari gasped. She surged to her feet. "I'll be right back," she said. "Don't touch any of my books," she called as she strode out of the room.

Well, the temptation was just too great.

I stood up and perused the shelves that lined the study walls. She never said I couldn't look. I paused in front of a title that grabbed my eyes. *The Wyld Hunt: A History*. My fingers itched to leaf through its pages, but I resisted. The Keeper would not be amused if I disturbed her precious tomes.

I leapt away from the bookshelf as Amari entered, probably looking guilty of much more than I could take credit for.

She barely noticed. "Ambrose, this is Riku."

A little fox entered the room just behind her, its lustrous pelt shining red in the firelight. Strangely, the fox had two tails. The intelligence in its eyes as it assessed me was further proof that this was no ordinary woodland animal.

"Riku is the one who kidnapped Caerus, the griffon baby."

"Oh," I said, startled. I looked from the fox to Amari, not sure how to respond.

"It is true," the fox said, his words tinted with a Japanese accent. I blinked in surprise. "Shame lies heavy on my heart."

"You will have the chance to redeem yourself, my friend," Amari said. "Ambrose has found the buyer, and perhaps your mate as well."

"Amiko? She lives?" The sudden spark of hope in the fox's clever eyes pulled at my heartstrings.

"Um, yes," I said. "She's... blue?"

Riku nodded, his tongue lolling out in a foxy grin. "You will take me to her?"

"Ambrose doesn't know where she is right now, Riku," Amari interjected. "But he will let us know as soon as he finds her. Until then, you should stay in the Repository."

The fox bowed its head. "I will do as you say, Amari-sama."

Amari returned her attention to me. "You'd better spend the night here, Ambrose. Let's get rid of that cold completely. You can renew your search tomorrow."

"Thank you," I said. I followed her out of the study, catching a last glimpse of the two-tailed fox as the heavy oak door of Amari's study closed behind us.

Our footsteps echoed loudly as we walked through the corridors towards the residential wing. Finally, I could no longer hold my tongue. "How do you know you can trust him?"

Amari nodded. "A valid question, Ambrose. I didn't, at first," she admitted. "And kitsunes have a reputation for being devious, but we both know the stories can't always be believed. I've gotten to know him. He was coerced. Everything Riku did, he did to ensure the safety of his mate. I trust him."

"Alright," I said, not entirely convinced, but with no real reason to argue. Amari would know better than I who could be trusted. And what on earth was a kitsune? Father's stories had never mentioned one of those.

We reached the door to the room that had been mine the last time I had spent the night inside the Repository. I turned to face the Keeper.

"One more thing, Amari. There is a blood moon tomorrow night –"

"A black market," Amari said, her jaw clenching.

"Yes."

"Then you must hurry, Ambrose. Find Caerus. Find the buyer. For all our sakes, we must protect them. At all costs."

I didn't need her to tell me who "them" were. I knew the stakes.

I nodded grimly.

✖ ✖ ✖

Shit.

I had been so sure that the siren's drawing was a depiction of the Circus Maximus, the huge racetrack where chariots had competed in Julius Caesar's time. It was the right shape, sort of oval, and I had assumed the concentric rings she had drawn referred to the stands surrounding the track where the spectators would have watched the drama unfold.

But now that I looked down upon what was left of the Circus, I knew immediately that this could not be the site of the black market. It looked like nothing much more than a gravelly plot of empty weed-grown land on the corner of a busy intersection. Lots of space for a market, but not the kind of privacy one would want for trading secretly in mythical creatures.

I ran a hand through my hair, exasperated. This was my only lead. Even if I had the time to go in search of the siren again, there was no guarantee that she could give me better information. And what if she had never even referred to the market? It's not like we had actually discussed my mission. This could all be a wild goose chase.

"Well, this is quite disappointing," a voice echoed my thoughts. I turned to see an elderly couple standing close to me, frowning at the track below us. "First the Colosseum and now this. I have to tell you, Frank, Rome is not living up to my expectations."

"I told you we should have gone to London instead..." the man replied, pulling a water bottle from his backpack and taking a long sip.

"What's next on our list?" the woman asked, pulling a guidebook from her handbag. "The Fountain of the Four Rivers. It's that one from the movie. Do you remember, Frank?"

"Don't bother," I said. The couple looked at me, startled at the interruption. "It's being renovated," I explained. "Completely closed off under scaffolding."

The man threw one hand in the air. "Of course it is. This entire city is one enormous construction site."

"First the Colosseum, now this? We might as well pack up and move on to Florence," the woman exclaimed.

"What's wrong with the Colosseum?" I asked. I'd been there at the start of my stay in Rome. Although parts of it had been covered up for renovation, it had still been one of the highlights of my time in the city. Rome might not have delivered on my expectations of mythical creatures until just yesterday, but I had certainly checked off a few of my must-see bucket list items while I'd been here.

"Closed," the woman replied. "Completely shut to the public. You can still view it from outside, of course, but I didn't travel halfway around the world to see things from outside."

I froze. What an idiot I was!

The Colosseum was closed to the public? The oval-shaped amphitheatre that rose two or three levels in concentric circles, complete with a series of cages under ground level custom made for keeping dangerous animals in?

"Sorry about that," I said, suddenly filled with adrenaline. "Try Castel Sant'Angelo instead. It was in that movie too," I called as I started sprinting, leaving the two tourists staring after me.

It didn't take me long to reach my destination, and I stared at the queue in front of the Santa Maria basilica in dismay. I glanced at my watch. It was still only mid-morning, but I didn't have any time to lose – the blood moon was tonight.

I pushed past the queue towards the entrance of the church, where a security guard was limiting the number of people who could pass through the gate.

"Excuse me," I said. "I don't want to go into the church. I just want to see the Mouth."

"You and everyone in this queue, *signore*," the man replied irritably. "There are priceless relics inside the church, beautiful paintings, a chance to encounter the Divine Presence, but all everyone ever wants to do is recreate that scene from an old movie. You will have to wait your turn."

"But –" The guard's frown turned into a scowl and I decided to drop the matter. I skulked towards the back of the queue, anxiously checking my watch again.

It was close to an hour later that I finally stood in front of the Mouth of Truth, the marbled head of Oceanos. Him again. At some point, I was probably going to have to make my peace with the god of waters. But not today.

Legend said that if you put your hand into his mouth and said anything that wasn't true, you'd lose the hand. I had no intention of going anywhere near his mouth – too many legends turned out to be fact these days – but I sincerely hoped that what I was about to say would indeed be true.

I turned my back to the queue of people waiting their turn, ignoring the guard who watched me with eyes drawn together in a frown, and bent down to the statue's stony lips.

"The blood moon is best viewed from inside the Colosseum," I whispered, feeling like a fool. Was anyone even listening? Could I trust the listener? "I would highly appreciate some aid from the Green Grove."

I waited expectantly, for what, I wasn't sure. The Mouth obviously didn't respond.

"*Signore*, if you are looking for enlightenment, I suggest you step into the church now," the guard rumbled behind me.

I coughed, embarrassed. "Maybe some other time," I said.

I pushed past the guard and the next person in line and stepped back onto the street. I glanced at my watch again. Almost midday. I wasn't far from the Colosseum. If I cut through the Roman Forum, I could probably be there within thirty minutes. I started running.

A wall twice as tall as I was blocked my way.

Fine, I'd take the less scenic route. I jogged along the path running outside the Palatine Hill, dodging pedestrians and crazy drivers alike. By the time I reached Constantine's Arch, I was panting and sweating like it was high summer.

I stood with my hands on my knees for a second, catching my breath. When I had recovered enough to stand upright again, I had to blink to make sure my eyes weren't playing tricks on me.

Monique was here, talking to the security guard who stood watch over the entrance to the Colosseum. He nodded and let her past, much to the dismay of the other tourists milling around the entrance. Surprisingly, there was no scaffolding, nothing to indicate that the old amphitheatre was unsafe for visitors, and yet no one was allowed inside.

No one but Monique.

My heart started racing again. I was at the right place this time.

But how was I going to get past the guard and into the Colosseum? From a little closer, he looked suspiciously like one of the two henchmen from Marco's boat. I couldn't risk asking him for entrance.

I surveyed my surroundings. There was a manhole cover just a few feet from me, but I didn't like that idea at all. I'd seen what crawled around in the pipes of Rome and I wasn't eager to come face to face with it again. The arches running around the bottom of the Colosseum were all fenced up, way too high for me to try to scale. And besides, there were too many tourists about to try something that would attract attention.

That meant I had to get past the guard somehow.

Trust the luck, is what Daniel would have said. Bloody leprechaun.

I picked up a pebble and, sauntering towards the guard, tossed it at the wall of the Colosseum, hoping the noise would draw his attention and give me a chance to slip past him. I must have misjudged my aim, and if I'd known I had such a good arm, I might have tried out for my local cricket team. The pebble smacked against the ancient stone of the Roman arena and, to both my horror and fascination, a large piece of brickwork came loose and toppled down just as the unsuspecting guard walked underneath its path. It hit him squarely in the head. The man fell to the ground and stayed there, unmoving.

A cry went up from the surrounding tourists and bystanders rushed to the prostrate man's aid. I ran to his side too, guilt a heavy ball in my stomach. I breathed a sigh of relief when I saw the guard's eyelids fluttering. He was going to have a bruise and a nasty headache, but he'd live.

While everyone's attention was on him, I took the opportunity to slip away and ducked into the Colosseum. It was cool and completely empty inside. Light falling in through the stone arches cast strange, creepy shadows everywhere. It was disturbingly quiet.

I nearly jumped out of my skin as the sound of an electric saw shattered the silence. Carefully, I walked through the corridor and towards the centre of the arena where the noise was coming from.

I had to clench my jaw to keep it from falling open. The entire arena floor, which was open to display the subterranean hypogeum below it when I had last visited, was now covered in wood. A small platform had been built on the far side from where I was standing, and a team of carpenters were busy constructing what looked like a rudimentary lift system above one of the shafts leading down into the cages.

I needed to get below ground.

Creeping through the hallways, I looked about until I found the stairs that led down into the tunnels below the arena. There was a gate with a no-entry sign, but that had never stopped me before. I pushed it open and stole downwards.

Below, a long passage curved out of sight. It

was dimly lit, with exposed light bulbs swaying from the stone ceiling. Doors were set into the walls at regular intervals. The first door on my left was slightly ajar and I could hear voices coming from it. I was about to sneak past it when I heard a familiar French accent coming from inside.

I suppressed a yelp and stepped backwards just in time to avoid Monique wrenching the door open. She turned back towards the room and said: "You'll cooperate eventually, James. Whether that's over Ambrose's dead body or not is up to you."

She slammed the door and stalked off down the passageway, leaving me paralysed. I stood in the shadows, wondering if I'd heard her correctly. Then, slowly, as if wading through a mound of snow, I walked towards the door. With shaking hands, I tried the handle.

It turned!

In her fury, Monique had forgotten to lock the door behind her. I opened it, holding my breath.

The room was tiny, a cell really, with no windows and only an iron grate near the ceiling to let in a bit of light. There was a desk in one corner with a shallow bowl of water on it and an empty chamber pot next to it. A rusty iron cot was shoved up against one wall.

My eyes burned as I stared at the man sitting on the bed. He was hunched over, holding his head in his hands, staring at the floor.

"I told you," he said in a voice that covered my skin with goose bumps. "I'm done. You won't get anything more from me."

When I didn't respond, he looked up, and his bloodshot eyes caught my own. It felt like time had come to a standstill.

"Ambrose?" he said, his voice filled with disbelief.

I swallowed back the lump in my throat.

"Father."

James Davids was on his feet in an instant, and the next we were hugging each other in a tight embrace. My father's body felt fragile, not as rock solid as I remembered him. When we pulled apart, I noticed the lines around his eyes and the silver in his hair.

"You're alive," I said, touching his arm again just to make sure.

"Look at you!" Father exclaimed, his eyes shining with unshed tears. "You don't know how many times I wished I could see you and your sister's faces again. You've turned into a man, my boy." Sadness welled up in his eyes and he coughed, as if just clearing his throat.

My own throat felt a bit raw, too. Here was my father, alive after we had thought him dead all these years.

"What are you doing here, Father?" I asked. I couldn't help but wonder if he was in league with Monique, if he had been working with Marco all this time. He'd been gone almost four years. Surely he could have tried to escape in that time. Surely he could have tried to contact us.

His face hardened, and a hint of anger entered his voice. "I'm their prisoner, Ambrose. They've used me..." His gaze dropped to the floor again. "They've used me to do unspeakable things."

I touched his hand and he looked up at me again. "We'll make it right," I promised him.

A fire lit behind his eyes and I saw his resolve return. "Yes," he said, as if making a promise to himself. "Yes, we will. I was right, you know." His gaze was intense, eager to see if I understood.

"I know," I nodded. "And Cassie knows too."

Father's face lit up. After all these years, he had finally found the validation he'd been seeking for so long. Then his brows furrowed again.

"We need to get out of here. Something's happening tonight."

"The black market," I replied. I hesitated. There was still something I didn't understand. "Why are you really here, Father? What happened that night when you disappeared?"

"Can't this wait, Ambrose? The French woman could be back any minute now."

"I need to know, Father."

He sighed. "I see. It's a matter of trust."

I shrugged uncomfortably.

"Fair enough," Father said, sighing. "I owe you that much." He leaned up against the desk and I sat down on the rickety cot. Its springs creaked under my weight.

"That night I was in the wrong place at the wrong time," Father began. "I was walking over Tower Bridge, just thinking. I was angry. I'd received another scathing rejection. I stopped and leaned over the railing, just staring across the Thames. I didn't know what to do. My reputation was in tatters. No respectable university would hire me. I had lost your mother; I was afraid I was going to lose you and Cassie, too. I didn't know what to do." His eyes looked far back into the past as he recalled that fateful night.

"And then, I saw something, under the bridge, near the edge of the water. A boy emerged from the river, naked as the day he was born." He shook his head at the recollection. "I stared, wondering what the hell had happened to him. And then a man appeared from the shadows. Tall, long blonde hair, dressed in leather, with two swords strapped to his back, like a kid who'd seen one too many Jackie Chan movies. But he wasn't playing. He threw a net over the boy, and I didn't even think. Took the stairs down two at a time and threw myself at him. Impulsive, Jenna always used to call me, and I guess she was right."

I smiled. At least now I knew where I got it from.

"I grabbed the man by the arm. 'You have no idea what you're getting involved with,' he growled at me. 'I guess I'll find out,' I said. Must have been the beer I'd had earlier talking. I'm not usually that brave." He smiled, and I motioned for him to continue.

"And then, right before my eyes, the boy shimmered. He shimmered, Ambrose!" Father was pacing the floor now, totally engrossed by his own tale. "The boy was gone, and a seal wriggled out from under the net. The man yelled and tried to push me aside, but I held on to him. I held on long enough to give the seal a chance to escape. As I watched it disappear into the Thames, it finally hit me. A selkie." Father's voice still held all the awe he must have felt that night.

"I knew in that moment that I had been right all along. No matter what they all said, I knew I was right. That thought still dazed me when the man threw the net over me. And then there was blue fire all around us and the next thing I knew, I was in a tiny cell. That's when I met Marco."

Father grimaced. "He told me all. There were still magical creatures in the world, hidden among us. He told me he collected them and studied them. He wanted my help in identifying them, and the magical properties they possessed." Father's eyes were feverish when he turned to me again.

"You must understand, Ambrose," he said, clasping my arm tightly. "Not only did I have the chance to see all the creatures I'd been dreaming of my whole life, I'd also get to study them! He didn't have to ask me twice. I agreed immediately. It was only later that I learned the horrible truth. That he didn't only collect them, but he traded them too. For years I studied everything he brought to me, giddy with excitement and the thrill of learning what each creature could do. I didn't know he'd be using my knowledge to sell them to the highest bidder, or that he would use them to make potions and charms with." He shuddered visibly as he said that. "By the time I realised what was really going on, it was too late. I was in too deep. I refused. He threatened me with your life, and Cassie's. I had no choice."

"I had no idea…"

"You do seem to be clueless about many things, Ambrose." I jumped to my feet as Monique stepped through the door. Her smirk sent chills through my bones. "You do like to play the hero, don't you? You almost make it too easy."

She quirked a finger at the door and the guard I had felled with my lucky throw earlier walked in. I frowned. I'd thought he'd be out of action for at least a day or two.

"Fabio," Monique purred. "If you would, please."

The guard grunted as he pulled a pair of handcuffs out. My fists clenched and then unclenched as I forced myself to relax when Monique pulled her gun out and levelled it at me.

"Go on, Ambrose. Try something."

The goon clamped a cuff around my wrist. A whiff of something herbal clung to him. Did he smell of green tea? I grit my teeth as he locked the other cuff around my father's wrist. Father seemed resigned to his fate and didn't offer any resistance, but I itched to do something. I had visions of turning into a big green rage monster and breaking the cuffs, the gun and the goon all in one fit of anger, but then I saw Monique's watchful gaze on me, and I slumped down onto the bed instead.

"*Au revoir*, boys," she said with that sardonic

smile of hers. "I'll leave Fabio here with you, just in case you get any clever ideas."

She waved cheekily at us and slammed the door behind her. The key clanged in its hole as she locked the door. We were trapped.

I stared at Fabio, wondering how we were going to get out of this mess. I glanced at Father and saw a smile playing across his lips.

He winked when he saw me watching him. "Everything isn't always what it appears to be, Ambrose." He inclined his head at the guard.

When I looked again, the goon was gone and in his place stood the little two-tailed fox Amari had called Riku. A shapeshifter!

"The kitsune," Father breathed almost reverently. *"Konnichiwa."*

Riku bared his teeth at my father. "Where is Amiko?" he growled.

"We will find her, Riku," I said quickly. "This is my father, James."

"We've met," Father said, pulling me off the bed as he took a step back from the angry creature.

Riku turned to me. "I came to help you, Ambrose-san, but this man is my enemy. He is the one who captured Amiko."

"That's not true," Father said hastily as I turned to him. "I was there when she was captured, yes, but I didn't set the trap. I only advised –"

"Father!" I glared at him. "Are you responsible for this?" I gestured at the arena around me.

Father's shoulders slumped. "I suppose you could say so." He turned to Riku. "I'm sorry about what happened. Truly. I will do whatever I can to help rescue Amiko."

The kitsune growled again, but then his snarl faded, leaving only a frown on his foxy face. He nodded. "We will make a bargain. Your freedom for Amiko's. Do I have your word?"

Father nodded, and I said: "Of course. And we must find the baby griffon. I assume that's why Amari sent you?"

I wouldn't have believed it possible, but I could've sworn the red-furred little creature's cheeks turned a deeper shade of crimson. "Amari did send you, right?" I asked.

"I am in great debt to Amari-sama," Riku replied. "But she is not my master."

I smiled. I liked the kitsune's guts.

"Can you get us out of these cuffs?" I asked.

The kitsune nodded and swished one of his two tails my way. A key slid across the floor towards me. I picked it up and quickly unlocked our bonds. Father rubbed his wrists as I tucked the handcuffs into my pocket. Who knows, I might need them again.

"How are we going to get out of this cell?" Father asked, trying the handle. "The door is locked."

The kitsune shimmered. I gasped as an enormous brown bear reared up on its hind legs. It placed one paw on the door and pushed it right out of its hinges.

Father and I both gaped at the open doorway.

Father was the first to recover. "Well, that's one way of doing it," he said, poking his head out and surveying the empty corridor. "Coast is clear. Come on." He slipped out of the room.

A howl rent the air just as I stepped into the passageway. The hairs on the back of my neck stood on end.

"Werewolf," Father confirmed. "That means the moon is out."

"We're out of time," the kitsune said as he shifted back into his true form.

"Let's split up," I said, trying my best to ignore

the thought of a werewolf within howling distance of us. "Father, you go upstairs and see what's happening. If you can, try to delay the proceedings until we've rescued Amiko and Caerus. Riku, you go left and I'll go right. Whoever finds them first, signal the others. Then we'll get the hell out of here. I have a bad feeling about this."

The others nodded and we parted ways, Father taking the stairs back up to the ground level, and Riku disappearing around the corner. They were both out of sight before I realised we hadn't agreed upon a signal.

Shit. Too late now. We'll just have to wait and see what happens.

The first few rooms I encountered were all closed behind locked doors, but then I found another door that was slightly ajar. Carefully, I peered in through the gap.

Marco, mercifully dressed this time in a white suit that made him look as sleazy as a mobster in a bad B-movie, stood next to Monique. Both he and the French thief looked displeased.

Across from them stood an Asian woman I had never seen before. Her black hair had wisps of grey in it, and it was neatly tied in a bun behind her head. A thin white scar ran from her one eye down to the corner of her mouth. In her one hand she held the cage containing the little blue fox, Amiko. The woman's other hand was stretched out towards Monique, as if waiting for her to hand something over.

Monique scowled, but she pulled a blue amulet out from around her neck and deposited it into the stranger's hand.

The Asian woman's smile turned my bones to jelly.

Then blue fire flared, and the woman and the cage were gone.

"Merde!" Monique swore. "How are we going to manage without the fox-fire?"

Marco grimaced. "We have a trove of magical creatures at our disposal. One of them will have the parts we need. You just have to persuade James to cooperate again."

I swore under my breath as they started walking towards the door. I darted around the corner as if hell hounds were on my scent, whooping quietly as I saw another flight of steps leading even further down into the bowels of the arena. I took the steps down two at a time and then paused to listen for footsteps.

Nothing. They were probably headed toward Father's cell. They may already know that we'd escaped. I'd better get a move on.

It was darker down here, the light bulbs dangling from the ceiling flickering intermittently. My nose scrunched up as the smell hit me, a combination of stale air, feathers and faeces. I pushed forward, expecting the worst, and then lumbered to a halt when the passageway opened onto a series of barred cages.

They were all filled with mythical creatures.

A chimaera paced along the bars of the first cage, its goat's head bleating at me while the lion's head watched me with hungry eyes. Its serpent-headed tail whipped its flanks impatiently. I shuddered and moved on.

The next cage contained a group of scantily dressed young women lying on the floor, their eyes dull and their hair oily. "Help us," one of them called in a hoarse whisper, stretching an arm out through the bars. I took a step backward. Won't catch me fool enough to touch a nymph again.

Something snarled behind me and I spun around to see a tangle of arms and fur that looked like it had stepped straight out of someone's nightmare glaring at me. Its razor-sharp teeth glinted in the dim light. I had never been so glad for something else to be behind bars before.

Which raised the question – what was I going to do with them? I couldn't just set these creatures free and let them run loose in the streets. They'd leave a trail of blood in their wake from here to wherever they could find a place to hide.

I didn't have much of a choice. I'd have to let Amari handle this.

"Ambrose."

"Shit, Riku," I swore, turning towards the little kitsune standing beside me, my heart beating like a drum. "Don't sneak up on me like that!"

The kitsune's tongue lolled out in a ridiculous grin. "I have found the baby griffon. The French woman has him. I saw her taking the lift leading up to the arena. There is a crowd gathered there already."

I swore again. "I have bad news for you, too. Amiko is gone. An Asian woman took her. They disappeared in a flash of blue fire."

Riku's foxy grin faded. "The woman had a scarred face?" I nodded, and both his tails swished nervously from side to side. "I must go, Ambrose-san."

"Wait," I said. "Caerus needs your help. He's here now, and he's only a baby. Help me rescue him."

The kitsune tilted his head slightly as he looked at me. Then he nodded. "He is my responsibility, too. I will stay."

"Thank you. Now come on, let's go see what's going on upstairs."

✕✕✕

A low buzz filled the arena of the Colosseum.

There were more people here than I had thought there would be, more people who knew of the existence of mythical creatures than I had thought possible. Most of them had their faces covered in masks, as if this were a masquerade ball. The blood moon hung large in the sky above us, casting a strange orange glow over the stadium.

"If you will permit me…" Riku said before shimmering into the shape of a tiny white songbird. He fluttered into the air and alighted on my shoulder. For a moment, I wished he had turned into something a little more macho, like a raven or a buzzard. Even a parrot would have sufficed. At least then I could have pretended to be a pirate. Now I just felt like an idiot with a little bird on his shoulder.

I took a deep breath and plunged into the crowd. I followed the press and flow of the people to the front, where I quickly found Father. He had obtained a hat somewhere and was lounging nonchalantly with his back towards the bricks of the Colosseum, close enough to the stage to see what was going on without being spotted himself. He beckoned me over and I went to stand by his side.

"Nice hat," I said. It was a woven white straw fedora with a black band tied around the head. I wouldn't have been surprised if he felt a little like Indiana Jones right then.

"Nice bird," he grinned back at me.

Riku chirped, and I wished a hidden shaft would open up and swallow me whole.

Father nudged me and I turned towards the stage, where Monique was ascending the steps. She tapped on a microphone that had been set up at the centre of the podium next to a display table, and then said: "Ladies and gentlemen, we are about to start. If you would take your places,

213

please."

The people shuffled around me and I had to elbow a few out of the way to make sure they didn't block my view. When all had quieted down, Marco appeared from the shadows of an archway and made his way up the stage. Monique handed him the microphone before taking the steps down and taking her place beside the lift I had seen being erected earlier.

I sensed Father tense up beside me. I didn't need to look at him to feel the hatred he had for this man who had held him captive for so long. I planned to have a few choice words with the Italian about that if I ever got the chance.

"*Benvenuto*, ladies and gentlemen," Marco said, his voice amplified throughout the arena. "Welcome to the blood moon market. We have some very special wares for you tonight. Who am I kidding, our wares are always special, am I right?" he joked, and my fists bunched as the surrounding people laughed on cue.

"Without further ado, let's start with our first item."

He nodded at Monique, who pulled down a lever that opened a trapdoor in the arena floor. The lift creaked as an enormous cage slowly ascended from the cells of the hypogeum below. I watched with bated breath to see what creature would be revealed.

The crowd gasped and my breath caught in my throat as the animal became visible. It was an elephant, of sorts. It was white as pure snow and had five heads and ten tusks that gleamed in the moonlight. It lifted its multiple trunks into the air and trumpeted mournfully, a sound that caught at my heartstrings. I wanted to sit down and sob.

"The airavata," Father said sadly. "Last of his kind, I think. If we lose him, the world will no longer know the need to protect a loved one."

Heat flooded my body. I wanted to grab the people around me and shout in their faces. Did they not know what the consequences were? Did they not care?

"Behold!" Marco's voice reverberated. "A mount worthy of the gods! The bringer of rain, the destroyer of armies – ladies and gentlemen, the airavata! Bidding will start at one million euros."

A woman close to us prodded the man standing next to her. "I want those tusks, darling," she drawled in an accent that could only have been cultivated in America's deep South. "They would be just right for the necklace I want to commission for our anniversary party."

"Now, honey," the man said, a hint of annoyance in his voice. "We can get ivory anywhere, but those heads will be the talk of the town hanging on the wall of the den." He lifted a numbered paddle up, and Marco's voice rang out: "One million. Do I hear one million fifty?"

Bile rose in my throat and I had to breathe deeply to keep my soaring blood pressure in check. This was a travesty. I hadn't understood Amari's desperate need before, but I did now. I had to stop this.

"What's the plan, Ambrose?" Father asked.

The pace of my breathing increased as voices called out larger and larger numbers. My skin was prickling, itchy, and my head felt fuzzy. I had to stop this. Now.

"No time for planning," I answered. Riku flitted from my shoulder as I pushed through the crowd and jumped onto the stage. I grabbed the microphone from the startled Marco and shouted into it.

"Are you all out of your minds? Don't you

know how special these creatures are? They are magical! They are not yours to own or chop up into pieces. The world needs them."

I gazed out at the sea of masked faces before me. I didn't know what I had expected to happen, if I'd thought they'd rise and join my cause, like I was some charismatic liberator, but their silence baffled me. Next to the lift, Monique's crooked smile was a knife through my soul.

"Thank you, Ambrose," Marco said for my ears only as he took the microphone from me. "You've just increased the value of my wares tenfold."

He turned towards the audience again and said: "Sold! To the gentleman in the stylish cowboy hat."

Arms grabbed me roughly from behind. I looked over my shoulder to see the second goon from Marco's boat glaring at me. I tried to wrench myself from his grasp, but all I got for my efforts were bruises on my arms. The man prodded me down the stage and held me captive by the edge of the crowd.

I watched with a sinking feeling in my stomach as the cage containing the five-headed elephant was lowered back underground. My eyes were riveted to the hole in the arena floor. Another cage was slowly being hauled upwards. It was much smaller this time and covered with a black velvet cloth.

Monique brought the cage up onto the stage and placed it on the table next to the microphone.

"Ladies and gentlemen," Marco said. "As our friend rightly said, these animals are indeed special. But fear not, they may be rare, but they are not extinct, and here's the proof." He nodded at Monique, who slipped the velvet cloth off the cage. The crowd breathed out a collective ooh.

Inside the cage was what looked like a lion cub, except it had pristine white fur, with blue feathered wings and an indigo crest on its head. It snapped at the cage with its hooked beak and Monique jumped back, swearing softly in French.

Marco laughed. "It may just be a baby, ladies and gentlemen, but a griffon is as fierce as a lion and as proud as an eagle. Still young enough to be trained! Imagine yourself soaring above the clouds on the back of this magnificent animal! The bidding will start at ten thousand euros."

Caerus! Amari would never forgive me if I let him slip through my fingers.

I dug my elbow into the stomach of the guard standing behind me and suppressed a surge of satisfaction as I heard him grunt. His grip slackened just enough to let me break free. I turned around to punch him in the face, but before the hit could land, he grabbed my balled fist in his hand, smiled maliciously, and planted his other fist in my ribs. Pain flared through my solar plexus as I staggered back. The crowd surged around me as I stumbled to the ground, gasping for breath.

The guard bent down beside me and picked up the handcuffs that had fallen from my pocket. Then he grabbed my jacket and yanked me back onto my feet. The cuffs clicked shut around my wrists before I had my breath back. The guard shoved me up against the wall of the Colosseum, the warning clear in his eyes.

I looked up and caught sight of Father's worried face peeking through the crowd, who had already returned their attention to Marco. I nodded grimly to show I was okay and saw him sigh in relief. A white bird fluttered up to me and landed on my shoulder.

"Ambrose-san," Riku twittered in my ear. "We

217

have to set the prisoners free."

"No," I whispered urgently. "They're too dangerous. There has to be another way."

"Sold!"

Riku launched himself into the air as my head whipped up to see Marco's triumphant smile. The villain smirked down at me before addressing the audience again. "Hold your breath, ladies and gentlemen, for you are about to see one of the greatest legends of all time come to life!"

All eyes swept towards the lift, where the next cage was already being hoisted up. It was covered in red velvet. Marco waited until the arena was completely silent. I could almost hear my heart thumping in my chest. And then he nodded at Monique. She swiped the cloth off the cage in one flowing movement.

Awe filled every fibre of my being.

A thunderous roar lifted from the crowd. No one needed Marco to tell them what they had in front of them.

Inside the cage was a bird the size of a large peacock. Its crimson plumage sparkled in the full moon's light and its long shimmery tail swept across the floor, almost like an irate feline's. Its eyes blazed angrily. It flapped its magnificent wings once and screeched, a sound that set my teeth on edge.

Marco's voice blared across the loudspeaker, but I wasn't paying attention. The little white bird flittered in front of the cage door.

"The bidding will start at –"

The cage door flew open and the crimson bird surged from it, shooting straight up into the air with an ear-shattering shriek. The crowd gasped as the bird hovered above them, right in the centre of the arena, shining as bright as the sun.

Then it burst into flame.

Cheers turned into screams as fire rained down from the sky. People pushed towards the exit. My guard grabbed my arm and started steering me along with the crowd.

A howl ripped through the noise. My head whipped in the direction of the sound and my heart lurched into my throat. A creature bounded into the arena. Black fur covered its entire body and its enormous fangs gleamed red in the light of the blood moon. It swiped cruel-looking claws at the unfortunate man nearest to it, and the man crumpled to the ground in a spurt of blood.

The werewolf!

All hell broke loose as everyone tried to flee and found their exits blocked by creatures of fangs and scales and teeth and claws. Riku must have taken matters into his own hands. The captive creatures had come to fight for their freedom.

Heaven help us.

"Ambrose!" Father yelled. He was trying to push against the surge towards me. A woman ran across his path, chased by the chimaera I had seen earlier. She tripped over something and fell to the ground. The creature was on her in an instant. Her cry for help ended abruptly.

I turned my head from the gruesome sight to see the airavata barge into the arena. Two people were immediately impaled upon its tusks as the creature stampeded through the chaos, trampling anyone in its way.

And then the floor started shaking.

With a deafening roar, the Army of the Green Grove charged into the Colosseum. The centaurs stormed through the arena, spears and swords thrusting indiscriminately, their hooves crushing everything underfoot. Commander Gaius was in the lead and, incredibly, Sarah was astride him, clinging to his armoured torso, her eyes wild.

"Sarah!" I yelled. I was both relieved to see her here, unharmed, and anxious, here in the middle of what had effectively become a battlefield.

She waved at me and slid from the rampaging centaur's back, but was immediately lost within the throng.

My guard suddenly grunted and released my arms. I spun around to confront the man. His face was ashen, his eyes already losing focus. Behind him stood a nymph, one arm turned to wood, a branch protruding from the man's stomach. A trickle of blood ran down the corner of his mouth as his head slumped forward.

I took a step backwards, bile rising in my throat.

The nymph's eyes glowed green as she shrugged the body from her arm. She inspected the wood, wiping the blood away with her human hand. Then she turned her gaze on me.

A silver whistle was at my lips before I had time to think about it. I blew it, hoping I'd picked the right one in my haste, and scrambled backwards as the nymph reached for me.

A searing white light blazed between us. Amari stepped into view.

"Look out!" I shouted, pushing her off her feet. A shaft of wood shot over our heads as we tumbled to the ground.

Amari swore. She pushed me off her and jumped to her feet. She yelled a Word and a ring of fire suddenly flared around the murderous wood nymph. The creature shrieked and pulled her appendage back towards her body, cradling the now-human arm against her chest. The smell of burnt timber filled my nostrils.

"What the hell, Ambrose?" Amari said, her eyes wide as she looked beyond the circle of fire and took the entire scene in. "I sent you to retrieve a cub, not massacre a city." She glared at me. "Tell me you've found Caerus at least."

"He's here," I said. Somewhere. I held my cuffed hands up at her. She touched the metal with one fingertip and whispered a Word I almost recognised. With a click, my bonds fell to the ground. She held out a hand and helped me to my feet.

"Is that…?" Amari's frown turned into a look of wonder. I followed her gaze to where a group of centaurs were facing the airavata, spears levelled at the creature as it raised itself up onto its hind legs. It trumpeted its defiance, and lightning flashed from the sky.

The Keeper looked at the chaos raging around her, the awe fading from her face. "This is beyond me," she said. She pulled her mobile from the pocket of her jeans, hesitated for a second, her finger hovering over the keys. Then the werewolf's howl rent the air again, and she pressed a button. "I have no choice. I'll have to trust them." She turned to me again. "They'll be here in a minute. Where's Caerus?"

"I'll find him," I promised, just as shafts of light appeared throughout the arena.

"The Council is here," Amari explained. "Go, Ambrose!" She ran towards her allies, shooting me a worried look over her shoulder.

I glanced around me. People were still dashing about, frantically trying to escape or hide from the mythical creatures they had come to buy, now out for their blood. I saw my father in the middle of the arena, crouching down to pick something up. He'd lost his hat and looked a little dishevelled, but well enough under the circumstances.

Sarah was harder to find, but I spotted her off to one side, facing Monique. The two women were circling each other warily. Monique had a knife in her hand and Sarah was wielding one of the centaurs' discarded spears. Much as I wanted to intervene, I knew Sarah could handle herself. I'd probably just get in her way.

There! I saw Marco slipping through one of the Colosseum's arches. He had Caerus' cage with him! I ran after them, neatly sidestepping a pillar of fire shooting past my face and ducking as something soared just over my head. I pushed my way through the press of people, evading two centaurs harassing the humans trying to escape, and sprinted through the gates of the Colosseum.

It was dark outside. All the electric lights in the area seemed to have short-circuited, and only the eerie orange glow of the blood moon lit the night. It was also strangely quiet, as if the outside world was oblivious to the mayhem taking place within the walls of the ancient arena.

Footsteps on paving stones echoed through the stillness. Marco was running towards the entrance of the Roman Forum. I raced after him. I'd never find him in there again. There were just too many places to hide.

"Hey!" I shouted.

Marco skidded to a halt next to Constantine's Arch and turned towards me. If looks could kill, I'd be ten feet under right now. "What do you want, Ambrose?" he yelled.

"Hand me that griffon, and I'll ask the Keeper to go easy on you," I replied.

"You think the Keeper scares me," Marco sneered. "She's a pawn, Ambrose. Just like you are." He held a hand out towards me, as if he wanted me to shake it. "I have powerful friends, more powerful than your precious Keeper can ever dream of being. Join me and we can start fresh."

A wind suddenly gusted and the cover of the

manhole close to the Arch quivered. I took a step backwards. I knew what this heralded.

Marco plucked a gun out of his pocket and aimed it at me. "Join me or die!" he shouted.

The ground rumbled beneath us. The cover shot into the air and a foul smell spewed from the open sewerage drain. The bissabova burst from the pipe, roaring, its monstrous maw wide open, needle-sharp teeth glinting in the moonlight.

Marco shrieked. He dropped Caerus' cage and gripped his gun with both hands. They were shaking as he aimed at the creature. The bissabova reared up to its full height, towering above us almost as tall as the Arch, before darting towards the Italian with reptilian speed. It lunged at the man, engulfing his entire upper body in one big gulp. The shriek cut off and I averted my eyes, leaning towards the gutter to heave.

When I had nothing left in my stomach, I stood up, wiping my mouth on the back of my sleeve. My heart nearly failed when I realised the creature was right next to me, its head eye level with mine. I tried very hard not to look at the gore encrusting its lips.

It stared at me with unblinking eyes.

I kept as still as a statue.

It flicked its tongue at me.

"What?" I said flippantly, no longer able to handle the monster's gaze. "I don't have any more *gelato*, if that's what you're looking for."

The creature snorted, almost peevishly, as if to say that it had done all the hard work of dispatching Marco for me and I didn't even have a reward for it. Then it twisted its sinuous body and dived back into the sewers, taking the remnants of Marco's corpse with it but leaving the offending stench behind.

A low breath escaped my lips. I couldn't

believe I was still alive. My life had turned bloody bizarre and there was no denying that.

"Thank you," I called after the creature, and was rewarded by a gust of foul air whipping through my hair.

A tiny mew reminded me of the little cub still trapped in its cage where Marco had dropped it. I ran over to see the baby griffon whimpering, curled up in the corner of the cage furthest away from the open manhole.

"Don't worry, little guy," I said. "I'll keep you safe."

I looked at the cage's lock. It was pretty sturdy, not something I could break by hand. Could I...?

I touched a finger to the lock and whispered the Word I had overheard from Amari. The mechanism clicked and the cage door sprung open. Ha!

The little griffon jumped out and into my arms. He snuggled into my chest, where he looked up at me with enormous eyes that immediately melted my heart. Carefully, I ran my hand through his silky fur. A small purr rumbled through the cub's tiny chest.

"Come on, Caerus," I said to the little griffon. "Let's go see about getting you home."

✕✕✕

The arena inside the Colosseum looked like the aftermath of a battle, which I suppose it was. Bodies littered the floor, both human and otherwise. I had to tread carefully not to slip in patches of blood, or worse, as far as I went.

The Council seemed to have everything under control now. A stern-eyed woman was talking to a group of traumatised human survivors, all huddled together in a far-off corner of the arena.

Amari was moving from one captured creature to the next, whispering something that set them to sleep one by one. Probably the easiest way to get the creatures transported to the Repository.

The Army of the Green Grove was stationed next to the lift leading down into the hypogeum. They watched, stamping their hooves and flicking their tails nervously, as Gaius talked to a man in a pinstriped suit off to one side.

"There you are!" Sarah came striding towards me, relief plain on her face. She came in for a hug, but I stopped her at arm's length.

"Careful," I said, opening my jacket a little so she could see the griffon snuggled beneath it.

Her lips formed a silent "oh" and she gave a step backwards.

"Are you alright?" I asked. She had a bandage wrapped around her arm where Monique had slashed her yesterday. A small patch of blood had soaked through it. Her hair was a mess, but her smile was triumphant.

"Yes," she replied, nodding her head. I followed her gaze to see Monique cuffed to the side of the stage, her arrogant sneer replaced by a petulant pout. She wouldn't get away this time. "What happened to you, anyway? I was worried sick when you disappeared like that."

"It's a long story. My phone's dead and I didn't know how to get hold of you."

"You did in the end," Sarah said, her green eyes sparkling. "I was with Gaius when your message came through. I knew you were okay then."

"And who is this charming young woman, Ambrose?" Father asked, joining us. He held both hands cupped together and had his body turned so that his back was towards Amari and the Council.

"Sarah, this is my father, James Davids," I

introduced them.

"Your father!" Sarah said. "I thought –"

"Not dead, just misplaced," Father said, grinning. "Pleased to meet you, Sarah. I was quite impressed with how you took that French woman down. Nasty piece of work, that one, but you were more than up to the challenge."

I chuckled as Sarah's cheeks turned rosy.

"What have you got there, Father?" I asked, pointing at his cupped hands. He opened them to reveal a wrinkly baby bird nestled in his palms.

"That phoenix belongs with me, if you would, Mister Davids," Amari said, striding towards our group.

"Shit," Father swore softly, before turning towards Amari. "You must be the Keeper. I've heard many things, but I'm afraid none of them did you any justice," Father said, charming as ever.

"Amari Kerubo," the Keeper introduced herself, flashing a smile at Sarah. "Mister Davids, I must really insist –" She paused, looking at the lump underneath my jacket. Then she squealed: "Caerus! Oh, Ambrose, you found him!"

I opened my jacket and reluctantly handed the griffon over. The Keeper and the creature nuzzled each other affectionately. "Look how big you've grown!" Amari said. "I'll have to make you your own enclosure one of these days."

"We will need to discuss that, Miss Kerubo," another voice joined our group. It was the man in the pinstriped suit, accompanied by Gaius. The man had a refined English accent and the kind of handsomely rugged looks you only saw in expensive wristwatch adverts. I took an immediate dislike to him.

"Commander Equustos and I have had a very interesting discussion. It seems we have not been fair to the sentient creatures in our care. We may have to reconsider our policies."

Amari's jaw tightened as she looked from the man to the centaur and her grip on the griffon became protective. "The Repository is a safe haven, Chairman. At least, it was always meant to be, and I will make sure it is again. Commander Equustos and his men are welcome within its walls as well."

The centaur snorted and I shared a look with Sarah. We both knew Gaius would not willingly be locked up in the Repository.

The Chairman held a placating hand up towards the bristling centaur. "The Council will meet to discuss all our options. For now, Commander Equustos has agreed to a temporary lodging of all the mythical creatures detained here today, until we can determine what's best for them. If you would, Miss Kerubo. I'd rather you personally oversee their safe transport from here to the mountain."

Amari opened her mouth as if she wanted to say something else, but she seemed to think better of it and nodded instead. "Of course, Mister Chairman," she said. She glanced at me, shaking her head in a movement so small I wouldn't have noticed if I hadn't been paying attention. Was she giving me a warning? Or did she just disagree with the Chairman's plans to review their policy?

"Come, Keeper," Gaius intoned. "I am eager to see what you have planned for your new guests. I want to make sure they don't come to any more harm under the Council's care."

Amari and the centaur strode off together, her arms wrapped protectively around the griffon cub as if she were afraid someone was going to take him from her again.

The Chairman watched them go, his face an unreadable mask. Then he turned towards us again. Father immediately offered his hand.

"James Davids," he introduced himself.

"Oh, I've heard about you, Mister Davids," the Chairman replied. "When we have more time, I'd like us to discuss your options with the Elder Council. I suspect we could come to some sort of an agreement that doesn't involve an academic paper."

To me, his words carried a hint of threat, but Father's laugh was genuine. "We'll have to see about that."

"Ambrose," the Chairman said, turning to me. "The Keeper thinks highly of you. Apparently, we have you to thank for uncovering this market tonight. The Council is in your debt."

"I didn't mean for it to turn into a bloodbath," I said, feeling a sharp pang of guilt in my chest.

"Don't worry," the Chairman replied. "Where myth meets the mundane, there's bound to be conflict. That's the reason the Repository was created in the first place. To keep the magic confined."

I frowned. "Amari told me it was to protect the magical creatures from the world."

"Of course! And us from them. It's a mutually beneficial arrangement," the Chairman replied, smiling.

"What will happen to the centaurs?" Sarah asked.

The Chairman turned to her. "They will be free to go as they please. Of course, Commander Gaius will have to make amends for the loss of human life his army is responsible for today. The Council will handle it. Miss...?"

"Detective Inspector Miller," she replied, shaking his hand. "I'm just here for the thief."

"Ah, yes, the French woman." The Chairman frowned. "We will detain the other humans for questioning. Would you like us to take care of her too?"

"Take care?" I blurted. "Permanently?"

The Chairman chuckled. "Nothing so sinister, Ambrose. We just have to find out how much they know and how they found out in the first place. The existence of mythical creatures is supposed to be a secret, after all, and yet here we have an entire Colosseum full of people who came to buy them. How did this happen?"

"What are you going to do with them once you've questioned them?" Sarah asked.

"We'll just give them something to help them forget," the Chairman said, shrugging. "And then they can go back to their normal lives."

I frowned. That sounded very easy and convenient. Too easy.

"Fair enough," Sarah said, obviously not sharing my fears. "The thief is coming with me, though. She's wanted by Interpol. We'll handle it."

"As you wish." The Chairman nodded at all of us. "Now, if you'll please excuse me. Lots to be done." He walked off towards the woman overseeing the survivors.

"What do we do now?" I asked.

"Well, I don't know about you, but I would kill for a cappuccino," Father replied. "Metaphorically speaking, of course," he added as Sarah and I stared at him.

"You go ahead," Sarah said. "I'll catch up later." She gave my hand a squeeze and flashed me a quick smile. "I'm sure you have lots to talk about." She pulled her mobile phone out as she walked towards the stage where Monique was still confined.

"Come on, Ambrose," Father said. "Let's go before they remember I still have this little one with me." He placed his cupped hands against his chest, hiding the little fledgling phoenix he had rescued from the flames.

I laughed, shaking my head.

Besides everything that had happened, it felt like the world was almost right again.

✖✖✖

The sun painted the Thames in shades of orange as I stood at the railing of Tower Bridge, enjoying the last rays of its heat on my face. In the end, Rome had not been too bad. But it was good to be back home again.

My new phone bleeped. I glanced at the text message scrolling across the display. It was from Amari.

--Do you happen to know where Riku is? I haven't seen him since before the blood moon.--

--Sorry, no.--

I tucked the phone away again. It wasn't a lie; I hadn't seen the kitsune since he'd set the phoenix free at the Colosseum. But I had a good idea what he was doing now. And I hadn't forgotten our bargain either.

I glanced at my watch. It was almost time to meet Mother and Cassie at my favourite restaurant. I had a surprise for them tonight.

Movement drew my eyes towards the shoreline just under the bridge. An incredulous laugh escaped my lips. What were the odds?

"There you are, Ambrose," Father said, joining me at the railing. He put his hand on my shoulder. "Sorry I'm a tad late. What are we looking at?"

I pointed wordlessly.

Father inhaled loudly. "Let's go say hello."

I followed him down the steps that led down to water level. We stopped in front of a drainage pipe and waited. A few moments later, a golden-haired teenager wearing baggy jeans and a black hoodie stepped into view. I recognised him immediately. He was the boy I'd encountered in Hyde Park so many months ago, a lifetime ago, who wouldn't dive into the water to save the asrai.

Clever guy.

"Hey, I know you," he said, relaxing his wary stance as the suspicion in his eyes was replaced by recognition. He took a step towards Father and then wrapped his arms around him in a tight embrace. "Thank you," the boy whispered, his head against my flustered father's chest.

I watched the emotions play out on Father's face. I knew what he must be feeling: surprise at first, then regret for all the lost years, and finally relief that it was all over. He hugged the boy back and they stood like that for a few minutes.

I coughed awkwardly. "Should I let you two have a moment?" I asked, biting my lip to stop the smile from spreading across my face.

Father and the boy pulled apart. The boy's face was flushed, but Father's eyes twinkled happily.

"I'll see you around," the boy said gruffly, trying to hide his embarrassment. He nodded goodbye and sprinted up the steps and out of view.

"Come on, Ambrose," Father said, wrapping one arm around my shoulder in a half-hug. Happiness filled my heart like a seed of sunshine had taken sprout there. "Let's go surprise the ladies."

PART 5

SPRIGGAN'S QUEST

H yde Park had changed since the last time I'd been here.

My breath had frosted in the air then. It had been dark and cold and damp, the perfect metaphor for my life at the time. And, of course, a girl had tried to drown me.

Things were different now. No one had attempted to kill me tonight.

Not yet, at least.

The night was still young, though. So young that it wasn't actually dark yet. The air was cool, but not chilly enough for the tweed jacket I carried slung across one shoulder. The promise of summer hung thick in the air, the intoxicating scent of budding blooms and green shoots filling my nostrils. A duck quacked off to the side, and someone screamed.

Startled, I stopped in my tracks. Had I imagined...? There! I ran towards the sound. I pushed past shrubbery and stumbled to a halt, my mouth pulling into a thin line at the scene confronting me.

The scream had come from a boy who looked to be about eight or ten years old. He had short curly brown hair and skin the colour of dark wood. I gaped in surprise. Correction: his skin *was* wood. As I watched, his arms blistered into rough bark and twigs started sprouting from his head. His eyes were acorn brown, and filled with an all too human terror.

I recognised the man looming over him immediately.

He was around my age with blonde hair pulled back into a half ponytail that trailed down his back. Twin katanas were strapped to the back of his sleeveless black vest, and he held a weighted net in one hand.

It was the rogue hunter Father had told me about, the one that had taken him captive when he'd saved the selkie so many years ago.

"Hey, you!" I shouted, adrenaline surging through my veins as I stepped out of the shadows. "Pick on someone your own size."

The man turned towards me, a sneer marring his handsome features. Although we'd never met before, he somehow seemed vaguely familiar. His green eyes blazed as he looked me over.

"Mind your own business," he finally growled at me.

"This is my business," I replied, swallowing down my first instinct to run. I wasn't going to let this predator touch the boy, human or not. Especially since the boy clearly wasn't human.

I pulled Amari's silver whistle from around my neck. The man's eyes were drawn to it as it caught the fading sunlight. His scowl deepened.

"This one's mine," he said. "Find your own prize." He turned towards the boy again. The lad cowered in on himself, his feet literally rooted to the ground. He was more tree than boy by now. Leaves rustled as he shook with fear.

"Didn't you hear what happened to Marco?" I said. The man paused, his back suddenly rigid. He glanced at me. Maybe he hadn't heard. "He was eaten by one of his so-called prizes."

The hunter's face was all hard lines and tough angles. "How do you know?"

"I was there," I replied, suppressing a shudder. Too many teeth. Too much blood. I pushed the memory away and forced my focus back towards the man in front of me, probably just as dangerous in his own right. "In Rome, on the blood moon, not even a week ago. And so was the Keeper. If I blow on this whistle, she'll be here in a second, and believe me, you do not want to face her wrath."

The man pursed his lips as he considered my words. Then, his movements so fast I didn't have time to react, he drew one of the swords and surged towards me. I swallowed carefully as he pressed the point of the katana's blade against my neck. His green eyes bore into mine.

"Marco is a fool, but he's not stupid. How do I know you're telling the truth?"

"You can ask the Keeper yourself," I said, inclining my head slightly towards the whistle I still held in my hand. "I'm sure she'd love to catch up with you."

"Fine," the man growled after a few agonising seconds. He stepped back and re-sheathed his sword. "This one's all yours. But if I find you've lied to me, I will come for you and I'll take what's mine."

He pressed his left hand against an amulet hanging around his neck. Blue fox-fire blazed, and then he was gone.

I exhaled slowly. Good thing I wasn't lying, then. The last thing I wanted was for a creepy sword-wielding bloke to be stalking me.

I turned towards the boy. "You're a spriggan, aren't you?" I said, remembering an entry I had read in Father's notebook recently. He had hinted at two types of spriggans: the first a nasty troll-like creature that liked to play cruel pranks on humans, the second a demure tree sprite that preferred to stay hidden and kept to themselves. Looking at the petrified boy, it was probably safe to say I was dealing with the latter kind here.

The boy nodded, eyeing me warily.

"Don't worry," I said, tucking the whistle back under my shirt. "I'm not going to hurt you. I'm not like that man. I just want to get you home safely."

Some of the tension left the boy's stance.

"My name's Ambrose," I said, sitting down on the grass in front of the boy. Hopefully, he'd find me a little less threatening this way. "What's yours?"

He cocked his head at me, a small frown furrowing his mossy eyebrows. After a long moment, he finally answered. "Thomas."

"Is your mum nearby, Thomas? Can I take you to her?"

"Mum said not to trust strangers with silver whistles."

"And your mum is probably right," I agreed. "But you can trust me. I'm not going to use the whistle."

"But you hunt... us? Like that man? He didn't have a whistle, but he's a bad man."

"Stalker?" I scoffed, improvising a nickname. "I'm not like him."

I paused, considering. Was I like him? I ran a hand through my hair. "I've never actually hunted anything down," I confessed. "It just sort of happens to me."

"But you can find something if I asked you to?" Thomas' eyes were keen as he watched me.

"I suppose I could," I admitted. I certainly had enough contacts to track something down if I needed to. Hell, with my luck, I'd trip and accidentally fall into some dragon's lair right here in the heart of London. That's how all this had started in the first place. Tripping over my own feet. "Who do you need me to find? Your parents?"

"Nah," Thomas shrugged. His limbs slowly

softened back into flesh and the leafy twigs that had sprouted from his head dropped to the ground until he looked just like a normal boy, dressed in jeans and a Spider-Man t-shirt. Mythical creature or not, I'd still feel much better if I knew he was somewhere safe.

I climbed back to my feet. "How can I help you then?"

His eyes gleamed mischievously. "I need a few things. I can pay you."

"What kind of things?" I asked, narrowing my eyes. If this was some kind of prank, I'd better be careful. He didn't look ragged and homeless, so he probably wasn't after something as mundane as drugs or a good meal.

"Just a few things," Thomas said. "But I need it soon. Before the end of the week. If you can bring me what I ask for, I'll give you my treasure."

I snorted. "I've been offered treasure before, young man. Is this the kind that vanishes when the sun comes up, or something like that?"

"No," the boy replied, pouting. "It's real. But if you don't want to help me, I'll find someone else."

"Wait," I said, holding my hands up in surrender. "I never said I didn't want to. I'll help if I can."

To be honest, I could do with some treasure. After my decision to no longer hunt creatures for the Council, there was no way of knowing when I'd see a decent pay cheque again. I had enough in the bank to live comfortably for another few months or so, but it wouldn't last forever. My financial career was still in ruins and, let's face it, I wasn't going to pay the rent by writing the odd article about mythical creatures. I was fresh out of ideas.

Thomas beamed at me. "Great. I need three things: the wings of a water-leaper, a tear from the

Ceann-Cinnidh, and a lucky four-leaf clover. Not just any one – a lucky one!"

"Woah, there," I said. "I don't even know what half those things are. Why do you need them?"

Tears started welling in the boy's eyes and his lower lip quivered. "To change my life," he replied, sniffing.

I didn't know how to react. Should I hug him? Pat him on the head? Offer him a hanky?

"Are you in trouble, Thomas?"

He wiped at his eyes with the back of his hands and when he looked at me again, anger had replaced all traces of sadness. "Are you going to help me or not?"

"Yes," I said. "But only if I know you'll be alright while I look for these things."

"I'll be fine," he said, thrusting his hands into his pockets. His lower lip jotted out in a pout. "But I need them before the end of the week, or the deal is off."

"Alright." I pulled out my mobile and quickly jotted it all down. "Any hints on where to find these items?" I asked, frowning at the list. One of them should be easy enough, but I had no clue about the others.

"You'll figure it out," Thomas said.

"Fine," I agreed. "I'll do what I can."

Thomas' ire disappeared as he stepped forward and wrapped his arms around me. I stiffened until I realised he was just giving me a hug. "Thank you for saving me from that man," he said, his voice suddenly soft and vulnerable, reminding me that, mythical creature or not, he really still was just a little boy.

I put my arms around him, a little awkwardly. "No problem, kid. Now go home."

He released me, flashed me a cheeky smile, and then darted off into the bushes.

I looked at the list on my phone. I might have my work cut out for me. Luckily, I knew just who to call to help me out. I sent off a quick text.

Daniel's response came almost immediately.

--Not on me, but I know where to find some. We'd need to go to Ireland.--

Ireland? Well, why not? I certainly couldn't expect to walk into a Tesco and just buy what I needed. I texted him back.

--Gatwick at 6am tomorrow? Trip's on me.--

--Sure, see you there.--

I grinned. Daniel was always up for an adventure. This was going to be fun.

✳✳✳

A pang ripped through my heart as I looked at the boards displaying departing flight information in the waiting area at the airport. Paris was at the top of the list, and I had conflicted feelings when I thought about the City of Love, even more so now that the Notre Dame was in smouldering ruins. Paris was where Sarah and I had fallen in love, but it was also at the heart of all our troubles. We may have moved past our misunderstandings in Rome, but our relationship was still fragile.

I needed to get my life back in order if I wanted to make things work with Sarah. Problem was, to fix things, I'd need to fix the mistake I had made that had cost me my career, and I had no idea how to do that. Not unless I could suddenly get my hands on millions of pounds.

Perhaps Thomas' treasure was the answer I'd

been looking for. Perhaps this one last fling with the mythical world was what I needed before everything could go back to normal.

I exhaled loudly.

Would things ever be normal again? I knew too much now. I'd seen too many strange things. Hell, did I even *want* things to be normal after all of this?

"It's way too early in the morning to be looking so glum, mate," Daniel said, holding a steaming cup of tea in a takeaway container out at me. I accepted it gratefully, inhaling the fragrant aroma as he sat down beside me with his own cup of black coffee. "Penny for your thoughts?"

I took a sip, scalding my tongue on the warm beverage. "Just wondering if my life would ever be normal again," I replied, taking the plastic lid off the cup to cool the tea down.

"I hope not!" Daniel laughed. "I'm sure I don't fit into your definition of normal, and I've got rather fond of our adventures. Speaking of... Not that I mind an impromptu road-trip, Ambrose, but what's this about? Why do you need a four-leaf clover?"

"A lucky one," I reminded my best friend. "The boy was very specific about that."

"What boy?"

I quickly filled him in on my encounter with Thomas in the park last night. He looked alarmed when I told him about Stalker, but didn't seem surprised when I described Thomas and the state he was in when I had intervened. He just nodded when I explained the boy was a spriggan, clearly finding nothing unusual about the situation. And why would he? I read out the list of items the boy had requested.

Daniel took a sip of his coffee, considering. "That's quite the shopping list," he finally said.

"The Ceann-Cinnidh? Those were his exact words?"

"Yes. You know what it means?"

The redhead nodded. "Let's worry about that when the time comes. A water-leaper, though? Doesn't ring a bell."

"Damn," I swore. "I'd hoped you'd know what it was. I couldn't find anything in Father's book."

"Don't worry, we'll figure it out. There's an extensive library at the farm. We might find something there."

I blinked in surprise. "We're going to a farm?"

Daniel grimaced. "Been in my family for generations. The old ways still hold true there. I couldn't get away from the place fast enough."

"Anything I should be prepared for?" I asked, suddenly alarmed. Daniel might look and act human enough to fool anyone, but he was a Tuath, one of the Good Folk, and I'd heard enough stories to know that I'd better tread carefully. Especially if I was going to a place still steeped in old traditions. I might not even be welcome there.

"I wouldn't want to ruin the surprise for you," Daniel replied, his expression neutral. "That's us," he said, standing up, and I realised the boarding sign was flashing next to our flight number. I grabbed my duffel bag and joined him in the queue.

As we walked through the gate towards our plane, I noticed Daniel scowling. Even though it was a cloudless morning, a rainbow was hanging low in the sky. Normally I would have found my friend's irritation humorous, but for some reason, all I felt now was trepidation.

✕✕✕

We rented a small nondescript car at Dublin

airport and, with Daniel behind the wheel, headed inland. I'd never been to Ireland before and stared out the window at the verdant countryside, speckled with white sheep munching lazily behind low stone walls. The sky was a sombre grey, except for Daniel's ever-present rainbow stretching out before us like a multihued way marker.

My friend was strangely subdued as we drove, and it made me nervous. I needed to lighten the mood.

"Is there a pot of gold at the end of that?" I joked, pointing at the rainbow.

"Several," Daniel said, perfectly serious. "But don't go looking for them. It's rude."

"Oh," I said, taken aback. I'd never really given his mythical heritage much thought. I knew he was different, of course, but he was Daniel – the guy I played squash with on Tuesday nights, who'd listened to me moan about Rachel and gush over Sarah. Not some clichéd little prankster in a green suit with a pot of gold, but a real flesh and blood man who had to pay rent and make a living, same as me. We hadn't known each other that long, but I couldn't imagine my life without him.

Which led me to another thought.

"Hey Daniel, what trait would be lost if there were no more leprechauns? Hypothetically speaking, of course," I added quickly as his expression soured.

"Isn't it obvious?" he asked.

I hesitated. He was already in a bad mood. I didn't want to make things worse.

"Come on, Ambrose. Say it. I won't be upset."

"Greed? I'm just guessing because of the whole hoarding gold thing..."

"Close," Daniel admitted. "Avarice, actually. Why do something in half measures?" His tone had turned jocund, but I sensed it was something that gnawed at him.

I frowned. That was not a word I would have associated with my best friend. Maybe with myself before I'd lost my job, but not with Daniel. He spent his days quietly mending shoes in that little shop of his, trying his best not to stand out. He was probably the most frugal person I knew.

I said as much, and Daniel nodded. "I try to be different. Why do you think I set out on my own? But you'll see. We're nearly there."

He turned the car's indicator on and we turned off the highway and onto a bumpy dirt road that slowed our pace down to crawling speed. I'd paid little attention while we were talking, but I now saw a fog had rolled in, obscuring the view of everything further than a few feet from the car. I swallowed down a sense of claustrophobia. Nothing ominous about this visit at all.

"Here we are," Daniel said as he parked the car next to a small stone cottage.

I climbed out and stared at the building. It was roughly half the size of my apartment in London, with a thatched roof that looked patchy in places and moss growing on the crumbling stone walls. I know Daniel had said the farm wasn't very modern, but this was not what I had expected. Certainly not from a family who had several pots of gold at their disposal.

"It's... quaint," I said, trying not to be offensive. He might not love this place, but it was still his childhood home.

Daniel chuckled. "That's the shed, Ambrose. This is the house."

I turned around and felt my jaw drop as the fog parted to reveal a manicured lawn with a stepped pathway leading up towards a grand three-storey manor house. It looked like the kind of place you'd read about in a Jane Austen novel. It probably had special corridors just for servants. And a huge library, as Daniel had claimed. I bet they even had a parlour reserved for making music in.

I stared at Daniel. "This is your house? It looks like the Queen's summer home!"

Daniel shrugged. "Come on," he said. "They probably know we're here by now."

My stomach gave a twist and all my worries returned as I followed my friend up the path towards the house. What kind of welcome would I get? I vaguely remembered some of Father's old stories warning mortals not to eat anything offered by the Fae. Good thing I'd had that muffin on the plane then. I patted my pockets, trying to remember if I had anything made of iron on me.

The door opened and a woman stepped out to greet us. Her auburn hair was lined with silver and tied into a neat bun at the nape of her neck. Her dress was turn-of-the-century, with lace at the wrists and a high neckline. Thin laughter lines crinkled around her mouth as Daniel enveloped her in a hug.

"Daniel!" she exclaimed. "What a pleasant surprise!"

The redhead's smile was genuine when he let her go again. He might not be happy to be here, but he was happy to see this woman again, at least.

"Ma, this is my friend, Ambrose Davids," he introduced me. I could see the family resemblance around the eyes when she turned to greet me.

I shook her hand. Her grip was firm but gentle. "A pleasure to meet you, Mrs Brady."

"Oh, an Englishman," Daniel's mother said, a small frown appearing between her brows.

"Just by birth," I quipped.

Her smile returned immediately. "Any friend of Daniel's is welcome here, Ambrose. You may call me Mary."

Before I could thank her, the rest of Daniel's family spilled out of the front door. I immediately knew they were family, because I had never seen so many gingers in one place. I counted five brothers and one sister who looked so much alike I could hardly tell them apart, much less remember their names. They were all hugging him and slapping him on the back like they hadn't seen him in years. Perhaps they hadn't.

Daniel's father was a rotund man with ruddy cheeks and a handshake that almost bruised my fingers. "Patrick Brady, my good man," he introduced himself. "Anyone who can get Daniel to come see his old Da is welcome in this house." I grinned, relieved. Perhaps I'd been worried over nothing.

"Why *are* you here, Daniel?" his sister asked. She looked around Cassie's age, two or three years younger than me. Her slim figure was enveloped in a frilly Victorian dress and a mop of wild red hair framed her freckled face. Although she was smiling, her blue eyes held a hint of sadness as she looked at her brother.

"Do I need a reason to come visit my family?" Daniel asked, laughing.

"You're not fooling anyone, lad," Patrick replied jovially. "I'm sure you didn't bring Ambrose just to show him around the farm."

"Actually, we're here to see Bessie," Daniel admitted. "Anyone fancy helping us —" He hadn't even finished his sentence before his siblings started laughing and making excuses.

"You'll get no help from this bunch of hooligans, Daniel dear," Mary said with a twinkle in her eye. "You boys better get to it, if you want to be done in time for dinner. The field's been harvested recently. You might be out of luck today."

"We'd better go look anyway," Daniel said as he watched his brothers disappear back into the house. "We only need one."

"One's likely all you'll get," Patrick said. "Best of luck to you. We'll see you later." He patted his son on the back again, before holding the door open for Mary and Daniel's sister to enter the house. He nodded to me and followed them in.

"Come on, Ambrose. Let's go find that clover."

We climbed over a low stone wall and walked through a green pasture. The fog was lifting, revealing glimpses of a cerulean sky above. A single black and white cow mooed at us as we neared her.

Daniel walked up to the cow and slapped her on the rump. "Hello girl," he said whimsically. "Mind if we rummage through your lunch?"

The cow mooed again. "Bessie says she doesn't mind." Daniel grinned at me.

I looked around the field. It was entirely covered by clover. This wouldn't be as easy as I'd thought. In my mind's eye I'd seen a greenhouse with the tiny plants potted and labelled, perhaps by magnitude of luck, carefully nurtured by someone who was part librarian, part gardener.

I guess not.

"Please tell me you have a better way to find what we're looking for other than scrambling around on our hands and knees," I said, and winced when Daniel shook his head. We both dropped down on all fours and started looking through the clover. "How will I know if I find a lucky one?" I asked.

"You'll know," was all Daniel said.

I snorted. Bloody leprechaun.

At first, I inspected every tiny little plant, carefully counting each leaf on each stem. Always three. Three, three, three. Never four. The clouds parted and sweat started to collect at the nape of my neck. Three, three, three. The sun moved as hours passed. My vision started blurring. Every plant looked the same. Had I inspected these yet? Did it matter? They all only had three leaves, anyway. Three, three, three. Not four. Bessie mooed, her tail whipping back and forth, flies buzzing around her. Flies buzzed around me, but I didn't have a tail. Three, three, three.

Four!

"YES!" I roared, holding the clover aloft like the hero holding a sword to the sky on the cover of a fantasy novel.

"Not lucky," Daniel said.

Shit.

Disgusted, I tossed the offending plant away and continued my search. Three, three, three. Dirt under my fingernails, sweat rolling down my back, cow mooing, flies buzzing. Three, three, three. Lips dry, parched, dehydrated. Needed water. Cow mooing. Knees sore. Back aching. Three, three, three. Not four. Three, three, three.

Finally, I pushed myself up and sat back on my haunches, surveying the field, the endless green expanse, the impossible task. I knew it. I was under some faerie enchantment. This was purgatory, and I was trapped here forever. This is what happened when mortals messed with mythical creatures.

Bessie mooed again, right beside me. In a daze, I turned towards the cow. She was grazing on a patch of clover I hadn't inspected yet, and right beside her lips, something sparkled.

I blinked.

"Bessie, no!" I bellowed, diving towards the cow. Startled, she stepped backwards. I folded my body in a dome across the plant.

"Ambrose, mate," I heard Daniel say. "Are you alright?"

I rolled over onto my side, my one hand cupped protectively around the sparkling clover. It had four leaves. "Lucky?" I asked.

Daniel grinned. "Lucky."

I fell over onto my back, sighing with relief. Nine rainbows glimmered overhead. It was the prettiest thing I had ever seen.

"You'd better grab that clover before Bessie does, Ambrose."

Right. I rolled back over and plucked the four-leafed stem. Then I took the hand Daniel offered me and he pulled me to my feet. I held the clover up between my forefinger and my thumb for him to see.

"A fine specimen," Daniel said, a teasing grin on his freckled face. "Better keep it safe."

I pulled a little re-sealable bag out of my shirt pocket and carefully placed the plant in it. "I came prepared," I said as I tucked the bag back into my pocket.

"Good thinking," Daniel approved. "Let's go clean up. I don't know about you, but I could certainly do with a pint right about now."

I couldn't agree more.

✖✖✖

"I hope your room is to your liking, Ambrose dear," Daniel's mother said as she set a serving dish down onto the huge dining table, already filled with more platters of food than I could easily keep track of. My mouth watered at the smell of it all. There was enough mutton stew, cabbage, carrots, and boiled potatoes to feed a small army. Daniel's sister filled my glass with dark golden beer before taking her place opposite me.

"Yes, thank you," I said, surreptitiously loosening my belt a little in preparation for the feast. In truth, my room had caught me somewhat by surprise. It was lavishly decorated with gilded furniture and expensive brocades, but there had been a candle on my bedside table and a copper bathtub in the corner that a servant had filled with hot water from a bucket. The chamber pot underneath my bed had also been a novel experience for me. I suspected that when Daniel had complained about the farm being stuck in the old ways, he'd meant that quite literally.

Mary sat down too, smiling at Daniel beside me. At the head of the table, his father also beamed at him, before shushing his brothers at the other end of the room.

"Tonight, we're grateful that the whole family can be together again," Patrick said and I sensed Daniel stiffen for a moment, before relaxing again. "We're thankful for new friends and for the bounty that has been laid out before us." The rest of the family rumbled their gratitude in unison and then there was a brief pause before everyone went for the food at once.

I sat back, grinning at the spectacle. This was a far cry from Mother's civilised soirees.

"Dig in, Ambrose," Daniel said. "There'll be nothing left if you wait too long."

I reached for the potatoes, and remembered my earlier fears. My hand hovered in the air for a few seconds.

"Something wrong?" Mary asked, seeing my hesitation.

"I'll bet he's worried about the stories," Patrick said, winking at me. His cheeks were rosy as he took a draught of his beer and smacked his lips in pleasure. "No food or drink must cross his lips, lest he be enslaved forever. Am I right, Ambrose?"

A giggle went around the table, and even Daniel looked amused. I felt my cheeks warming in embarrassment.

"So the stories…?"

"Are all true," Patrick said, shrugging. "If you were dealing with the Good Folk. We Tuath are not so forbidding. We have no use for slaves."

"And besides," Mary added kindly. "You're a friend of the family. Here." She took my plate and started scooping pork sausages onto it. "You look hungry enough to eat a horse. I'll not let anyone have a rumbling tummy under my roof."

My stomach used that moment to growl loudly. If I hadn't been blushing before, I certainly was now. Daniel guffawed and his mother handed me the plate, her lips twitching. I didn't waste another second and tucked in. The food was delicious! Simple, but hearty, and just as tasty as anything Mother could have served.

"Did you find what you were looking for?" his sister asked when I stopped to take a sip of my beer.

I nodded. "We were lucky."

She sniffed. "Luck is very overrated."

I studied her for a moment. There was an air of melancholy about her. She was like the heroine of a Brontë novel. I could almost picture her stumbling along a lonely moor, weeping quietly. "I'm sorry, I didn't catch your name?"

"Caitlynn," she responded. "I don't expect Daniel has ever mentioned me."

"No," I admitted. "I knew nothing about his family until we arrived. He doesn't speak about himself that much."

"I'm not surprised," Caitlynn said. "Every story that tells about a Tuath meeting a mortal ends badly for the Tuath. But you're different." Her large blue eyes studied me as if I were a puzzle. "Daniel says you had the chance to deliver him to the Council, but you decided not to. Why?"

I took a large bite to give myself time to think. Even though the room was noisy with conversation, I had a feeling everyone's ears had perked up at that question.

"We made a deal," I finally said, deciding on the truth. "At the time I didn't know who the Council was, and Daniel had offered me his pot of gold when I really needed the money."

"And now?" Caitlynn asked.

"And now he's my best friend. I'd never think of selling him out to the Council."

Caitlynn took a sip of wine from a crystal glass while she studied my face. Why had I never heard of female leprechauns before? It seemed like there were quite a few details the myths conveniently left out.

"Can I come with you to London?" Caitlynn suddenly asked.

"Over my dead body," her mother said before I could answer.

"But Mum –"

"I do not need my only daughter risking the mortal world. No offence, Ambrose," Mary said in a voice that brooked no argument. "You're safe here and that's the end of it."

Caitlynn opened her mouth as if to protest, thought better of it, and closed it again. She dropped her gaze and started playing with her food, but I saw her glancing at me from beneath lowered lashes. She had spirit. I had a feeling her mother wouldn't be able to keep her cooped up on the farm much longer.

"Daniel mentioned you had an extensive library?" I said to lighten the tension.

"Indeed," Patrick replied. "Anything specific you're looking for?"

I nodded. "We're looking for a creature called a water-leaper."

"Doesn't ring a bell," Patrick said, scratching at his sideburns. "But you're welcome to have a look. Never was much of a bookworm myself, although Caitlynn practically lives in there. I'm surprised she hasn't moved in yet."

I looked at Daniel's sister, but she shook her head slightly. Damn it.

"What about the Ceann-Cinnidh? Daniel knows something, but he's keeping it to himself."

"Oho!" Patrick laughed. "Without a doubt." He turned towards his son and said: "Give the old Mor my regards. I haven't seen him since your sister's naming day. I'll bet he's getting fed up with the whole situation by now."

"I'm sure he is," Daniel said. "And before Ambrose gets even more frustrated by our secrecy, I'd better give him a clue."

Finally! I was about ready to resort to physical violence. "Yes?" I prompted.

"You'd better get that fancy phone of yours out and book us a flight to Inverness for tomorrow morning," Daniel replied.

"Scotland? All the way up north?" I asked, reaching for my phone.

"Do you have to leave so soon, Daniel?" Mary asked, a small tremble in her voice. "It's so rare that you come to visit us."

"I'm afraid so," he replied, reaching for the carrots and ladling some more stew into his dish. "We're on a bit of a deadline and we still need to find the water-leaper."

"I hope you're not on a hunt for the Council..." Patrick frowned.

"No, sir," I said quickly, looking up from the list of flight times on my phone. "It is a hunt of sorts, I guess, but it's a personal quest. I don't work for the Council anymore."

"Good," he said, relaxing again. "In that case, you might want to ask the Mor. If this creature you're looking for is aquatic, the Mor should have some idea."

"Good idea, Da," Daniel replied.

"You'll stay the night, at least, won't you?" Mary asked.

"First flight out is at eight o'clock," I supplied. "Booking the tickets now."

"It would be easier if we slept over in Dublin —"

"Nonsense, Daniel," his mother said. "You can get up early tomorrow morning. I'll pack you a breakfast."

Daniel didn't object, but his face settled into a resigned expression. His mother was strong-willed and he probably knew he wasn't going to win this argument. They may be leprechauns, creatures from myth, but deep down, their family was just like mine.

I shrugged. I didn't mind the delay. With the clover in my pocket, we were still on track to meet the deadline. It had been a long day and I wouldn't mind getting a good night's rest before we set out again.

"Join us for some whiskey in the parlour, Ambrose?" Patrick said as Mary and Caitlynn started collecting plates.

"Actually, if you don't mind, I'd like to see the library."

"Of course," Patrick replied. "Third door on your left. Holler if you need anything." Then he turned to Daniel. "Come, my boy, your brothers and I would like to hear everything about your life in London. Have you met the Queen yet?"

I grinned as Daniel was ushered out of the room, his brothers all clamouring around him with questions. I picked up an empty dish to carry into the kitchen, but Mary wagged a finger at me.

"Leave that to us, dear. To the library, off with you now."

Sheepishly, I stepped out of the dining room and into the corridor. I could hear the men talking behind the first door as I passed. The second door was open and I peeked inside quickly. A grand piano stood in one corner with chairs placed around the room. I knew it!

The third door led into the library. Three of the four walls were fitted out with shelves filled with old, leather-bound books and a soft carpet covered the wooden floor. A comfortable sofa lounged underneath a window looking out onto the garden. The light was fading outside. I didn't have much time if I wanted to get any reading done. There was no light hanging from the ceiling and, come to think of it, I hadn't seen any in my room either. Probably no electricity in this old manor house.

I wasted no more time and wandered along the shelves, perusing the books. The collection was not as impressive as Amari's, but it held a respectable amount of esoteric books written exclusively by Celtic authors. I grabbed a dust-covered tome without a title on its spine and settled down on the couch, squinting by the little light coming in through the window.

The text inside was handwritten and archaic, but I could make sense of some of it thanks to Father's tuition in my early years. It was an old English dialect, written by someone in the late seventeenth century, if the preface was to be believed. I flicked through the first few pages until the phrase "wyld hunt" drew my attention. I read with rapt attention about the Cŵn Annwn, or "hounds of hell" as the author called them. Apart from the fact that he had correctly identified them as hounds, he had remarkably few other details right. I knew from close personal experience they did not have forked tails or horns on their head. And I'm pretty sure I would have noticed if a rift into hell had opened in their wake.

I was rolling my eyes for what seemed like the hundredth time when the library door opened and Caitlynn slipped in. She seemed a little breathless, as if she'd been running. A strange look flashed across her face when she saw me - something like fear and relief mingled together. Then she closed the door softly behind her. She turned back towards me and held a flickering candle out at me.

"I've brought you this," she said. "It's getting dark in here and you don't want to ruin your eyes."

"Thank you," I replied, expecting her to bring the candle closer, but she just stood there at the other end of the room, watching me. I remembered Patrick saying she practically lived in here. This was probably her way of ushering me out of the room.

I shot to my feet, a little flustered. I smacked the book closed and coughed as dust rose from its pages.

"What were you reading?" Caitlynn asked as I returned the old tome to its place on the bookshelf. She seemed nervous. Her free hand clutched onto her dress as she stood perfectly still, watching me.

"A fairy tale." I smiled, trying to set her at ease. It was clear she didn't get out much. She was probably not used to being alone in the dark with strange men.

"I hope you don't believe everything you read in old books, Ambrose. The truth isn't always as black and white as they make it seem."

I snorted. "You don't have to tell me. I've seen

it for myself."

Caitlynn nodded, and from the way she jutted her chin out, it seemed like she'd come to a decision. She walked towards me, the light from the candle casting flickering shadows on the library walls. Her blue eyes were very bright when she stopped in front of me, all traces of nervousness gone.

"Take me with you, Ambrose," she said, the sadness I had sensed earlier replaced with an excited tension. "Tonight, right now. When you and Daniel leave, let me come with you."

"I…" Can't, is what I wanted to say. Not against her mother's wishes. Not over her mother's dead body. Those had been her words. I took a step away from her, but Caitlynn reached out and grabbed my hand.

"Please, Ambrose," she said, her grip tightening. "I don't want to be trapped here anymore. I want to be free, like Daniel. I'll do anything you say." She bit her lower lip, hesitating, and then blurted out: "I'll give you my pot of gold!"

Knowing what I did about a leprechaun's lust for wealth, I understood exactly how desperate her request was. Her brother had offered me his in exchange for his life, or so he'd thought. I couldn't help but feel that Caitlynn was doing the same.

Before I could answer, the library door opened. Caitlynn dropped my hand, startled, and stepped away from me. Her mother came in, her smile wavering as she saw the two of us together.

"You have an early morning tomorrow, Ambrose," Mary said, slipping her smile back on and her arm into mine. "Come, I'll show you to your room. This is a large house and guests often get turned around in the dark."

I let her lead me out of the library, casting a last

glance over my shoulder. Caitlynn stood in the flickering candlelight in the middle of the darkened room. Her face was a mask, but her eyes were pleading silently.

Mary led me up the stairs and to my room at the end of the hall. I bid her goodnight and flopped down onto the large four-poster bed, staring at the ceiling.

Caitlynn's eyes haunted me. Should I take her with me? Could I risk the wrath of her mother, and maybe Daniel's as well? Or should I leave her in a place where she was safe, but clearly unhappy?

I tossed and turned in that great four-poster all night until a dreamless sleep finally claimed me in the wee hours of the morning.

❊ ❊ ❊

Daniel's entire family came to see us off before the sun had properly risen, bleary-eyed and yawning. Only Caitlynn was absent.

I felt a twinge of jealousy, looking at them and knowing that my own sundered family would never be together like this again. Mother had been less than thrilled to see Father, judging by the look on her face when we had surprised them at the restaurant two nights ago. At least she'd been civil enough. Cassie... Well, Cassie's eyes had lit up when she saw him at first, but then she'd withdrawn from the conversation and had been unusually silent all evening. What with the rush to embark on Thomas' quest, I hadn't had a chance to talk to her since then. She was probably fine. Likely just overwhelmed by Father's sudden return.

Mary squeezed my hand, bringing me back to the present, while Daniel was busy saying goodbye to his brothers. "Take care of him, Ambrose," she said, a little catch in her voice. "The outside world is dangerous for our kind. I can't imagine how he's managed on his own for so long."

"I will," I said, feeling awkward. I glanced at my friend, engulfed within a big bear hug from his father. So far, Daniel had been the one helping me out of trouble, not the other way around. He'd always seemed quite capable and confident on his own. Perhaps it was just a mother's worry for her son, although I doubt mine was as concerned for me most of the time.

"Thank you for your hospitality," I said, switching places with Daniel and shaking his father's hand.

"You're always welcome here, Ambrose," Patrick replied. "Give my regards to the old Mor. Tell him I said not to eat you."

I laughed with him. He was joking, of course. He had to be.

I climbed into the passenger seat while Daniel started the car. As we drove off, waving goodbye, I noticed Caitlynn staring at us from a window on the second floor. Her face was pale and she didn't wave.

"Can I ask you a question?" I said as the little rental car bumped down the dirt road and past the dilapidated cottage I had mistaken for the family house at first. "Why don't you come visit them more often?"

Daniel's eyes were bloodshot as he squinted to see in the pre-dawn darkness. The blanket of fog encircling the farm probably didn't help either. And I was pretty sure he was nursing an epic hangover.

"Because it's so hard to say goodbye every time." His hands tightened on the steering wheel. "But I can't stay here. We can't hide from the world forever. I want to be free to live life on my own terms."

"Your sister seems to feel the same way."

Daniel glanced at me, frowning. "Did she say something?"

"She begged me to take her with us today. She was... very insistent. But I couldn't be responsible for a family feud." I fiddled with my seatbelt, guilt still wracking me. "She probably hates me now."

"Ma will never let her leave," Daniel said as we merged onto the main road and started speeding towards Dublin. The sun was an orange splinter on the horizon, the pre-dawn light a pale glow. "Six boys and one girl: those are good odds for Tuaths. She's too precious to risk."

"I suspected as much," I replied.

"But it's not fair to Caitlynn," Daniel continued. "She deserves her freedom as much as I do."

"Would you rather I'd brought her with us today?"

"No," Daniel said after a brief pause. "No, you did the right thing. When this is over, I'll have a chat with Caitlynn and see what we can do. Perhaps if she came to live with me, Ma wouldn't be quite as upset."

We travelled further in silence, each lost in his own thoughts.

A few hours later, as we boarded the plane heading for Scotland, I was still thinking about Daniel and Caitlynn's wish for freedom. I remembered what he had said to me the first time I had met him, when he had thought I might deliver him up to the Council: I'd rather be free than safe.

Perhaps that was a choice everyone had to make for themselves.

⋇⋇⋇

It was a miserable day in Inverness. The sky was overcast and gloomy, transforming the River Ness into a shadowy serpent slinking through the city. With Daniel behind the wheel again, we left the castle on the hilltop behind, speeding past the brightly painted houses and the rustling trees lining the riverfront.

I couldn't take the suspense anymore. "We're going to Loch Ness, aren't we?" I asked.

Daniel's grin was mischievous. "Took you long enough."

"You know the Loch Ness Monster isn't real, right?" I scoffed.

"How sure of that are you?"

"Wait, what?" I gasped. "Are you saying the Ceann-Cinnidh is... Nessie?" My mind reeled at the thought. Years ago, when Cassie and I were still kids and our parents had still been together, we came to Scotland on holiday. The Loch Ness visitor centre had been on the itinerary, and if the informative exhibition had accomplished anything, it was to firmly convince our family of believers that there was nothing of supernatural interest living in Scotland's largest lake.

"We should stop to take a gift," Daniel said. "He'll be much more amenable if he's not hungry. And don't call him Nessie, or a monster. That really annoys him."

"Him?" I spluttered as Daniel stopped the car next to a Tesco's.

"Wait here," he said, jumping out of the rental. I sat, stunned, still trying to come to terms with the fact that not only was the Loch Ness monster real, but also male. Daniel was back within minutes, carrying something pungent wrapped in brown paper. "Haddock," he said when he noticed my enquiring gaze. "Let's keep the windows rolled down, shall we?"

The stench of fish was thickly ingrained into my nostrils by the time we left the city behind and took the highway running along the length of Loch Ness. I stared at the loch through my window, clenching my jaw to keep it from chattering in the cold air wafting in. The water of the lake was choppy and gloomy. I could see why so many people believed a prehistoric beast could be hiding in its depths.

Could it actually be true?

It didn't take us long to reach Urquhart castle, a picturesque ruin on the shores of the loch. The sight of it immediately stirred my imagination. Old castles had that effect on me. They had so many stories to tell.

Daniel parked the car in the empty parking lot. By now, the sky was a deep grey, threatening an impending downpour, and the wind whipped through my hair as I stepped out.

"The castle's closed," I called out, disappointment a sour taste in my mouth, not unlike the smell of the haddock Daniel was carrying in one hand. A metal chain was stretched across the length of the bridge straddling the dry moat that defended the castle from the mainland. A homemade sign hung from the chain. The words 'CLOSED ON ACCOUNT OF THE WEATHER' were handwritten on it in red ink.

"Perfect," Daniel said. "Means we have the place to ourselves. Come on." He climbed over the chain and strode across the bridge.

Shrugging, I followed my friend. Wasn't the first time I'd trespassed somewhere I wasn't supposed to.

As I followed in the wake of the fishy stench Daniel's parcel left behind, something on the ground caught my eye. It was a pen with the words LOCH NESS painted in bold letters on it. I picked it up. One half of it was made of clear plastic through which I could see a creature with a long neck floating in a blue liquid. When I tipped the pen downwards, the familiar rounded humps of Nessie's body stuck up out of the water. A souvenir someone must have dropped in their haste to get away before the rain came.

"You coming?" Daniel called.

I pocketed the pen and followed my friend along the footpath through the gatehouse to where a partial wall with a locked wooden gate led to stairs down to the water's edge. Daniel and I stepped over the ruined wall, bypassing the useless gate, and walked down towards the water.

I stopped a few steps away from the shore. I'd rather not get too close to the water, especially if there was something lurking there that might want to eat me. "What is a Ceann-Cinnidh, anyway?" I asked, eyeing the dark surface of the loch warily.

"The Chief of Chieftains," Daniel replied. "You'll see soon enough. If you're sure you want to do this? The Mor can be... a little irritable, if you catch him in a foul mood."

I swallowed, my throat suddenly dry, but I nodded. "I am. If you are?"

"Why wouldn't I be?" Daniel asked, unwrapping the haddock and placing it so that one half of the fish was on dry land, the other half in the water.

"Well," I said, fiddling with the pen I had picked up. "The way you reacted when you found out I had unicorn blood in Cardiff, I thought you'd have a problem with taking a tear from Nes–, I mean, from the Mor."

Daniel guffawed. "Believe me Ambrose, if he doesn't want you to have a tear, you won't get one. Let's let him decide."

"Alright..." I agreed, unsettled by Daniel's

unconcern. I looked at the fishy offering, glad that it was the bait and not me. "And you're sure that fish is all we need to summon him?"

"Oh, he knows we're here. The fish is just to entice him to come chat with us. Haddock's his favourite, and you won't find any in this loch."

I glanced at the ominous sky and felt a light drizzle on my face. Great. I hope we didn't have to wait long for Nessie to show up or we'd get soaked to the bone. I thrust my hands into my jacket pockets, wishing I'd brought a raincoat with me. I looked at the loch again. Small drops were plonking onto the surface, causing tiny ripples in the choppy water.

And then I noticed the large ripple moving towards us.

A thrill of fear ran through me as Daniel turned to me.

"You remember Angharad, right?" he said, a hint of anxiety finally in his voice.

"Of course," I nodded, swallowing nervously. How could I forget? The memory of the Welsh dragon's gaze and her fiery breath would stay with me until my dying day.

"The Mor demands the same respect," Daniel said.

Suddenly, the water churned at our feet. I took a step backwards as a massive head reared up out of the loch, followed by a long neck and the top half of a sinuous body. Deep blue scales glinted in the pale light as a webbed claw grabbed the haddock and tossed it into a great maw, teeth as long as my arm ripping the morsel to shreds. I gaped at the creature.

The Loch Ness monster was an enormous water dragon!

"*Latha math*, Kentigern Mor!" Daniel greeted the creature in Gaelic. The dragon turned its head towards us. I could feel the weight of his storm-grey eyes on me. "My father sends his respects."

The dragon snorted. A deep rumble rose from his belly, and when he spoke, his voice sounded like thunder crackling. "You brought a mortal to my shore, little Tuath? You know how I detest these humans. All day and all night, with their boats and their noise and their trash. They never give me a moment's peace."

"This is my friend, Ambrose Davids. I'll vouch for him, great Mor."

The dragon's head swooped in, so close I could poke him in the eye if I dared. He smelled a little fishy, not unlike the haddock he had devoured a few minutes ago. I tried to hold my breath as unobtrusively as possible. It wouldn't do to offend something that could bite your head off on a whim.

"Have you come here to reveal my secret, Ambrose Davids?" Kentigern Mor asked, his rumbling voice activating every flight instinct in my body. It was all I could do not to cower to the ground. "Are you going to bring your scientists here, now that you know how to find me?" the dragon continued. "Are you finally going to chase me from my home?"

"No," I stammered. "I came to ask a favour."

"Ha!" The dragon reared back and I breathed a sigh of relief. An enormous irate dragon looming over you, although not ideal, is infinitely better than an enormous irate dragon within biting distance from your face. "And what favour have you come to ask of the Ceann-Cinnidh? Speak!"

"A tear, great chief," I said, and flinched as the dragon roared.

"You think I don't know about the clever machines you humans have?" Kentigern Mor growled. "The ones that can determine what something is from a piece of a creature's body? They swept every inch of this loch, not long ago. I saw them poring over their electrical gadgets. They will come for me if I give you this tear. And I will not go down without a fight!"

The water surged as the great creature roiled, its sinuous body arching over itself in never-ending loops. Daniel and I both stepped backwards before we could get caught up in the dragon's frenzy.

"Peace, great Mor!" Daniel called, holding his arms up in a placating gesture. "The scientists won't come again. They've done their DNA tests. They think the lake is filled with giant eels."

"Eels?" the dragon bellowed, clearly offended. "They think I'm an eel?"

"The scientists won't come again," I said quickly. "But the believers will. They won't need a tear to prove that you exist. They'll keep on coming until the day that someone finds you. And when they do," I paused for dramatic effect. The dragon stopped thrashing, his head as still as a snake about to pounce. His eyes bored into mine. It took all my willpower not to turn and run. "When they do, you will have no peace. They will build high-rise hotels on the shores of the loch. They will send boats of tourists out every few minutes, people diving and snorkelling, nightly search parties. There will be camera crews hunting you night and day. You will be on display like a goldfish in a bowl for all the world to see."

The dragon gnashed his teeth, his two front paws clenched so tightly that the muscles in his powerful forearms bunched together.

"I can't change that," I continued, although my mouth was dry with fear. "But I can offer you an alternative."

"Ambrose..." Daniel said in a warning tone.

I held my hand up. "He deserves the choice, Daniel."

Slowly, Daniel nodded, his lips pursed. He didn't like it, but he couldn't argue with me. He believed in freedom of choice above all else.

"Speak, human," the dragon demanded.

"The Keeper will welcome you to the Repository," I said. "She will give you a loch twice as large as this one and, better yet, she will make sure that you're left alone."

The dragon's large body receded into the lake until only his head was visible. His enormous eyes didn't blink as he considered my offer.

"You want to lock Kentigern Mor up in a zoo?" Daniel finally exclaimed, unable to hold back any longer. "On display like some dumb animal, at the Council's mercy?"

"It's not a zoo," I said. "It's a haven. Trust me, the Keeper will make sure he's safe there." I turned to the dragon again. "I'm not trying to trick you, great dragon. I want to help you."

Kentigern Mor rose out of the water again, his stormy eyes never leaving my own. I gulped as he moved closer. I felt like a deer in the headlights, too afraid to run, but desperately needing to.

"I believe you, Ambrose Davids," he finally said, and I breathed a sigh of relief. Beside me, Daniel sighed in resignation. "I will give you a tear in exchange for my freedom. Make it so."

I pulled the silver whistle out. Turning to Daniel, I said: "You might want to stay out of sight."

Daniel nodded and sprinted up the stairs, ducking behind the ruined wall. I made sure he was not in view before blowing the silent whistle. A few minutes later, Amari stepped out of a shaft of white light.

"What is it, Ambrose? I'm quite busy —" The

Keeper stopped mid-sentence and her jaw dropped. I suppressed a laugh as her eyes nearly popped out of her head. A look of sheer wonder filled her face.

"Keeper," I intoned formally. "May I introduce Kentigern Mor, Chief of Chieftains. Great Mor, Amari Kerubo will assist your transition to the Repository."

Amari shot me a surprised look, but she quickly recovered and inclined her head respectfully at the dragon. "I would be honoured, great chieftain," she said.

"Ambrose has promised me solitude, Keeper," the dragon rumbled. "Can you deliver?"

"Of course," Amari said immediately. "I will build you an enclosure that will rival this lake for splendour, and you can decide who may come and go as you see fit."

The dragon swept his head from side to side, taking his home in. "Can you replicate this castle?" he asked, a note of wistfulness entering his voice.

"Of course," Amari said, a little taken aback. "Ruined or...?"

"As it is now," Kentigern Mor replied. "It's rather poetic in its current state, don't you think? I never liked the humans who lived here, anyway."

"It will be as you wish, great dragon," Amari said. I was pretty sure she would have agreed if he'd asked for a lifelike replica of Edinburgh castle. She was handling the situation well, but I could see the excitement bubbling underneath her calm facade.

"Then let us proceed, but first..." The dragon turned his head towards me again. "A tear for you, Ambrose, as agreed."

I plucked the little glass vial I had brought along from my jacket pocket. The Ceann-Cinnidh lowered his head to my height. A single droplet rolled from his enormous eye. I caught it and quickly stoppered the bottle, tucking it safely back into my pocket.

"I'll have that," Amari said immediately, holding her hand out at me.

I sighed. I should have seen this coming. "I need it –"

"Haven't we had this discussion before, Ambrose? No parts out in the world, even if freely given. It's just too dangerous."

"I agree, but –"

"What would you do with it, anyway?" the Keeper asked, quirking an eyebrow at me.

I didn't think she'd find my reason nearly as compelling as I did, and it meant I'd have to tell her about Thomas and risk having her insist I bring him in too. I shrugged. "Never mind," I said, handing the bottle over. I'd have to figure out a way to get it back from her later.

Amari frowned at me as she pocketed the vial. "We'll discuss this later," she promised. Then she turned back towards the dragon. "Ready?"

"Ready," Kentigern Mor replied without hesitation.

I shielded my eyes as a bright light filled my vision. When I looked again, Amari and the dragon were gone.

"What have you done, Ambrose?" Daniel said, stepping out from behind the ruined wall.

"It was his choice," I said.

"A bad one," my friend growled.

My temper rose. I hadn't tricked Kentigern Mor. Why couldn't Daniel understand that? "Just because you prefer to be free doesn't mean he does," I snapped. "Clearly he'd much rather be left alone, and there is no safer place for him than inside the Repository."

Daniel's face turned red as he bristled at my

argument. He opened his mouth as if to retort, but then his shoulders slumped and the fight went out of him. "I know, you're right," he said. "I still don't like it."

Thunder clapped and we both jumped. As if a sluice gate had been opened, heavy rain suddenly poured from the dark clouds above. Abandoning our dispute, we sprinted up the steps and across the already muddy moat. Daniel fumbled with the car keys. By the time we were in the rental, the windshield fogging over, we were both drenched.

"Ah, bollocks," Daniel said.

"What?" I dipped a hand into my jacket pocket to make sure the bag containing the four-leaf clover was still safe. Luckily, it was still there, along with the pen I had picked up.

"We forgot to ask him about the water-leaper."

I flopped back into my chair. Shit.

✷✷✷

"Why don't you ask the Keeper if she knows what a water-leaper is?" Daniel asked as we sat in a pub in Inverness, eating dinner later that night. It was still pouring down outside, but at least we'd had a chance to change clothes and dry off at a bed-and-breakfast in the centre of town. We'd decided to stay put until we knew where we would be going next before we tried to get a flight out of Scotland.

"I've considered it," I replied between a mouthful of haggis and blood pudding. My nose wrinkled. I thought I'd give this traditional Scots meal a try, but now I wished I'd stuck with fish and chips. "The problem is, if she knew I was going after the creature, she'd expect me to hand it over once I've found it. I don't want to create an expectation I can't keep."

"Fair enough," Daniel said, nodding. "Is this how you're going to handle this dilemma, then? Give them the option to choose? What about something that isn't smart enough to give you an answer?"

"I don't know," I admitted. "Guess I'll cross that bridge when I have to. I'm not actively hunting for the Council anymore. I never was, to be honest. I literally fell into this situation, as you well know." Daniel grinned at me, nodding. "By the way, I've been meaning to thank you."

He quirked an eyebrow at me.

"The shoes," I said, lifting one foot into the air to display a white trainer. "You were right: they really are lucky. They've saved my neck a couple of times."

Daniel laughed. "We make our own luck, Ambrose." He stood up. "I'll be right back."

Daniel disappeared for a few minutes before returning with two pints of dark lager. He placed one in front of me before taking his seat again. He took a long draught of his beer, draining the glass almost halfway. "Ah," he said, smacking his lips appreciatively. "Have you tried ogling it?"

I blinked at him. "Excuse me?"

"The water-leaper. Have you tried ogling it on that fancy phone of yours?"

I laughed. "You mean Googling it? No, I didn't even think about that. Let me have a look quickly." Now why hadn't I thought of that? I quickly opened a browser on my mobile and did a quick search. "Daniel, you're a genius," I said as images of a strange hybrid animal popped up. It looked like a frog with wings, alarmingly also equipped with the tail of a scorpion. I showed the pictures to Daniel.

"Ugly little critter."

"Says here it's a creature from Welsh mythology. Preys on fishermen, apparently."

"Welsh fishermen must be very timid, then," Daniel quipped. "Takes more than a funny-looking amphibian to scare an Irishman."

I quickly changed my search and whooped as Google brought back a series of recent articles from the *South Wales Echo*. "We're in luck. Apparently, the lake at Roath Park in Cardiff has been closed all week because of a series of unexplained accidents. Three fishermen have been found drowned, and their bodies show signs of being gnawed on." I grimaced as that gruesome image popped up in my mind's eye. "The local authorities are baffled."

"Lucky for us, not so lucky for the fishermen." Daniel shuddered. "To Wales tomorrow then?"

"Yeah," I agreed, pushing my plate of haggis to one side. My stomach was churning enough as it was. "Train or plane?"

"How many days do we have before you need to find young Thomas again?"

"He said end of the week. Two days from now."

"Plane then," Daniel said. "We can't afford a day on the rails with such a tight deadline."

"Agreed," I said, snagging us a couple of last-minute tickets on a low-cost airline. "I didn't think I'd be going back to Cardiff any time soon," I admitted, shuddering at the memory. "The last time nearly did me in."

"At least this time, we know what we're in for," Daniel said, downing his beer.

A shiver tingled down my spine, almost like a premonition. I didn't relish the idea of going after something that preyed on people from the water. My track record wasn't promising.

But if Daniel was right and we really did make our own luck, then I'd damn well make sure I was better prepared this time. This time, I would be the hunter instead of the hunted.

※※※

It was late morning by the time we reached Roath Park and, although there were cars parked along the streets next to it, the area was deserted. The yellow police line that spanned the park's perimeter probably had something to do with that. A police officer stood at one corner, keeping an eye on the empty street. His gaze turned to us as we walked closer.

"You take care of him," Daniel said, nodding at the officer. "I'll go find us some fishing tackle." He swerved off and I found myself walking alone towards the copper, whose frown deepened the nearer I came. He was a burly man with a glower that seemed permanently etched on his face. A salt and pepper moustache curled along his cheeks.

"Morning," I said. "My friend and I were just –"

"Park's off limits," the policeman interrupted me. "No civilians allowed past the line." He pointed a thumb at the yellow line as if I hadn't noticed it yet.

"But we –"

"No exceptions, young man. Off with you now." His hand strayed towards the baton at his waist.

I backed away. The officer was clearly spooked, and he might become suspicious if I insisted. I really didn't want to get caught up in another murder investigation.

Which gave me an idea.

I pulled out my mobile and dialled Sarah. She answered almost immediately.

"Ambrose!" My heart warmed at the sound of

her voice. "If you're calling about coffee, then tonight at five o'clock would be great."

I laughed. "That *would* be great, but I'll have to take a rain cheque. I'm in Cardiff at the moment."

"Cardiff?"

"It's a long story," I said. The sudden silence on the other end startled me and I realised my mistake. "I'll tell you all about it over coffee, I promise, but I need a favour right now."

"Are you on Amari's business?" she asked, sounding more curious than angry. I should have confided in her from the start. It would have saved me months of heartache.

"Sort of. It's nothing that will get you in trouble, I promise."

"I'll take your word for it, but you'd better come clean when I see you again. What do you need?"

I grinned, hardly able to believe how lucky I was to have her on my side. I really needed to sort my life out. Right after this business was settled. I quickly explained the current situation to her.

"I'm on it," she said. "Give me five minutes. And Ambrose?"

"Yes?"

"Whatever you're doing... be careful."

A warm rush filled my chest. "I will," I promised. "At least long enough to make good on that coffee."

She laughed and ended the call just as Daniel came back, carrying two fishing poles and a small cooler box, presumably filled with bait.

"Not letting us through, is he?" my friend asked.

"No, but he will. I pulled a few strings."

The policeman's walkie-talkie crackled, and I couldn't help a grin from slipping across my face. I knew I could count on Sarah.

"Come on," I said to Daniel as I started walking towards the police officer again. The man's bushy eyebrows were drawn together in an angry V as he put his walkie-talkie away. He said nothing as we strolled past him, but I almost drowned in the waves of distrust rolling from him.

"Officer," Daniel greeted him politely, a telltale twinkle in his eyes. The man's moustache drooped lower as his mouth turned down into a scowl, and I quickly hurried my mischievous friend along. The corners of Daniel's mouth were twitching, and I had to fight to keep my own smile from breaking through.

We ducked underneath the yellow tape and found a secluded spot next to the lake. I glanced around. The foliage and thick trunks of trees around the perimeter of the park hid us from view of the surrounding houses. A cluster of ducks swam past as Daniel hooked something squiggly onto a fishing pole.

"Know how to fish?" he asked as he handed me the pole.

"No," I admitted. "But how hard can it be?"

Daniel laughed. "Good thing we're not actually trying to catch a fish then."

I shuddered as an image of a bloated body with gnaw marks popped into my head. Just for once, why couldn't the fairy tale creature I'm after be something nice and cuddly that didn't want to kill me?

"Let's stay vigilant," I said, casting my eyes across the calm water of the lake. "We don't know for sure if it's a water-leaper that killed those men. But whatever it is, it's dangerous. Even if it is a flying frog."

Daniel showed me how to cast my line and, for a few minutes, we stood together in silence, nervously watching the surface for any suspicious ripples. The ducks swam past again, quacking nosily, and I expelled a breath I hadn't even realised I was holding. It should be safe enough if the birds weren't worried.

"Officer," Daniel said.

I turned my head just in time to see the police officer's body disappear behind a tree again. "Checking up on us?" I asked.

Daniel nodded. "I'd like to think he's concerned for our safety," he quipped.

I snorted. I doubted that was the real reason he was watching us. I don't know what Sarah had told his superiors, but the man must surely be wondering who would pull those kinds of strings just to come fishing for the afternoon.

"What are you going to do with the money, Ambrose?" Daniel suddenly asked. I stared blankly at him for a moment, confused by the question. "Young Thomas' treasure. It's not just about the adventure, is it? Why do you want the treasure so much you're willing to risk life and limb for it?"

"Oh, that money," I said. I sighed, rubbing a hand across the back of my neck. "I thought I might use it to try to fix the mistake I made at work. It's something that's been bothering me for months now. I can't move on with my life until I've made things right again."

Daniel nodded. "What really happened? I always got the impression you didn't want to talk about it."

"Because I'd been such a fool," I replied, a tingle of irritation running down my spine as the memories resurfaced. "I was the golden boy of the company, before it happened." The more I talked, the more it felt like a floodgate had opened, spilling out all the resentment and shame I'd been bottling up for so long. It was time to finally come clean. "I was in charge of the company's largest hedge fund. I made my clients rich overnight by following my gut and investing creatively. Just lucky, I guess. But then the pressure kept increasing. They wanted more money and they wanted it now. I took bigger risks, and fortunately they always paid out, but it was never enough."

A sour taste filled my mouth as I recalled those days. I had been stressed out, constantly searching for ideas, chasing the next big thing. I had told myself I loved the pressure, the challenge, the rush of success. I knew better now.

"One night," I continued my tale, "I was in my local pub, just trying to take the edge off. I'd had one too many beers, I guess, when a guy sat down next to me. In retrospect, I should have wondered why he'd wanted to give me financial advice, but at the time, I was too far gone to care. I took the bait. I gambled millions, and I lost it all." I shook my head in frustration. "They fired me the next day. I never had a chance to make things right."

"I'm sorry, mate," Daniel said. I glanced at him to see that his face had gone as pale as a White Lady's eyes. The thought of losing millions must be devastating to a leprechaun.

I grimaced. "I'm not sure how Thomas' treasure can fix what I've done, but perhaps I could use it to – I don't know – repay some of my clients. At least if they got back what I'd lost, I might feel better about myself again."

"These things happen, Ambrose," Daniel said. "They gambled that money as much as you did. You shouldn't beat yourself up too much about it." He lifted a hand in greeting again. "Officer."

I swivelled just in time to see the policeman duck out of sight again. That man was really starting to work on my nerves. Can't a guy be left alone to fish in peace? There was nothing to worry about here. The ducks were still... Where were the ducks?

"Ambrose!"

I stumbled backwards as something lunged out of the lake. It had the slick body of an amphibian, but two transparent bat-like wings propelled it forward. It was enormous! At least as big as a small cow! Monstrous fangs latched onto Daniel's leg and swept him into the water.

My friend had time to yell a curse before he was pulled under.

"Daniel!" I yelled. I hesitated, frozen in shock. And then I plunged in after him.

My eyes stung as I opened them under the murky water. Sand kicked up from the bottom clouded my vision and panic rose in my stomach. The weight of the water pushed me downwards. An image of cold hands reaching for me sent a shiver through my body. Air! I needed air!

A hand suddenly clutched my arm and I gulped water in a silent scream. The hand was pale, but dotted with freckles. Daniel! I grabbed his arm and pulled, kicking furiously towards the surface.

I gasped as my head cleared the water. Struggling, I heaved Daniel to the shore. His body was remarkably heavy. His face was contorted in pain and he was swearing profusely in between splutters.

"Get it off me!" he yelled.

I recoiled as I realised the water-leaper was still attached, its jaws clamped firmly around my friend's leg. A trail of blood soiled the wet grass.

Adrenaline raced through my veins as I surveyed my surroundings, looking for a weapon. My eyes landed on my fishing pole. I grabbed it and started beating the monster over the head with it.

The water-leaper let go of Daniel's leg and the

momentum pulled me off my feet. I fell onto my back. Gasping, I rolled away just in time to avoid the creature's scorpion-like tail darting at me.

The thing lurched into the air, hovering above me on its ridiculous bat wings. It let out a cry – half croak, half screech – and the hair on my arms came erect. Its monstrous fangs glinted in the sunlight as it suddenly dived towards me.

Instinctively, I held my fishing pole out in front of me. I heard a sickening squelch and the creature screamed as the tip of the pole pierced its eye and lodged into its brain. It dropped out of the sky and landed on me like a piano.

I grunted as it knocked the breath out of my lungs.

I lay there on my back, the monstrous water-leaper pinning me to the ground, trying to catch my breath again.

"Are you alright?" Daniel asked.

"Fine," I panted, dropping the fishing rod and giving him a thumbs up. "You?"

"I've been better. I think this may leave another scar."

"I hear girls love scars."

"Yes," Daniel said lightly. "Nothing says 'sexy' like a limp and an angry red welt down your leg."

He groaned and the weight of the water-leaper lifted as Daniel rolled the dead creature off me. He held a hand out to help me up. I winced as I struggled to my feet. My ribs were blazing in agony. I'd probably bruised or broken a few of them.

Hunting myths was not for the faint-hearted. Or the easily-maimed.

I gasped as I looked at my friend. His leg was a bloody mess where the creature's serrated teeth had torn into it. He was leaning heavily on the other fishing pole and his face was even paler than it had been before.

"We need to get you to a hospital," I said.

"Probably," Daniel agreed. "But what are we going to do about this?"

We both stared at the corpse of the water-leaper. Thomas had wanted its wings, but I hadn't come prepared to butcher anything. I'd expected wrapping something no larger than my hand in a freezer bag and passing it on intact. People would surely notice if I tried to lug a monster the size of a small cow onto the train.

"I'll take it off your hands, gentlemen."

I spun around, expecting the see the policeman confronting us. Instead, Stalker held an unsheathed katana casually in one hand as he walked closer. He wrinkled his nose as he stopped next to the corpse and prodded it with one steel-tipped boot.

"I prefer my targets alive, if only to avoid the smell."

"You can't have that," I said.

"Who's going to stop me? You?" He smirked at me. "Or your injured friend?" He made a little mocking half-bow, his eyes never leaving us, watchful for any sudden moves. "Luckily, my new employer doesn't care too much about the state of my finds. Saves them the effort of upkeep, I imagine."

His new employer? I didn't think he'd find someone else to work for so soon. Maybe there were more players in this game than I had thought. I wondered if Amari knew that this rogue hunter was still at large, and what she would do about it if she did?

"Leave us the wings, at least," Daniel said. "I bled for that."

Stalker snorted. "What kind of amateur do you think I am?" Then he placed one hand on the water-leaper's slimy torso. He grinned at us again. "Gentlemen." The blue fire flashed.

"Son of a –" Daniel lunged, but his injured leg gave way when he put weight on it. I caught his arm just in time to stop him from falling.

"Take it easy," I said.

Daniel growled, frustrated, staring at the empty spot where Stalker and the dead water-leaper had disappeared. "If he'd left us something, we might have been able to use it to track him. Now he's gone. And we don't know who he's taking that thing to."

Disappointment was bitter in my mouth. "And we've failed our quest."

Daniel nodded. "Doubt we'll find another one of those monsters in time for the deadline. And neither of us is in any state to take another one on if we did. What do you want to do now?"

"Let's get you cleaned up first. At the very least, you'll need some stitches and a tetanus shot. Then we'll worry about the rest."

A thought suddenly occurred to me as we were limping back towards the rental car. "What trait do you think was associated with that thing?"

"Officer," Daniel nodded as we stumbled past the police officer. His eyes widened at the state of us. His hand went for his walkie-talkie. I could probably expect a call from Sarah soon.

"I'll bet it's exaggeration," Daniel finally said as I helped him into the car. "Fishermen all across Wales must have been blaming it for years for the one that got away."

"I wouldn't be surprised," I scoffed. "That thing was as big as a house."

Daniel blinked at me, and it took me a second to realise what I'd done. "Well then," my friend said. "I guess there must be at least one more water-leaper out there."

I nodded, relieved that I hadn't killed the last of its kind, and also a little disturbed to know that there were more of those monsters somewhere out there.

※※※

We were both quiet as we watched the landscape shooting past on the last train from Cardiff to London that evening. I grimaced as I shuffled in my seat, trying to get comfortable with three bruised ribs wrapped tightly in bandages. Daniel's usually jovial face was sombre, for once not an effect of the rainbow mocking him outside the window. He'd needed stitches and, as it turned out, my friend really didn't enjoy needles.

"Of the three things we had to find, we only have one," he said, turning towards me. "I'm afraid our quest has failed, my friend." From his tone, I could tell he was thinking of more than just the quest. Now that he knew what it really meant to me, he was just as disappointed as I was.

My mobile rang and I looked at the caller ID. Sarah.

"Are you alright?" she asked. I loved that *that* was the first thing she wanted to know.

"I'm fine. Daniel's in worse shape, but he's being stoic about it. I hope we didn't get you into any trouble."

"Not me, but I had to talk fast to keep you out of it. Seems like the officer on duty thought you were involved with the murders somehow. Reliving the euphoria of the crime, or something dire like that. I told them you were independent consultants investigating the case and that I would vouch for you. I guess it helped that you came out bleeding yourselves, although there must be a better way to prove your innocence."

I shrugged. "If anyone asks, we had a fishing accident. It's true enough."

"Right. And you'll tell me all about it..."

"Tomorrow," I promised. "There's just one more thing I need to do first."

"Alright, Ambrose. I trust you. See you tomorrow."

I put the phone down and turned back to Daniel. "Do you want to come with me to go see Thomas? Even if we don't have what he asked for, we can at least let him know what happened."

"Of course," Daniel said. "I started it with you, I'll finish it with you too."

"Thanks," I said, turning back towards the window and watching green meadows giving way to rows of stocky brown houses. The ray of hope talking to Sarah had given me was fading quickly as I mulled over the events of the past few days.

I'd failed. Again.

The bitter taste in my mouth was becoming all too familiar. First my job in finance, then my contract with the Council, and now Thomas' quest.

It felt like I was destined to make a dog's dinner of everything I touched. But this time, at least, I had a chance to admit my failure and try to make amends somehow. It was the least I could do.

※※※

The sun was low on the horizon as we hobbled into Hyde Park. Thomas was waiting for us under a cluster of trees, a collection of sheets spread out on the surrounding grass. A pair of scissors and a half empty bottle of glue, along with an assortment of colourful pens, completed the picture. He looked up as we drew closer.

"Did you get it?" he asked.

"I'm sorry," I said, shaking my head. My heart lurched as his face fell, disappointed.

"But you promised!" he pouted. "Now I'm going to fail this assignment, and Mum will send me to holiday school to catch up on my grades." His face rumpled as tears started rolling down his cheeks.

"Wait," Daniel said. "This is for school?"

Thomas nodded. "I need to do well. I don't want to spend my summer in a classroom!"

I sat down on the grass next to the boy. "What is your assignment about? Can I help?" I looked at the pieces of paper spread out in front of the boy. The first page was coloured in red, with pictures of volcanoes, the sun and a phoenix drawn across it. The boy was a talented artist. The other sheets were painted blue and green, and the last one was white.

"Are these the elements?" I asked, gazing at the blue paper. It was covered in pictures of a waterfall, rolling ocean waves, and water drops. "This is water, and the red one is fire. I'm guessing the green is earth, which would make the white one —"

"Wind," Thomas said, wiping the tears from his cheeks. "I didn't really know how to draw it."

"This is amazing," I said, admiring the tornado he had inked in. "It looks like you have everything you need for your assignment already. Why did you want all the things you asked for?"

Thomas shrugged. "I thought I'd get some extra credit if I had something to show for each element."

"The tear was for water," I said, realisation dawning.

"And the clover is earth?" Daniel guessed.

Thomas nodded.

"That would make the water-leaper's wings...

air?" I added. "But what about fire?"

"I have that one already," the boy said excitedly. He pulled a stick from his pocket and pressed his thumb against it. A small flame ignited at the stick's tip. It was a novelty lighter in the shape of a wizard's wand.

I pinched the bridge of my nose, closing my eyes for a moment. We had just spent three days traipsing all across the country, in real danger of being eaten, to find things that could have easily been replaced with more mundane magic.

I took a deep breath. It wasn't the boy's fault. He just wanted to have the summer off. For an eight-year-old, that was certainly life-changing and important enough to send someone off on a quest. I should have asked more questions. The promise of treasure had consumed me so much that I had been so eager to go on this quest I hadn't stopped to think if I should. And now that I *did* think about it, I wasn't even sure that the treasure would be anything of value. What would a child value? What would a spriggan value?

"We can't give you the wings or the tear," Daniel said, understanding dawning on his face too. Instead of being annoyed, he looked amused. "But what if we helped you find something else to demonstrate the elements with?"

The boy considered the offer for a second, and then nodded. "How?" he asked.

Putting my disappointment aside for the moment, I looked around for ideas.

"How about this for water?" I asked, pulling the pen I had found at Urquhart castle out of my pocket and handing it to Thomas. The boy's face lit up as he played with it, making Nessie appear and disappear underneath the liquid inside it.

"And perhaps this for air?" Daniel said, bending over to pick up a stray duck feather. He blew it and Thomas giggled as it floated towards him and landed on his head.

"And finally, for earth, this four-leaf clover," I said, taking it out of the bag I had been keeping it in and handing it to the boy. "It's lucky, but I don't think you'll need luck to do well in this assignment." I winked at him.

The boy jumped up and threw himself into my arms. "Thank you! I'll have the best assignment in class now!" I ruffled his hair, happy to see the kid so excited.

"Thomas?" a female voice called.

The boy pulled away from me. "Gotta go," he said, scrambling to get all his papers and supplies together. He was just about to dash off when he stopped and looked over his shoulder at me. "Look under the old oak tree. Take a shovel."

My heart lurched as the boy skipped away. I looked at Daniel. His eyes were as wide as my own.

"Let's go get it," he said.

✕✕✕

I pressed a hand against my sore ribs. Digging this hole hadn't done me any favours, but it had been worth it. An odd sense of satisfaction rolled across me at the sight of the treasure sparkling in the moonlight.

"Woah," Daniel said, leaning against his shovel, wiping sweat from his brow. "This was not what I'd expected. How had Thomas got hold of it? It must be worth a fortune now."

I nodded. "Probably even more than your pot of gold."

Daniel nodded in agreement. To my friend's everlasting credit, there wasn't even a hint of greed in his gaze. "What are you going to do with it? Too bad Monique's languishing in jail right now. She'd be able to take care of this for you."

I snorted. "Monique is exactly where she belongs. And this..." I looked at the treasure, hardly able to believe my eyes... "This belongs in a museum."

"Yes..." Daniel agreed, his voice sounding somewhat wistful. He gave himself a little shake, as if his thoughts had been far away just then. "I know someone who works at the British Museum. If that's really what you want to do with it, I can arrange it."

"Yes," I said immediately. An idea sparked and my insides lurched as excitement bubbled up. "But let me make a phone call first..."

※※※

I hung my jacket across the back of the chair and rolled my sleeves up. Then I took a sip of my tea, savouring the rich aroma. The late morning sky was clear blue and in the distance I could see the telltale rainbow hanging over Daniel's shoe shop. It was a beautiful day in London, the kind postcards were made of.

"Would you like a scone with your tea, sir?" the waiter asked me.

"Please."

My mobile beeped and my eyes widened as I read the text. A rather large sum had just been deposited into my account, with Amari's name as reference. The thought of being paid for bringing Kentigern Mor into the Repository's care had never even crossed my mind. I hoped the old dragon would at last find the peace he'd been looking for there.

The phone beeped again. Another message from the bank and my heart lurched: the finder's fee. Daniel's friend had wasted no time at all. She'd been thrilled when we showed her what we'd found, her hands shaking in excitement as she'd taken the treasure from me. The exhilaration of recovering something so precious had probably kept her up all night.

"Thank you," I said as the waiter placed a plate of scones in front of me, as well as a jar of strawberry jam and a large cup of whipped cream. "Do you mind if we turn the telly on? On Sky News, if you would."

The waiter obliged and I turned towards the television. The news was on and, as I'd expected, the treasure Daniel and I had dug up last night was the main headline. Subtext scrolling across the bottom of the screen declared it "a lucky miracle".

The reporter's cheeks were flushed with excitement as he stood underneath the iconic glass ceiling of the British Museum. "The historical community is abuzz with excitement as the British Museum revealed what has been confirmed as the rediscovery of the Cross of Calais, lost nearly a year ago during a robbery during an exhibition at the Notre Dame in Paris. The legendary Cross, said to be able to heal any ailment, has sparked a renewed interest in mythical artefacts and believers and non-believers alike from all across the country are showing up to see the relic for themselves."

My phone beeped a third time. A text from Jake, my old colleague, popped onto the screen.

--Bloody hell, Ambrose. How did you know? The investors are pleased. Your tip was worth millions!! Expect a phone call from the partners.--

A self-satisfied smile tugged at the corners of my mouth. The last-minute investment in various antiquities currently up for sale had done the trick, as I'd hoped. Maybe I hadn't lost my touch, after all.

"I'd like to hear how you pulled all of this off, Ambrose Davids."

I looked up to see Sarah standing in front of my table, one hand resting on her hip as she stared at me over the rims of her black hipster glasses. Her foot tapped in mock annoyance, but the corners of her moss-green eyes crinkled as a smile hovered across her lips.

"Sit down," I said, offering her the chair beside me. "And I'll tell you all about it."

Her smile widened as she joined me.

"Your tea, miss," the waiter said, on cue, as he placed the cup I had ordered earlier in front of her. Sarah thanked him, sighing as she inhaled the aroma of her favourite blend. She added a dash of milk before turning her attention back to me.

I took the opportunity to take one of her hands in my own, looking into those gorgeous green eyes. "It all started the day I met a young detective who accused me of wasting her time in a murder investigation."

Sarah laughed, a rich, melodic sound, and I couldn't help but feel that – finally – everything was going to be alright after all.

THE END

(The adventure continues in *Myth Keeper*, the next novel in the Mythical Menagerie series...)

BONUS SCENES

THOMAS' TREASURE

T homas' leaves rustled in the breeze. He blinked, slowly waking from his nap. The sun was a red smudge low on the horizon, casting long shadows in the deepening twilight. He'd better get home, or his mum would come looking for him. How many times had she told him not to fall asleep in the middle of Hyde Park during the day?

Taking advantage of the wind, he shook his branches a few times, preparing his limbs for the shift. An indignant squawk sounded next to where his ear would be. Thomas froze. He peered at the Egyptian goose that had settled on one of his boughs. It glared back at Thomas with beady, orange eyes.

"Sorry!" Thomas said, his voice a vegetative whisper. "But I really need you to get off me now."

The goose ruffled its feathers, but stayed stubbornly put. It flapped its wings a few times, then wiggled its bottom and pooped loudly. If Thomas had had a nose, he would have scrunched it up. He stifled a giggle.

A deep voice swore below him, and Thomas swished in surprise. He looked down to see a man with a head as shiny as a duck's egg wiping at his bald pate with a handkerchief. The man scowled up at the goose. Then he stooped and picked up a large rock. The goose squawked loudly as the rock flew past its head, narrowly missing it.

Thomas bristled. This was not a nice man.

If there was one thing Thomas was good at, it was growing acorns. He sent his senses out until he found a flower in just the right place and with just the right amount of enthusiasm. It took only a bit of encouragement to see the flower bloom into an acorn and swell into the size of an apple.

"Tesserier." Thomas paused his aim to see the man putting his handkerchief away as a woman strode into view. She was dressed all in black and her long black hair was swept back into a ponytail. "Do you have it?" the man asked.

"Do you have the money?" the woman countered. Her accent sounded strange to Thomas.

The man nodded. "Of course," he said, taking out his mobile phone. "Show me the relic and I'll do the transfer now."

The woman hesitated, then reached into her jacket pocket and took out a velvet drawstring bag. Both Thomas and the man drew in a deep breath as she pulled out a golden cross, bejewelled and sparkling in the dim light. Grandpa would have loved that, Thomas thought, sighing wistfully as the woman quickly tucked the treasure back into its bag.

The man did something on his mobile phone, and the woman's phone pinged in response. Her smile was lopsided as she checked her message, before tossing the velvet bag towards the man. He grabbed it greedily.

"Pleasure doing business with you," she said, already walking away. *"Au revoir."*

The man looked around, as if making sure no one had seen the exchange. When he spotted the goose sitting in Thomas' boughs, quietly cleaning its feathers, a nasty sneer crossed the man's lips. He stooped and picked up another rock, much larger this time.

His aim was true. The goose screeched as it fell to the ground.

It felt like his branches had caught fire. Thomas roared, not in the secret language of trees, but loud as a storm rolling across the moors. His limbs turned to claws, his trunk twisted to show his face, contorted with rage, his acorns swelled to the size of footballs.

This was a bad man and he needed to be punished. He needed to learn some respect.

The blood drained from the man's face as he stared at Thomas. Terrified, he opened his mouth to scream, but no sound came out. Shaking, he took the golden cross out of its bag and held it out in front of him, as if it could protect him.

Thomas had no time for trinkets. Could gold ease suffering? With fury boiling in his vines, he lunged for the man.

The man shrieked and dropped the cross. He turned and ran, his expensive shoes slapping against the pavement as he disappeared from view.

Thomas grunted.

His limbs shifted as his body shrunk. He scratched at his arms as bark gave way to nut-brown skin. It didn't take long before Thomas looked like a normal boy again.

And he had bird poop all down the front of his *Lion Guard* jumper. His mum wasn't going to like that.

He turned toward the goose. It was lying on its side, but Thomas breathed a sigh of relief to see its little chest still moving. He bent down and placed a hand on the goose's soft feathers. The bird's orange eyes were clouded with pain.

Carefully, Thomas picked the goose up. "Mum will know what to do," he said, his voice soft and reassuring. "She's good at healing animals."

The goose didn't object.

From the corner of his eye, Thomas saw something glinting. It was the golden cross the man had dropped in his fright. Thomas scooped it up and tucked it into the pocket of his jeans. *I'll take this to Grandpa later*, he thought.

Then, gently stroking the goose's back, he went in search of his mum.

DIANA'S FIRST
WORD

D iana stifled a yawn. She rubbed her tired eyes
until lights danced in front of her vision like
playful pixies. Then she stood up, stretching the
ache from her shoulders, and walked over to the
fireplace. She stoked the smouldering coals and
added another log from the small pile stacked next
to it for the night's use. She rubbed some feeling
back into her hands as the fire grudgingly
spluttered back to life.

A tiny sound, like a suppressed sneeze, made
her turn from the fire and inspect her study. The
thick Persian carpet was soft underfoot. Her
antique mahogany desk dominated the centre of
the room, currently littered with open books and
scattered notes in her cramped handwriting. The
walls of the windowless room were covered in
shelves lined with dusty, ancient tomes.

Slowly, her heart rate returned to normal. It
was late and she was tired. Her imagination was
getting the better of her.

"Just a few more minutes," Diana muttered as
she lowered herself back into her chair. She'd been

wrestling with the Sumerian cuneiform in *Arashti's Heaven and Earth*, the vellum sheets so tattered she winced whenever she needed to turn the page. Squinting, she tried to decipher that last symbol. Was it an *el* or an *al* sound? Ablative or locative? Or did the transcriber's hand just slip when he had copied from the original clay tablet and inadvertently caused the headache that was now brewing behind her left ear, millennia later?

Diana's head whipped up, her blood-shot eyes wide with alarm. She'd heard a sigh then, hadn't she? The room remained the same, but the fire cast shadows across the walls that left Diana's mouth dry as a djinni's doorstep. There was a particularly dark patch in the corner furthest away from the hearth. Diana stared into it until her eyes started watering. Shaking her head, she wrenched her gaze from the darkness and focussed on the page once more. There it was again! Diana was on her feet, her hands balled into fists. She was safe in the Repository, wasn't she? She'd been here, locked inside the mountain, alone with the creatures, for almost a year now, and nothing worth mentioning had ever happened. Nothing the Council had felt worth mentioning, in any event. In those first few days, Diana had carried a cudgel with her everywhere she went. She wondered what had happened to it.

Silence. Nothing but the crackling fire and the thumping of her own heart, loud in her ears.

The chair creaked as she sat down. Forcing herself to concentrate, she stared at the writing on the page. The symbols looked like chicken scratches now. If only she could make out that last syllable...

Softly, she whispered the sounds to herself, her finger trailing each mark. She paused at the last sound.

"It's *ahl*," a voice suddenly said.

Diana yelped, the sound slipping from her tongue before she could stop herself.

Her head whipped towards the dark corner. Two piercing blue eyes held her gaze as the shadows faded to reveal the form of a winged monkey perched upon the topmost bookshelf.

"Congratulations, Keeper," the monkey said. "You've just learned your first Word."

"Who are you?" Diana demanded, rubbing her arms. They were covered in goose bumps. The Word lingered in the air, heavy with magic. Diana steadied her trembling hands, hoping the intruder didn't notice.

The monkey made a little comic bow. "Reese, at your service, my lady."

"The shapeshifter?" Her predecessor had mentioned the creature in his journals, but the enclosure allocated to it had always been empty when she'd visited. She'd assumed the creature had been a figment of the old man's imagination. So much for assumptions.

"What are you doing in my study? Hiding in the shadows?"

"Observing," Reese replied smoothly. "You've lasted longer than the others, therefor I have to assume you'll stay. I wanted to get to know you."

"There are better ways than spying on me."

"Granted. I wasn't planning on staying long, but your research intrigued me."

Diana glared at the winged monkey. She wasn't sure if she should feel grateful or annoyed that it hadn't helped her out sooner. She settled for mildly irritable.

"Do you know many Words?" she asked.

The monkey's face was sly as it smiled at her. "Perhaps."

Diana sighed. Nothing was ever easy.

"It's late," she said. "You should be in your enclosure."

The monkey launched itself from the shelf and hovered in the air before her. "You should get some sleep, Diana," it chattered. "You'll need your wits about you if you want to survive the Repository."

"Is that a threat?" she asked, surging to her feet.

"An observation. Good night." A glow surrounded the monkey as it shifted. A mouse dropped to the floor and ran towards the door. It squeaked in farewell as it squeezed underneath the heavy oak frame.

Diana blinked. This was a creature she had better keep an eye on.

Yawning, she walked over to the fireplace again. Perhaps she should just rest her eyes for a bit. She pulled the sheepskin blanket from across the leather-back chair positioned next to the fire and wrapped herself in it before settling comfortably into the armchair.

The warmth of accomplishment settled over her as she watched the flames dancing in the hearth. "My first Word," she mumbled as her eyes slid closed and her breathing softened.

ACKNOWLEDGEMENTS

This novel has taken a long time to complete and would probably have never seen the light of day if it wasn't for an amazing group of people who have cheered me on, checked my spelling and grammar, helped me work out niggling plot points and generally told me to HURRY UP AND FINISH IT ALREADY!

Thank you to the Dragon Writers writing group on Facebook! Your constant motivation, writing advice, expertise and friendship mean the world to me. Writing is a lonely and difficult journey, and you guys and girls have made it easier and a lot more fun.

Thank you to my team of beta readers: Cathy Dannhauser, Gavin and Debbie Green, Piet le Roux, Heather McDade, and Nico Swanepoel. Special thank you to Thalia Fourie and Mari Terblanche for going above and beyond and helping me make this the best book it can be.

To Schalk van der Merwe, who composed the fantastic theme music for the book trailer - I am in awe of your talent! Thank you for being my flash fiction alpha reader and coming up with outrageously creative ideas to help me improve my really short short stories.

Thank you to my bestie, Claudette van der Merwe, for cheerleading, chocolate, and cake when I need it most.

Most of all, thank you to my family for their endless support and belief in me, for babysitting when I needed to get out of the house to write, for helping me work out issues and for taking care of more mundane things while my head was in the clouds. A very special thank you to my mum and dad, Henda and Jannie le Roux, and my hubby, Gareth Jones, for your continued encouragement. I would never have had the courage to do this if you hadn't urged me on and supported me every step of the way.

WANT MORE?

Subscribe to Suneé le Roux's email list to receive a free flash fiction in your inbox every month. You'll also receive an exclusive short story prequel set in the Mythical Menagerie universe, only available to newsletter subscribers!

SUBSCRIBE.SUNEELEROUX.COM/KEEPEROFEXOTICANIMALS

WHAT WOULD YOU DO IF THE WORLD'S LAST UNICORN WENT MISSING?

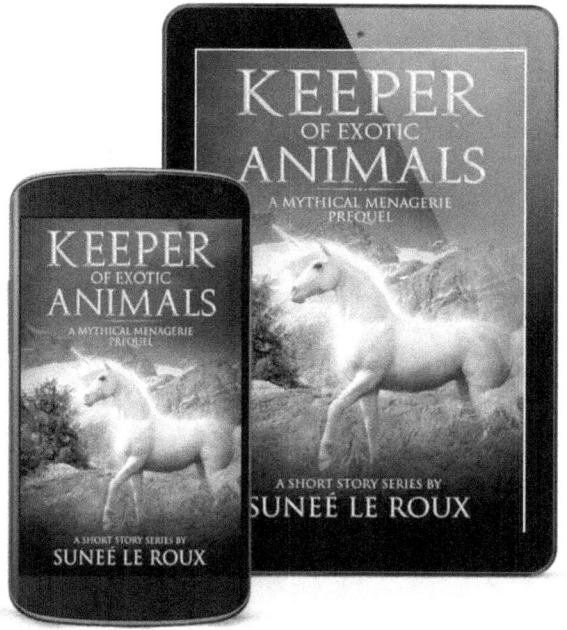

Claim your free e-book now!

PLEASE REVIEW

If you've enjoyed this story, please consider leaving a review on your online platform of choice and/or on Goodreads. Think of it as word of mouth recommendation. Independent authors such as myself need reviews for visibility and social proof, and to get those algorithms to place my books in the hands of other readers.

It doesn't have to be a long and in-depth review - one sentence, or even just a star rating, will do.

It would mean the world to me. Thank you!

ABOUT THE AUTHOR

Suneé le Roux is a South African author of contemporary and high fantasy stories that blend myth, magic, and adventure. She lives in South Africa with her Welsh husband and their young wizard-in-training.

She loves nothing more than to hear from readers. Connect with her here:

Website: www.suneeleroux.com

Email: contact@suneeleroux.com

Facebook: www.facebook.com/authorsuneeleroux/

Instagram: www.instagram.com/suneeleroux/

WWW.SUNEELEROUX.COM